WELCOME

TO

COOPER

TARIQ
ASHKANANI

Published by Thomas and Mercer, Seattle

www.apub.com

Amazon, the Amazon logo, and Thomas and Mercer are trademarks of Amazon.com, Inc., or its affiliates.

ISBN-13: 9781542031271
ISBN-10: 1542031273

Cover design by kid-ethic

Printed in the United States of America

WELCOME
TO
COOPER

For Lucy

They ask me to tell them a story.

Friendly words, spoken by tired men wearing crushed suits, over lukewarm coffee in a paper cup and a bagel that was cold long before it ever reached me.

Tell us a story.

A red-hooded girl visits her grandmother. I think they've heard that one before.

The problem is, I was never any good at telling stories. Never could work out the best place to start. *It's all about making an impact—see, I get that. Grabbing their attention and not letting up till you're done. I get that part plenty. I got that part spilling out my pockets.* Pick a moment, buddy, *they say, like we're friends. Like we're in a bar and not in a room with the blinds closed.*

I think back over everything that's happened these past few weeks. I remember the snow, snow up to my shins. Snow like ash, from a blackened sky to bury all beneath it. Flakes of the stuff gathering in my hair and in the folds of my ears. I remember watching as she stood at the window and stared out at me. She couldn't see me—even from where she was standing she couldn't see me, even from twenty yards away. I remember moving down her hallway, and the sound my wet shoes made on her wooden floors. I remember my hands didn't shake like they used to, like they had the first time. And I remember music playing, but don't ask me what it was. It was noise, and noise was good. I could hide in the noise.

Or maybe I should just jump straight to the end. Give these boys what they want. The forest and the early morning sun and the spot where I led a man to his death.

Only they don't want that story. They want history. They want backstory. *I can see it in their eyes, I'm losing them, and they interrupt with their questions, with their confusion.* Back it up now, *they say, like my memory's an old SUV with a busted axle. A hand pushes a fresh cup of coffee across the table to help me remember.*

So I'll take them back. Not to the very start, because I don't know them all that well just yet and, besides, most of that stuff isn't important to them. But I'll lead them far enough. Back to my arrival in town, back to the tall grass and the cornfields, and that long freeway, cracked and uneven, and the sign that read Welcome to Cooper *in bleached, looped writing.*

I push the coffee away, ask for something stronger. Glances all around but I keep my mouth shut, like I'd be happy keeping my mouth shut forever. Eventually someone shuffles out the door and I lean back in my chair to wait.

I think I'll start with the girl.

Chapter One

She was dead and dressed for dancing.

Face up, that's how they found her. On her back and stretched out across the grass like the only thing being killed was time.

I stood at the back door next to Joe and pulled on a pair of latex gloves. Snow drifted across her crowded backyard.

I thought about that sign on the way into town. Some welcome.

Her body was lying at the foot of a tree. Don't ask me what kind. Big and brown, with blossoms on the branches. White petals, whatever. Rachel would have known what it was.

A group of men had gathered. A murder like this, they always did. No-name men in chinos, from departments I didn't care enough about to ask. Bureaucracy, who gives a damn. They weren't here because they cared and I'm sure you all know something about that. As we got close I could see it in their eyes, in their bent heads, in the way they were talking, in the way they sucked back on their cigarettes, in the way they gazed down at her. Detached. Like she was a bad cut of meat. Like she was a problem.

I followed Joe across the yard and he turned to me and said he wanted me to take point on this, and I said alright. I figured he was testing me, and I guessed this was as good a way as any. I wasn't worried. I didn't much care what he thought of me. People sometimes say I'm emotionally closed off, but people say a lot of things. A woman once said I was an asshole and I reckon she was right.

The men shifted as we approached. I caught a glimpse of a bare arm in the fresh snow. Pale white.

"Who's your boy?" one of them asked Joe. I couldn't tell who.

"This here is Tommy Levine," he said. "Make him feel welcome."

I swept my gaze around the group, got a perverse pleasure that no one bothered to try. Joe slid a cigarette into his mouth. Waved me on as he lit up.

I pushed through to the center of the circle. Bodies shifting just enough to let me pass. Shoulders brushing, the tang of stale coffee and bad breath. When I emerged she was revealed to me in all her grotesque beauty, and when I stood over her it was like some tribal ritual.

Black shoe, the fancy kind, and only on one foot. Light-brown pantyhose. A thin black dress and a slim leather belt. Her legs outstretched, her arms tossed up above her head, her hands crumpled together. A dark, heavy necklace of bruises around her neck. Blonde hair, long and curled at the ends. She was young, maybe mid-twenties, and if whoever had killed her had left her eyes behind she'd have been pretty, too. Hell, you've seen the photos.

I felt it then. Uncoiling in my gut, warm and slick. That strange mix of feebleness and fury, like I wanted to throw up and beat my fists against a brick wall at the same time. Staring at a mutilated woman tends to do that to a guy.

"What do we know?" I said, hoping someone would answer.

Someone did. "Name's Kelly Frances Scott. Or at least, we're presuming so."

It was a bald man dressed all in white. I caught his eye. "This is Ms. Scott's house?"

"That's right."

I crouched down beside her. The circle of men around me tightened.

"Weather's going to bury this crime scene," I said. "We should get a tarp up."

"Already requested, Detective."

"Any sign of sexual assault?"

"Doesn't look like it. I'll need to do a proper examination when we get her back to the station."

I stood, paced slowly around her.

"Her hands," I said, pointing. "Any sign they were bound?"

"None."

"So he was strong," I said. "Held her down, pinned her arms with one hand, strangled her with the other."

"Maybe she was unconscious," one of them said.

I looked at him—paunchy and greasy-faced—then back down at the woman. I wiped at my nose with the back of a gloved hand.

"Maybe," I said, then found the man in the white jumpsuit. "You got a time of death yet?"

"Best I can do right now is sometime in the last eight hours."

"She's not dressed for bed," I said. "Her outfit, I'm guessing she was out last night."

"Robbery gone bad?" It was the greasy-faced detective again.

"Not sure. She's missing a watch." I pointed to a band of paler skin on her wrist.

"You think he took it?"

"Back off, Lloyd."

That was Joe. I turned and saw him standing at the edge of the circle. He was staring at the body.

"Kid says she's missing a watch," Lloyd said.

"It's not a damn robbery, Lloyd. You bothered to get your fat ass up those stairs, you'd probably find it on her nightstand."

5

"What did you just say?"

"I said he didn't break in to steal her goddamn TV. This is Homicide's. Besides, I've seen your stats. You guys don't need another red line this quarter."

I glanced back and forth between them. Lloyd's round face was reddening. He shook his head, hard, then turned away. "You can have it, you prick," he muttered as he pushed past.

Joe waited until Lloyd was gone, then stepped forward. Some people took a step back. "Her eyes," he said to me.

The flesh around her sockets was torn and jagged.

"He did them quick," I said, "there's no precision." I paused. "He was angry."

Silence. Then, murmurs and movement, cellphones and fresh cigarettes.

"Get a tent up," Joe said quietly. "And get it up now, you understand me? Christ, it's been snowing since we got here. We'll be lucky if we find anything."

He left then, snapping off his gloves as he went.

I took one final glance at the dead woman with the missing eyes, but she didn't look back. Everything around me seemed to melt away, her empty sockets widening into yawning tunnels, and I knew if I didn't turn away now they'd swallow me whole.

Chapter Two

I rode shotgun in Joe's beat-up Ford through the thickening snow, the crappy heater blowing cold air on my legs as I pictured Kelly Scott's sockets filling up with white.

I'd just met Joe that morning. I'd arrived in town late on Friday, spent the weekend unpacking and eating shitty egg foo young with my switchblade because I didn't own a fork, and then Monday morning rolled around and here I was.

Well, no. Truth was, I didn't have that much to unpack, and most of it was still in boxes. Truth was, I'd stayed in at my new apartment because I didn't want to leave. Didn't want to go outside, didn't want to walk the empty streets. When I lay in bed it was quiet. No cars, no voices yelling. Cooper was a different world from DC, and I guess maybe I didn't like that. But wasn't that the whole damn point?

Now, Joe's a big guy. You've seen him. Not fat or out of shape, just big. Bulky. The kind of guy you wouldn't want to face off against in a boxing ring. Like he'd had muscles, back in the day. Grey hair and grey stubble, crushed shirt, and a tie that'd probably had the same knot in it for twenty years. Large hands that squeezed the wheel tight enough to make it creak.

We drove for ten minutes before he spoke. I got the feeling that driving in silence was a habit, and that suited me fine. He asked me if I wanted a smoke and I said no, then he asked me if I minded and I said no to that, too. So he clumsily patted his long trench coat down with both hands, steadying the wheel between his legs. The straight road weaved ahead. He tapped out a cigarette on his forearm and slid it straight into his mouth. Lit it with a practiced hand.

"About back there," he said, then clammed up. He blew smoke out in a long sigh.

I stared out the passenger window, watched Cooper slide by. Single-story storefronts with broken windows; graffiti-tagged metal shutters; garbage spilling out of trash cans like moss. A thick blanket of snow would be a blessing.

"Weather always this bad?" I asked.

"Not usually in November."

"I've seen worse," I said.

Joe sent me a sideways glance as he cracked the window. "Sure you have," he said, maybe sarcastically, I couldn't tell. He knocked the end of his cigarette on the edge of the glass, sent hot ash to flutter and die.

We spent a couple of blocks like that. Joe turned on the radio. I figured it was easier than talking. Country music, Kenny Rogers in between bursts of static. I tapped out the tune on the window frame.

"You introduced me to everyone as Tommy," I said.

"What?"

"At the crime scene. I prefer Thomas, is all."

Joe nodded. Let the silence between us grow a little more. "You a religious man, Thomas?"

"Not really. Why?"

Laughter from the radio host. A grating squeal that punctured the static.

Joe said, "Only Thomas I ever knew grew up to be a priest. Went off to a big city somewhere. Phoenix, maybe." A pause as he flicked more ash onto the cold street. "Don't see the appeal, myself."

8

"Of Phoenix?"

"Of big cities. I heard you used to work in DC."

"Couple years."

"Cooper must be quite the change."

I thought of it again. Lying in bed, a pressure in the stillness. I hadn't realized how much I needed the noise to help me sleep.

"It's certainly quieter," I said.

"I'll bet."

"You ever been to DC?"

Joe took a draw, shook his head. "I check in on the news every four years, see who's in charge. That's enough for me. Why'd you leave?"

"I needed a change."

A grunt. He looked at me, swung his cigarette toward my chest. "Well, you still dress like you're in DC. Lose the suit."

"What's wrong with my suit?"

"You see anyone else back there wearing one?"

"I'm just trying to make a good impression."

"You want to make a good impression, you help me catch this guy. People around here see you wearing that on their doorstep, they'll think you're trying to sell them something. Save the fancy stuff for court."

"Thanks for the tip."

"Don't mention it. What you carrying?"

"My gun? Smith and Wesson Model thirty-six."

Joe's eyebrows peaked. "Revolver man. *Dirty Harry*. Didn't have you pegged."

"For a violent sociopath?"

"What, you didn't like that movie?"

I shrugged. "I seem to remember his revolver being a little bigger."

Joe grunted again, then tossed the remainder of his cigarette out the window and wound it back up. The car roared. I got the impression we were done talking.

◆ ◆ ◆

Cooper was small, but spread out. We followed the main street through the middle of town. I watched kids laughing on the corners, bumping fists filled with baggies like they'd seen on TV. Apartment blocks and convenience stores, and every so often a glimpse of the wide expanse beyond. Cornfields and cattle, scrubland, and farther out still the swelling embankment that marked the edge of the Pine Ridge and the Nebraska National Forest. I'd never been somewhere with this much open space. Ironic, maybe, that it would feel so oppressive.

It was nearing noon by the time we arrived. Joe said he had stuff to take care of, barely waited for me to close the door before tearing out of the parking lot. I spent the rest of the day at my desk. Paperwork and handshakes. The usual first-day bullshit.

Flicking through my morning's crime scene notes, I kept thinking of Kelly Scott. I couldn't stop seeing her eyes. Images of them sliding out of her head. A blade slicing at her optic nerves. I tossed my notebook and stood up. It was after six, and I needed a drink.

Stingray's was a small bar just around the corner from the station, all red leather and high stools. A neon sign flickered in the window. It was happy hour.

Inside, my shoes crackled on the sticky floor. The air was heavy with a strong, sweaty musk. A lone bartender was behind the counter, dressed all in black. She was slowly drying a rack of glasses. Her name was Mary, but of course I didn't know that yet.

She didn't look like a Mary. Not that first time. She looked like a goth, or whatever the word is nowadays. Dark hair with a fierce

10

streak of pink down one side, cut into a sharp bob that ended just under her chin. She didn't look up as I approached.

I tried to pull out a barstool, found them bolted to the floor. Yeah, it was that kind of place. Sliding onto the hard, worn padding I noticed a man sitting in the corner of the room by himself. Hunched over a plate of fried eggs and bacon.

"What can I get you?" the bartender asked me, slapping the rag she'd been using to dry across one shoulder.

"Bourbon," I said. "And a dinner menu, if it's not too much trouble." I smiled at her but she'd already turned away. She filled a shot glass, slid it across the bar.

"You're new in town," she said.

I nodded.

"Just between us," she said, leaning in close, "I wouldn't recommend the food."

I caught her perfume, something with orange. Her eyes were emerald green. She motioned with a tip of her head, her pink streak swaying. I glanced over at the man in the corner and together we watched him awkwardly wrap a piece of undercooked bacon around his fork like spaghetti. She raised her eyebrows.

"Bourbon will do just fine," I said.

She nodded and went back to drying glasses. I liked the way she leaned against the wall as she did. All casual, like she was just counting down the hours. It also gave me a pretty good view of her figure. She was toned, her T-shirt clinging to her flat stomach, her slim upper arms. I remember a sliver of skin where her shirt rode up above her black jeans, but you know what, that might just be my memory playing tricks. It's hard to get everything straight right now. Lot of stuff rattling around up there. So maybe there wasn't any skin. Maybe she wasn't even wearing a T-shirt. Maybe she was a blonde in a blue dress and I was at a cocktail lounge, though I sure as shit hope not, 'cause that would mean I'm in more trouble than I thought. So, we'll go with the goth look for now, and we'll have her leaning against the wall on one hip like she's doing it on purpose, and make her hair dark, make it jet black and splash that pink down one side. Yeah, just like that.

"What brings you to Cooper?" she said, her eyes flicking onto mine.

"You're the second person to ask me that today."

"We don't get that many newcomers."

I took a drink and let it settle through me. "I got bored with big-city life."

"Omaha?"

"DC."

She paused her drying for a moment. "You're a long way from home."

"Not anymore." I smiled and finished my drink, nudged the glass forward for another.

There was movement to my left and the guy from the corner appeared with a bundle of notes in his hand. I clocked a snub-nosed pistol tucked down the front of his pants. A woman's gun. Dumb prick must have thought it made him look tough. I thought about asking to see his permit. Maybe show him what a real gun looked like. He dropped the notes onto the counter and let his eyes linger on the bartender before dragging them onto me. I nodded a hello but my eyes said fuck off, and he walked away, pulling on a worn coat as he left.

"What was it about Cooper in particular that attracted you?" she asked, pouring another shot. "Our delightful population?"

"Your wonderful scenery," I said, tilting the glass toward her in thanks. "Care to join me?"

"Thanks, but I'll pass." She smiled, jade eyes shimmering in the dim light. "No one comes to Cooper by choice, Officer."

That startled me a little. Hid it by finishing my drink. "I didn't even need to show you my badge."

"Like I said, we don't get many newcomers."

I leaned back and dug out my wallet. Thumbed a couple of notes. Placed them on the counter, sat my empty glass on top.

"I'm Mary," the bartender said, picking up my glass but leaving the cash.

"Thomas," I said.

"See you around, Thomas."

"See you around."

The fresh air was cold and it stung my face like I was just done shaving. My apartment wasn't much warmer. The heating rattled as it came on. Above me I could hear canned laughter, blaring commercials for used cars and divorce lawyers, and a hacking cough that went on for nearly a minute. I'd seen the old guy upstairs over the weekend. Not for the first time, I considered introducing myself, checking in on him.

Instead, I forced myself to start unpacking. Spent the rest of the evening going through boxes as fresh snow started to fall.

I wasn't sure what time it was when I came across her photo, still in its frame and tucked next to a half-empty bottle of Red Stag. I took the bottle and left the picture and drifted off to sleep soon after, my dreams fueled by images of long roads, rising water, vast plains filled with faceless men, and women with pink hair and no eyes.

Early the next morning, a hammering on my apartment door. I opened it and Joe pushed his way inside. Just about knocked my coffee out of my hand.

"Morning," I said. "Can I get you anything?"

"No time. Bob pulled a print this morning. From her belt, Tommy. From her goddamn belt. Partial thumb, computer says it's a seventy-six-point-nine percent match to Foster. Good enough for any judge. Now, we're moving fast on this, but that's the way of it. I want to be first on the scene, alright? I want to be the one to kick that pervert's door down and drag him kicking and screaming all the way to the electric chair. Hell, I want to throw the damn switch."

"Who's Foster?"

"Get in the car and I'll tell you. And don't forget that revolver."

"Expecting trouble?"

"Always, Tommy. Always."

"Give me a minute to finish getting dressed." I checked my watch; just after seven. A shower could wait. I dumped my half-drunk coffee, remembered what Joe had told me yesterday, and pulled on a pair of khakis. Grabbed my coat and fixed my tie on the way out the door.

"Kevin Foster," Joe said, pulling out his car keys. "Convicted triple murderer, recently released on appeal. Liked to scoop young girls' eyes out with a spoon, leave them in their backyards. Sound familiar?"

"Rings a bell," I said, climbing in and remembering I'd forgotten to brush my teeth.

"And they said you weren't detective material."

I tapped my temple. "Steel trap."

The Ford started up with a roar and Joe pulled away from the curb. He reached down and stuck a light on the dash. Thing lit up blue and started spinning. Joe smacked the wheel as he ran a red. I chewed on some gum and felt my Smith and Wesson lying hard against my chest, and I tried to ignore the knot that tightened painfully in my stomach.

Chapter Three

Foster owned a place on the outskirts of town. The quiet edge, where the buildings shrank away into the cornfields. Where the long, flat line was broken by the distant rise of the Pine Ridge. I wondered if Foster could see it. From his bedroom window, maybe. Standing there staring at those tree-lined canyons like it was an escape route.

Anyway, you know where he lived. You've been all over every inch of that place. And I can guess your questions before they even come, but I'm not about to tell you that this was the start of it all. Truth is, it started long before that house.

Now, I don't recall Joe knocking when we got there. I remember his boot though. He kicked in that front door like it was personal. Wood—dark, rotten—caved in without much of a fight, pieces of it flying up and settling on the white snow. I drew my gun then. My Smith and Wesson Model 36 revolver. It's important you remember that.

Together we stepped across the threshold and into the house. A front room with the curtains drawn. Slivers of streetlight through the cracks. I paused to let my eyes adjust.

"Cooper PD!" Joe shouted. "You hear me, Foster?"

I'd tracked snow into the foyer. Dirty white mush smeared across the dark carpet. I could feel flakes floating in behind me, past my face and neck and making my hairs stand on end. Cooper spreading its feelers into Foster's home.

"Come on," Joe said.

The room was bare. A couch against one wall, a small television against the other. No sign it had really been lived in; Foster couldn't have been long out of prison. We moved slowly, our guns raised. Joe clicked on a small flashlight and swept the beam forward.

"Check the other rooms," he said. "I'm going upstairs."

Back in the foyer there was a side table with a phone; the handset lying on its side, a woman's voice telling us to please hang up and try again. A mirror hung above it, smeared with so much dirt my reflection was a murky blur.

The kitchen and bathroom were empty. A half-used bar of soap by the sink; a couple of old Chinese takeout containers on the foldout table. I clicked on lights, threw open curtains. Anything to get rid of the gloom. By the time I made my way back to the foyer, a couple of minutes had passed. I paused. The woman on the phone repeated her request. Lifting the receiver, I sat it gently back in its cradle.

A sudden crash from above. Then silence.

"Joe?" I called.

Nothing.

I took the cramped stairs two at a time, squeezing my revolver tight. Followed the noise into a bedroom and Joe was standing there, his back to me. I moved closer, said his name. Saw the glint of something gold wrapped around the fingers of his right hand. Brass knuckles, and when he turned he drove them hard into my stomach.

I wasn't wrong about Joe's physique. The punch was heavy. I fell back. Landed against the wall, air escaping from my mouth in a long, slow gasp. My revolver clattered to the floor and I sank down after it. I couldn't breathe, my lungs stalled. Pain began to well up in my guts and for a brief second my vision clouded over.

When it cleared I finally spotted him. Foster. Guy was curled up against a radiator. Gaunt face, dark circles, scruffy beard. Wide eyes blinking rapidly.

Joe crouched down next to me. Slid the knuckles off and into a pocket. He reached out and I shrank back, but his hand found my shoulder and squeezed it reassuringly. He looked into my eyes. "Breathe," he said, inflating his chest to show me how. Like I'd never been sucker-punched before. "Your diaphragm's contracting. Give it a few moments to relax."

I stared at him. I couldn't do anything else. He watched me for a moment longer and then, apparently satisfied, picked up my gun. I tried to say something but it came out in a wheeze. Joe stood, turned my revolver over in his hands. Then he pointed it at Foster.

If the guy knew what was coming, he didn't show it. Didn't scream or beg for his life. Didn't try to run. He just kept on staring at me, kept on blinking. Held my gaze right up until the moment Joe pulled the trigger. Then the wall went red, and Foster's eyes rolled back until they were nothing but white.

So before we get any further, why don't we go around the room?

There's Tubby over there. Pasty white, with a sweaty forehead and a Kim Jong-un haircut. He's the notetaker. A completely redundant position given there's a recorder in the middle of the table. When he's not double-noting my words, he's tapping out a beat on his notebook with the end of his pen. Guy goes at it every chance he gets. Like some sort of compulsion. Couldn't tell you what the song is. I never cared much for music.

Sitting across from him is a bald black man. I think he introduced himself as Special Agent Comstock. Or Cocksock. Or Cumstain. Something like that. He has a notepad in front of him as well, but he only writes down the occasional word or two. He's the question-asker. He's the one who brings me back on point when I threaten to wander off-topic. He's the one who keeps having to remind me why I'm here. A series of bad choices, *he calls it.* It's so rehearsed it hurts. *A series of bad choices that put you in this chair, at this table, in this room eating that shitty turkey sandwich telling your shitty story.* Sometimes he has to remind me what I'm getting from all this, too. *Signed and sealed and on its way,* he says. *It's always on its way. It's an old trick, and I'm sure he thinks I'm dumb enough to fall for it. Only I'm keeping the final card close to my chest for the time being. Until I have it on* the table in front of me. Signed and sealed and in my goddamn hands, Cumstain.

There's a rookie kid who sits nervously on a chair outside the room. Sometimes I see his shadow moving across the glass in the door. Sometimes I wonder if he's even there. He's the one they send when they decide I've earned myself a coffee (which is usually when they decide they've earned themselves a coffee). I'm guessing he's just a local boy, drafted in to play with the big boys for a few days. Maybe in the evenings he tells them where's good to eat around here, or what local bars to avoid. Where to find the strip clubs that offer a little extra if you know where to tuck the right bill. Poor kid. This is probably the most exciting thing that's happened to him all year.

Chapter Four

It was nearly nine by the time I got back to my apartment. My stomach was badly bruised. I stood in the bathroom and stared at it in the mirror. As first weeks went, I'd had better.

At least I had time for that shower. A half-assed shave in lukewarm water and two aspirin from my glove compartment, swallowed dry as I coaxed my Impala to life. She didn't want to start and neither did I. The temperature had dropped in the night; the snow turned hard underfoot. She gave in on the third try, gurgling unhappily. I checked my cell as I scraped ice from my windshield. A missed call, the number unlisted.

I knew how she felt; by the time I got to the station I could feel it sitting high in my stomach, cresting and falling. I couldn't even make it to my desk. Hustled into the john, one arm across my chest to protect my tie as I threw up my guts into a cracked toilet with no seat. Dark eyes and a shaving rash stared back out of a dirty mirror. I rinsed my mouth with cold water, splashed some up on my face, too. The hand dryer was broken, so I dragged my palms down the sides of my coat and patted at my forehead with my tie. Took it off after and scrunched it into a pocket.

The station was old and looked it. It was the bullpen in the lobby, a chain-linked holding area for newly arrested assholes who littered the floor with crushed soda cans and food wrappers that no one bothered to clean up. It was the peeling walls and the nicotine-stained ceiling. The cracked windows. The cheap black-and-white-squared linoleum floor that made your shoes squeak.

Through the double doors and into the main office. It wasn't big; a scattering of desks, all of them covered in papers and files. A handful of cops were stood in a corner talking. I recognized a couple of them from the dead woman's yard. Greasy-faced Lloyd.

A coffee machine in the corner caught my eye. It rattled as it spat watery brown into a paper cup. I picked it up and hissed, my fingertips burning.

"Weak coffee in a cheap cup," Joe said. "Welcome to Cooper."

I turned and stared at him. He held my gaze for a moment, then pressed a button on the machine. Collected his cup with practiced ease.

"Don't worry," he said, "you'll get used to it."

"I don't want to get used to it."

"Suit yourself."

"We're going to sit down and have a conversation, you and me."

"Later," he said, taking a slurp. "Right now we need to talk to Bob down in the morgue about our new girl. You can finish your coffee on the way."

We met Captain Morricone on the narrow staircase down to the basement. It's an Italian name, right? *Morricone.* Like the guy who scored all those Westerns. But the captain didn't look it. Didn't have the thick swept-back dark hair or the tanned skin, but maybe I was stereotyping.

He looked like a science teacher. Tall and slim, wearing rimless glasses and a sweater vest. Each part of his outfit half finished. I wondered if he had a pocket watch. He smiled when he saw me, and his teeth shone in the dim light.

"Thomas." He announced my name like I was receiving an award. "At last we meet."

I actually can't remember exactly what we talked about, Joe and me and Morricone. The dead woman and the case most likely.

But if you're listening to this now, Captain, and I sure as hell hope you are, I'd just like to say you were decent to me. Back when most folks weren't. And you didn't deserve what happened and that's the truth. All this shit—all this paperwork—just dumped on your doorstep. Christ, I hope you come out of this better than I do.

Before he left though, and I remember this real clear, he gripped my shoulder and said he knew why I was in Cooper. Said he wasn't interested in any of it. Said I'd done the right thing.

No one had ever said that to me before. But if there's any decency in ratting out your fellow officers, I never found it.

Morricone said all he cared about was that I cleared my cases and kept my nose clean. "Don't think of this as a punishment," he added as he walked away, and I wanted to say, *But how can it be anything else?*

The entrance to the morgue was a doorway draped in strips of frosted plastic. Through the slivers I could see metallic grey and coldness. An abattoir. Chunks of meat hanging from hooks, white aprons splashed with red. Music drifted over from a computer, something classical.

Turned out Bob was the bald guy from yesterday's crime scene. He smiled when we entered. It was the warmest thing in the room.

The girl was waiting for us under a white sheet. Bob pulled a dangling chain and set off fluorescent bulbs that flickered and pinged above our heads. Everything went purple, and when Bob peeled back the sheet Kelly Scott's naked body was purple too. Her skin tight over skinny bones. Her lids open and her bare sockets exposed. They were larger than I remembered. I could have rolled a pool ball in there; spots or stripes, corner pocket.

Bob walked us through it. He didn't have much.

She'd been strangled. Her windpipe crushed. It happened between midnight and 6 a.m., and it happened outside. Dirt under her fingernails and booze in her blood; she'd been drinking. No drugs though, recreational or otherwise, and no sex either. Least not last night. No foreign DNA, no unexplained hair fibers. Killer had wiped her bedroom clean, right down to the book on her nightstand.

Joe said Bob was making him sound like a goddamned ghost, and Bob said goddamned ghosts don't need to climb through unlocked bathroom windows.

I stared down at that patch of pale skin on her left wrist and asked if anyone had found a watch but they hadn't.

Now, I want to pause for a moment and talk about how she died. Bob said she was strangled, and she sure had the bruises to prove it. For those that don't know much about murder let me say this. It's a difficult method, strangulation. It takes time, more than most think. It's not like in the movies, you don't accidentally strangle someone in a few confused seconds or in a moment of rage or passion. The human brain can survive without oxygen for over four minutes. That's two hundred and forty seconds of keeping that pressure tight; of holding them still; of not changing your mind. You ask me, killers who strangle are a hell of a lot more evil than some frenzied stabber or shopping-mall shooter. With them, it's more than simple intent, it's a state of mind. And it scares the hell out of me.

Joe said, "Tell me about the eyes," and Bob did. Called them a rush job. Angled a small lamp downward to show us why. Killer used something blunt, he said. Maybe a spoon. Damaged a lot of the surrounding tissue but he knew what he was doing.

I asked about the print, and Bob looked at Joe in a way that I didn't like.

"Pulled it from her belt," Bob said. "Seventy-six percent match."

"Seventy-six-point-nine," Joe said.

"When did you pull it?" I asked.

"Just before midnight."

"You always work that late?"

"We're understaffed."

"And now they've got a second body to deal with," Joe said to me.

Foster was already on ice. Bob pulled his tray from the freezer. He was even skinnier than Kelly Scott.

"Gunshot wound to the face, point-blank."

I gazed at the clean hole in his forehead. Pictured the messier one at the back. The red on the wall, his eyes rolling up white. My morning coffee slithered in my bruised stomach.

"Suicide?" Joe asked.

"'Fraid not."

"Pity."

Sure was.

Joe pointed to the bullet. Bob said it was next on his list. Said it looked like a .38.

"Or a thirty-six," Joe said.

"We'll know more when the results come back from ATF." Bob snapped off his gloves. "One more thing."

He grabbed a chart, flipped a couple of pages.

"I found evidence of advanced lymphoma," he said. "Guy's armpits were swollen to all hell."

Joe stared at him. "He was dying?"

"Maybe he fancied taking someone with him. Dying's a lonely business."

Bob sealed Foster's body away. I turned my gaze to Kelly Scott just as the lamp above her clicked off, and in that microsecond between light and dark I thought I saw her head turn on the table. I started to get the crazy idea that she'd been watching me the entire time we'd been down here. Waiting on me to put it all together. I remembered last night's dream, long roads and rising water and a sign that read *Welcome to Cooper*, and I wondered if she hadn't been waiting on me for a while now.

Chapter Five

I was halfway through my third Jim Beam when the door swung open and her scent said hello. Through the mottle I could see her; a shadow-figure with a pink edge. I emptied my glass and she was there when I put it down. The most colorful woman in the room.

"You wanna get out of here?" she asked.

"Sure," I said.

We walked the narrow alley behind the bar. Dirty brick hemmed us in on both sides. It was cold but the Jim Beam helped. Mary carried a garbage bag, and when the slender passage ended we emerged in a little pocket of green. Rubble sat along one edge, and beyond the knee-high grass there was a crooked fence, and birdsong, and the sound of running water.

Mary dropped the garbage in a can and then leaned against the wall as she took me in. For a moment it was like the first time I'd seen her, and once again I wondered if she was doing it on purpose.

"You looked like you could use some air," she said, her head tilted slightly.

I sniffed and wiped at my nose with the back of my hand. Nodded.

"You got a coat?" she asked.

"Inside," I said.

She shook her head, smiling. A pity smile. Disquiet etched in the creases of her skin. I pretended not to notice.

"What's over there?" I said.

Mary pushed herself off the wall and followed where I was pointing. "That's the river." She began to pick her way through the undergrowth and I followed. The grass brushed against our waists, and Mary held her palm out flat, letting it skim over the tips like the keel of a ship. When we reached the lopsided fence I went to lean on it and she put her hand on my arm.

"Watch yourself, it isn't in the best shape."

I said nothing, just nodded and peered down. The water was low right now, little more than a trickle, but dark streaks on the sides of the bank showed just how high it could go. Something about it was calming, and I felt myself relax. Mary took her hand back.

"Rough morning?" she said.

I looked over at her. Maybe it was written on my face. Maybe it was the fact that I was getting loaded the second night in a row. But Mary wanted to know what had happened and I guess you do too.

"It's not bad, you know," I said. "Out here."

Mary rolled her eyes. "You think?"

"Well, compared to the rest of town."

"You should take a trip out to the Pine Ridge," she said. "Hike a canyon, see a proper river. It's not far, you can just about see it from here."

"Land this flat, it's hard to miss."

"People think Nebraska is nothing but fields. There's beauty too, if you know where to look."

"Maybe I'll check it out."

"This time of year, only the pines have any color left." She smiled. "Tell you what, if you're still here in the fall, I'll show you. We time it right, the cottonwoods go orange. It's spectacular."

She closed her eyes briefly, and for a moment I lost her to the forest. When she returned she checked her watch. "Damn, I have to get back. Richard gets pissed if I don't take over on time."

I followed her back inside. My Jim Beam buzz was fading anyway.

◆　◆　◆

Let's rewind a little.

Back to this morning. Back to the house. Back to Foster. Joe's still got my revolver—a Smith and Wesson Model 36, in case you forgot. (Although I asked you not to. Take some fucking notes if this is too hard.)

I've been carrying a Model 36 since I first joined the force in DC. It wasn't that I resisted the change to something more modern—Glocks were the standard long before I started—but more of a personal choice. A childhood of Westerns and '70s cop shows probably had more to do with becoming a detective than anything else. And there's just something nice and physical about a revolver. About seeing the mechanics of it all; watching the hammer slide back as the chamber rolls. About making every shot count.

The Smith and Wesson Model 36 revolver holds five bullets. It doesn't work like a modern semiautomatic; it doesn't use magazines and it doesn't launch the spent clips out of the firing chamber when they're done. Instead, the empty cartridges remain inside the chamber until they're manually removed.

Which is what Joe did. Snapped open the barrel and emptied it into his palm. Pocketed the four unused bullets, held up the empty fifth shell casing for me to see. Held it long enough between fat finger and thumb to make sure I knew what it meant.

Leverage.

From where I was sitting now I could still see Mary. I caught her eye and held up my glass. Gave it a little shake. I'm back at Stingray's, by the way, for those that need some context for all this. It's late in the evening and I've been drinking pretty heavily by this point. It's still Tuesday.

It took me a while to catch my breath properly. You ever been slugged in the stomach? Really drilled? I had, and it hurt just as bad this time. Worse, even, on account of those damn brass knuckles.

I can still see him. Foster. Clear as day. Propped up against that radiator like it'd be uncomfortable. I can picture him now and I could picture him twice as good in that bar, just twelve hours later. Can still see that look on his face, too. Surprised, even after it was over. Guy like him, riddled with cancer, sometimes I wonder if he thought about what was waiting for him on the other side. How could he not? Sometimes I wonder if he got a glimpse, and I wonder if it wasn't what he was expecting. I wonder if it was nothing.

Mary was back now and holding up the bottle of Johnnie Walker. Said I've been hitting it pretty hard and this stuff's not cheap. I told her I'm good for it and spun the glass. She went on with her work.

"Now I'm betting you're pretty pissed at me, and that's alright." That was what Joe said to me at Foster's. "If you'd sucker-punched me in the stomach I'd be pretty pissed too."

He watched me with small eyes as he pocketed the shell casing, and my revolver along with it. His face was red, his breathing loud.

I climbed to my feet, an adrenaline buzz masking the pain in my gut. I thought about running at him. About grinding his face against the wall until his skin peeled. I squeezed my fists—a telegraphed move. Joe pulled his Glock and waved it at Foster's corpse.

"This asshole deserved what he got," he said. "He's a murderer and I won't lose any sleep over it. He's killed four women, Tommy. In cold blood."

"This is cold blood."

"This is justice," Joe said, and he sucked in air noisily through his nose. His chest swelled with self-importance. "And if you were from Cooper you'd understand that. Now, you're going to listen to what I say and you're going to do what I ask, and if you impress me enough you might get your gun and your shell casing back."

He pointed the Glock at me.

"Or we can just end this now and I can write up a report about how you busted in guns blazing, caught a bullet in the neck from Foster as he went down swinging. You might even get a medal."

"You prick."

Joe looked amused. "Easy there, partner. I hit you in the stomach so you wouldn't have to answer any questions about a black eye. You want to tussle, that's fine with me."

"Did Bob even find a fingerprint?"

"We'll take care of that later."

"Jesus, Joe, you just shot him!"

"With your gun."

"You really think anyone will believe it was me?"

"New cop, fresh in town." Joe shrugged. "They don't know you, son. Not like they know me. I'm Cooper born and bred. Who the hell are you?" He stepped closer, backed me up against the wall. I could smell his sweat. "Let's get one thing clear so we don't have any future misunderstandings. If I wanted to, I could stand up in church and shoot you dead and no one would bat an eyelid. *That's* who I am."

From outside there was the sound of sirens. Faint but growing louder.

Joe moved back. His face flushed. "Now, you've got about thirty seconds to decide how you're going to play this. You want to stick to your morals, that's up to you."

"Or?"

"Or you work for me."

"Go to hell."

Joe grinned. "You want to pretend like you're better than me? Son, I know what happened in Washington."

That hit me almost as hard as those damned knuckles.

I guess I was stupid to think I could start again here. As if I could just shrug off my past like an old coat and step away from it. Morricone had told me not to think of this place as a punishment, and maybe he was right. And maybe Joe was right too. Maybe this *was* justice. For Foster. For me.

Footsteps on the path outside, raised voices yelling our names.

"We're up here, boys!" Joe shouted, holstering his Glock but never taking his eyes off me. "Get Forensics on the phone, we've found a body!"

And so it went.

I finished my Johnnie Walker, and I looked around for Mary. Spotted her watching me from across the room. She was standing behind the bar like the first time we'd met and I wondered why she could never just stand up straight. Always leaning on something with one hip, with her ass tilted and her arms crossed. Even from here I could see those emerald eyes glinting in the dim light.

I held up my glass again. Fumbled, nearly dropped it. Started to pull cash from my pockets in case she needed convincing, all crumpled bills and loose change. She wandered over and placed two cans down on the bar. Took a stool next to me.

I looked at her, squinting through one eye because it was clearer, and when she pulled the tab on her soda it fizzed over her finger, dark and frothy. She tapped the can against mine.

"Cheers," she said.

Chapter Six

We talked for a while, although I couldn't tell you how long.

"Let me ask you something," I said.

"Alright."

"What's the deal with this place?"

"Well, it's not exactly an upmarket cocktail bar—"

"Not here. I mean Cooper."

"I know."

She was smiling. Playing with the tab of her can as she held it. "You feel it, don't you?"

"Feel what?"

"What this place really is."

I tried to sit up and the room swayed. I stayed down. Took a sip of my Pepsi and nearly choked on the fizz.

"You're lost," Mary said. In the dim light her eyes were near black, her pupils wide and all-encompassing. Like a solar eclipse. A moon with an emerald edge. "But that's alright. Everyone is when they first arrive."

"Speaking from experience?"

She blew air out the side of her mouth. "You kidding? Jesus, I was a mess. But you just get on with it, you know? You adapt. Cooper doesn't care about whatever shit was going on in your life before you got here. It'll chew you up and spit you out if you let it." She leaned in close and her perfume leaned closer. "So don't let it."

"You make this place sound . . ." I couldn't think of the right word.

"Otherworldly?" Mary said, her eyes narrowed.

I blinked. "Is it?"

She laughed. "It's just a town, Thomas. A shitty backwater that the rest of the world left behind a long, long time ago. The people that come here, they . . . they come here for a reason, you understand? They just might not realize it at first."

I raised my eyebrows. Took another drink. I must have looked funny because Mary laughed and tucked a strand of pink hair behind her ear. It wasn't a nasty laugh; I don't think I ever thought that about Mary. The opposite, in fact. There was something safe about her. The way she would sometimes half reach for me with concern, her fingers curling in before they got too far. Or the way she was always so calm, when it seemed that all around her were walking balls of rage just waiting to lash out.

Course, even Mary got angry. I once saw her nearly throw a guy out on his ass for slapping the old jukebox with his palm to stop it skipping. I found that amusing. Of all the things to get riled up about in this town, music was the thing that did it. I meant to ask her about that jukebox, but I never did. Guess now I never will.

"What did you do?" I asked her. "Before coming to Cooper, I mean."

Mary's smile faltered for a moment, and when it came back it seemed forced. "Is it important?" she said.

"Guess not."

"What we did before doesn't matter," she said. "Only what we do now."

Then she went quiet, drained her soda, and got to her feet. I felt a pang of dismay but didn't say anything to stop her.

"Pepsi's on the house," she said, smoothing out her apron with the palms of her hands. "'Fraid you'll need to pay for the Scotch, though."

It was a poor attempt to recapture the mood, but I half smiled just the same.

Then she said, "We've all done things we're not proud of, Thomas. That's why we're here."

She was right, of course, only I was too ashamed to tell her then. Too wrapped up in my own head to see the bigger picture. Besides, it was getting late. All this talk causing the past to resurface in me, and I wasn't sure I was ready for that. I dropped a bundle of cash onto the bar and pulled on my coat. Caught Mary's gaze and nodded goodbye before stumbling out into the cold Nebraska night.

Time passes.

My ass is killing me.

It's the chair, I'm pretty sure. Thing feels like it was bought in the '80s; must have about a millimeter of padding on it. I can't help but notice that Tubby seems to have cornered the only leather seat in the room for himself.

The clock on the wall says it's past six o'clock, which means for these boys it's quittin' time. Pack up the day's learnings and forget about it all for a few hours of rowdy, good old-fashioned Nebraskan nighttime fun before getting up at seven and putting on your somber face.

I wonder what the plan is for this evening. Whether Rookie has recommended somewhere nice. These guys, I reckon they'll be getting some attention. You don't make an arrest in a case like this without getting plenty. Waitresses flashing them the eye, lingering glances and phone numbers scribbled on napkins. Hoping to get their hotel room number because they sure as shit can't bring a man back to their mom's. Cumstain is already loosening his tie. Bottle of mouthwash and some Paco Rabanne in the car. You play your cards right, Tubby, and you might even get his leftovers.

Once they've left, Rookie comes in and I hold out my arms obligingly so he can handcuff them together. I'm led out into the hallway and down to the end of the corridor where I get to sit on another cheap plastic seat for a few minutes while he fills out some paperwork over at the front desk. Beyond that I can see through the glazed main doors and out onto the parking lot and, behind that, Main Street. It's not far to the Pine Ridge from here. I wonder how easy it would be to lose them in there. To let myself get swallowed up in the dense undergrowth. Course I'd need a car to reach the woods. And I've still got my hand-cuffs. But it's a start.

Rookie is talking to the girl at the front desk. She's pretty cute. Blonde hair tied up in pigtails and a few too many teeth for her mouth, but she's got a nice smile and she sure likes using it on Rookie. Christ, I bet that kid still hasn't even started on that paperwork yet. He's got his back to me, too.

Cumstain and Tubby emerge from the guys' restroom—probably been sucking each other's dicks—and the two of them push open the glass doors and walk outside. I hear one of them laugh and then cool air washes over me and I nearly buckle, nearly start running there and then.

Rookie takes me down another corridor and through some double doors. We pass a few cops on the way but it's quiet in here. Down a set of stairs and to a row of cells. All empty, 'cept for mine. The bars roll smoothly on their tracks until the lock kicks in, then I stick my hands through so Rookie can uncuff me.

He keeps his keys on a small metal chain on his belt, on his right side.

Chapter Seven

I didn't realize I'd fallen asleep until I woke up. Sprawled across my bed, still wearing my shirt and khakis. I couldn't even remember getting home. My clock read 5:26. A half-empty bottle of Gentleman Jack on my nightstand told me I'd been out for a while. I sat up and looked out the window and it was dark, and for that brief moment between dreaming and living I felt like everything might turn out alright.

I rolled my legs free of the tangle of sheets. Her photo was lying face down on the floor.

Rachel.

I bent to collect it; my stomach rolling. She smiled at me from a warm summer's evening. A little crumpled around the edges but nothing too bad. I smoothed her out as best I could. Went to sit her next to the bottle, found my backup pistol there already. A Taurus 850 snub-nosed revolver. Fully loaded and with the safety off. I flicked it on and stuffed it into my pocket. Rested the photo in its place.

Rachel never liked guns, never liked the idea of me carrying one, of me bringing it into our home. A point of view that couldn't have been further from my own. I didn't worship them or anything like that, I wasn't some sort of MP5-loving freak. Didn't go to gun shops on my weekends and ask to hold a Magnum. I respected guns, though that was as far as I'd take it; when you carry one every day it'd be foolish to do otherwise.

So anyway, Rachel didn't like guns. Which was fine, didn't matter to me either way. She understood it, of course. Understood that I had to have one, had to wear it when I was working, keep it somewhere safe when I wasn't. That was our agreement. Wear it when you're working, somewhere safe when you're not. What did I need a handgun for when I was sitting down to dinner?

They always showed it like that in the movies, though. The detective getting in from a long shift and dangling his holster off the back of a kitchen chair. Like he's just hanging up his coat. And no doubt some do that. We preferred to use a safe. Rachel used to say the only thing worse than me using a gun was someone breaking into our apartment and using it on us.

A switchblade, however, that was okay with her. I never really got it myself, but there was some sort of distinction in Rachel's mind. She bought it for me our first Christmas together, not long after I'd started working the late shift in some of the more disreputable parts of the city. Anacostia wasn't exactly DC at its finest. She told me she wanted to feel like she was helping protect me. I guess it was sweet.

Okay.

Where were we?

Oh right, the morning after my bender in Stingray's. The Wednesday.

I yawned, stretched my back out. Stood and slid my knife into my other pocket. Three years old and the most it had ever been used for was slicing the occasional apple, and that was fine with me. It had been so long now it was just another thing I carried. Keys, wallet, switchblade. I doubted it'd ever get used.

From somewhere in the sheets my cell buzzed. A message from Joe.

I'm outside.

I pulled out my Taurus again and spun it around in cool hands that didn't shake as much as I thought they would. I flicked the safety off and on, off and on, strode to the window where I saw an unfamiliar car parked across the street—running lights only, thing thrumming like a stealth sub—and pointed the revolver at it. I still remember the clink as the barrel touched glass. The room was dark so I knew he couldn't see me, and if I'd thought I could actually hit him from there I might've done it.

I wasn't thinking so clearly back then, you see. Not that I'm necessarily thinking any more clearly now, of course. I did always have a violent streak in me, but I was the sharing type and I reckon I thought about dishing out the same to myself, too. Sliding back that hammer and sticking the barrel in my mouth. A desperate idea turned good by lack of reason not to.

But giving up wasn't exactly my style. I might've been self-destructive, sure, but I was also a hypocrite. Besides, a bullet was too direct. I preferred the bottle.

My cell buzzed again. *We need to talk.*

I looked over at Rachel. The clock said 5:31. I could still smell orange, like lipstick on my collar. I'd wanted a reason to keep on moving forward, and maybe that was reason enough.

Now for this next part to make any sense, I'm going to have to give you some backstory. Joe said he knew what happened in Washington, and I guess you do too. Or at least you think you do. The highlights, maybe. And great, you've got a file, whatever. That isn't everything. That isn't *me*.

Like I said earlier, I worked Homicide back in DC. In a southeast part of the city called Anacostia. Crime rates were high;

39

someone once told me that nearly half the murders in the capital happened in this neighborhood, and I didn't disagree. Drive-bys, child prostitution, junkies cooking their babies in microwaves and stabbing each other for dimes. It was our beat. Me and Isaac, my partner. The dark corners, the real places where people went to die. That was our jurisdiction, what me and Isaac lived and breathed and absorbed through our pores every damned day.

And the stuff we'd find at these crime scenes. Bottles of pills, bags of coke. Heroin. Needles and half-melted spoons and rubber tubing. All of it just lying around for anyone to take.

And so that's what we did. We'd go through these places, these junkies' dens. Before Forensics arrived we'd comb it for drugs, leave with our pockets bulging. Nothing serious, just pills and weed, mostly. I had no interest in the hard stuff at that point. Guess I thought that made me smart. Whatever we found we split, and whatever I ended up with I'd split again with Rachel when I got home.

Course, like any other dumb idea, it grew. I found out Isaac wasn't keeping the stuff for himself—not all of it anyway. And before you call me a phony, I don't mean he was sharing it with his girl, like I was. I mean he was selling it. Was selling it to other *cops*.

When I found out, I flipped. I don't know what scared me more, Isaac selling to some IA asshole and naming me to save himself, or just losing my easy access to dope, but I went crazy. I thought I was going to have to beat him half to death to make him see sense.

Only it didn't quite work out like that. Turned out maybe I was a phony after all, because he persuaded me to get on board and I don't think I took all that much convincing. I reckon all it took was a whiff of the cash Isaac had made and I was only too happy to make the leap from dumbass to dealer.

I don't really want to get too bogged down in all this. I'm sure you can work out what happened next. Pills and weed became cocaine and heroin. Became beating down doors to shake down junkies. Became pointing my gun in their faces or blowing a hole in their sofa to make a point. It got so I wasn't even in it for the money or the drugs anymore. I was in it for the rush. One time I cut up a guy so bad, Isaac made me burn my clothes to get rid of the blood.

But in the end it was the pills that did it. I think I can still remember the exact bag. They'd been wedged under a dirty mattress that belonged to a woman who had just murdered her partner in the room next door. Some domestic dispute, I don't remember the details. She'd killed him with a yellow spoon. Jammed it in his throat as he slept. Funny, the things that stick in your mind.

It happened about a week after that. I'd kept the bag for myself. Me and Rachel had been planning on sharing some that night. Just popping a couple each and drifting off for a few hours together. Only I was late getting home, and she must have decided to run herself a bath. Maybe she thought she'd hold off on the pills until I came home. So I was God knows where and she's running this bath, and finally she decided she couldn't wait anymore and she got in and took the pills and she drowned. The water was still warm when I found her.

I tried to keep it quiet—where she'd gotten the pills from, I mean—but I couldn't. I told my captain, told him about everything. About the drugs, about the dealing, about Isaac. I turned on Isaac like *that*. Wore a wire for IA and got him to admit to all sorts of shit, handed him over without a second thought. Like he didn't mean nothing. And I was the one worried he'd name *me*.

Worst part was, I didn't even feel bad about it.

Hypocrite, remember?

I should have been fired—I should have gone to prison. IA gave me a couple of options instead. Get out of DC or find a new line of work. No cop wanted to work with a rat. My old captain knew Morricone from the academy, and for whatever reason Morricone liked the sound of me. Maybe he pictured me like Serpico. Cleaning up the station from the inside. Whatever. Guy offered me a ticket out from under all that shit and I practically bit his hand off to take it. I'm sure everyone back in DC was only too happy to see me go.

So keep all that in mind when I tell you what happened next. Remember that streak of self-preservation, and listen when I tell you that it never went away. If anything it only festered, and grew rank. And maybe don't be too surprised with the choice I made, or too disappointed with how easily I chose it.

Believe me, I'm not worth it.

Chapter Eight

She came to life as I approached. A meaty roar and the dazzle of headlights. I pulled my coat around me and felt the reassuring presence of the Taurus against my side. Joe watched me cross the hood from behind a darkened windshield, and when I put my hand on the door I checked the back windows to make sure we were alone.

He barely looked at me when I climbed in. There was a duffel bag in the footwell I had to straddle, and it clattered as we pulled away from the sidewalk. I belted up.

We drove in silence because I didn't want to be the first one to speak. Joe was listening to a cassette, and some woman sang about beers and heartache while the tape player warped her voice like she was melting. I wanted to tell him to turn it off but I kept my mouth shut.

We were headed out of Cooper, riding that single highway through the cornfields. Harvest time long over. Fields of bare stalks, most of them twisted and broken. Bent ends that fluttered in the breeze. I wondered what this place was like in the fall, when the tufts grew high above your head.

This early, the traffic was sparse. Our only companions the hazy lights of an occasional tractor, drifting through the fields alongside us for a short while.

Eventually Joe looked over at me. I could feel his eyes, like a physical pressure. He shook out a cigarette and lit up, not bothering to ask if I wanted one this time. The click of his silver lighter, a flickering glow, then a long and measured sigh and I could smell tobacco in the air.

"Here's the deal, son," Joe said. I wished he'd stop calling me that. "Bob and the boys back at the station fished your brain-coated bullet out of some drywall late last night." He took another drag. "While you were getting good and loaded, by the look of you."

"How long until it's *my* door getting kicked in?"

"Well now, that's where you're lucky. Cooper doesn't have a ballistics unit, see? That buys you some time. Not much though. At six a.m.—that's twenty-four minutes from now—that bullet is leaving Cooper in the back of a police transport headed north. To the Bureau of Alcohol, Tobacco, Firearms and Explosives down in Omaha. Once it gets there, that bullet is on record. You understand what that means?"

"Means all you have to do is hand over my revolver and I'm finished."

"That's right."

I suddenly had the crazy idea of jumping him. Did he have my Smith and Wesson on him now? If I could get it off him, I might be able to turn things around.

"Pull over," I said. "I need to piss."

"Not here."

"I've been drinking, Joe. I've been drinking all night and most of the day before, too. I'll piss my pants all over your nice seats if you don't."

"You piss your pants, I'll shoot you in the fucking head. We're stopping soon, keep it in till then."

I paused. "Where we going?"

"To kill two birds with one stone."

"What?"

"Open the bag, Thomas."

I glanced down at the black gym bag by my feet. "What's in it?"

"Christ, just open the goddamn bag."

I reached down and unzipped the duffel bag. A pair of clown masks grinned back at me; comical red lips and crisscross blue eyes. Two sawed-off shotguns were stacked beneath them.

Joe swung the car off the main road onto a curving single-lane track.

I rolled back in my seat, disbelief sapping my strength. "What are you planning to do with these? And whose car is this, anyway?"

"Doesn't matter whose car it is."

Joe slowed us to a gentle halt maybe fifty yards off the highway. He killed the engine, the car rattling into silence. I stared forward through the windshield.

Ahead of us was a body of water. Hard to see in the gloom, a thin shimmer of moonlight across its surface. With the heating off, the car quickly began to cool. I shivered.

"Where are we?" I asked.

"Cowan Reservoir. It's nicer in the summer."

"Joe . . ."

"Five hundred thousand dollars," Joe said, his eyes trained on the snowy highway alongside us. "Cartel drug money seized during a raid last month. It's being moved right now to lockup at ATF."

"The cartel bothers with *Cooper*?"

"No, the cartel bothers with *Omaha*. We just handle their product."

"Not very well, by the sound of it."

"Don't start that, Tommy. You don't have any idea what goes on around here."

"Dirty cops moving dirty money. I think I get the gist."

Joe turned and stared at me. He leaned forward, his bulky frame filling the dark car. "Son, you don't know what the hell you're talking about. You're not in the big city anymore. We're on the edge out here, you understand me? Sure, it's dirty money. And the man it belongs to is coming to town. He wants his money back. We get that done and we're squared away. But trust me, he isn't someone you want to piss off."

I looked out at the water. "You need my help to hit the van. You get your money, I get my bullet. That why you shot Foster?"

"Foster murdered that woman. He had it coming."

"Maybe I just let this guy whose money you lost roll into town, let him take it up with you. Maybe he solves my problem for me."

Joe turned back to the highway. "Trust me, he won't."

We sat there in silence for another couple of minutes. Then Joe said, "You help me snatch it, you can keep five percent."

"What?"

"You know how much five percent of half a million dollars is?"

"Twenty-five."

"It's twenty-five with a bullet, Tommy. So what's it gonna be? You want to make some money or you want to go to prison? Make up your mind, but do it fast. That van is due any minute now."

I glared at him. My mind racing through it all. I thought about pulling my Taurus. Handcuffing the bastard to the steering wheel and calling it in. I thought about the bullet, rattling around in its little case. And yeah, I thought about the money, too.

You know what's coming next. I told you already, I'm a selfish asshole. For me, it was never even a choice.

"When do I get paid?"

"Soon as we're done."

"You hold out on me, you try to play me, you pull a gun on me, I'll arrest you. You understand?"

Joe glanced at me with a smile on his face that screamed mistake. "Good boy," he said, and jerked his head back. "There's body armor in the trunk. I suggest you strap some on."

Chapter Nine

My mother used to say there's positives in everything. You just need to know where to look.

So I flipped down the sun visor and tried the vanity mirror and a laughing clown looked back. Cheap rubber, sealing my face in a grinning cocoon. My scalp tingled with beads of sweat and the sawed-off felt heavy in my hands. I'd thought they might tremble, but they didn't.

When Joe started the engine I thought of Mary. As we rolled back toward the highway with our headlights off I saw the sadness beyond the surface of her green eyes and I remembered what she'd told me. *What we did before doesn't matter*, she'd said. *Only what we do now.*

We slipped behind the police van, riding in its wake. There was a positive here, I just had to find it. Maybe it had already passed. Maybe it was standing on a riverbank and drinking a can of Pepsi. I could still feel her hand on my arm and then too soon the engine was roaring as Joe flicked on his high beams. I pictured the cops up front squinting. Too distracted to notice the spike strip up ahead.

As Joe pressed down on the gas pedal I sucked in air hard through the open mouth of the mask. I couldn't seem to catch my breath under this thing, the tight rubber making me sweat, so hot I thought I might pass out. My hands were trembling now and I grabbed at the door panel as the van's front and then rear tires blew with a sound like two rounds of gunshots.

The van swerved in the snow, the driver overcorrecting. With a slow, sickening lurch it slid sideways. Then the nose swung forward again and it left the highway. Came to a sudden halt facedown in the ditch. Ass in the air, back wheels spinning.

Joe brought us to a skidding halt by the side of the road. We jumped out into the snow, my hard breathing visible in the cold air. By the time we got down there, the driver's door was open. Guy was on the ground and climbing to his feet. Clutching the van's wheel for support. His face was bleeding badly and I saw his eyes go wide as we approached. He reached for his weapon but I'd already closed in on him and I didn't even think, I just swung the butt of my shotgun into his face. His head recoiled violently; I tasted blood in my mouth and it wasn't mine. The officer slumped to the snow and stayed there. When I turned I saw Joe watching me silently.

The other cop was bent over the dashboard. He wasn't moving and the windshield was red.

What you did before doesn't matter. Only what you do now.

Two large, black gym bags were in the back of the van, and when I unzipped them I found stacks of hundred-dollar bills. I felt bile rise in my throat and knew that if I was sick I'd choke to death in this mask. We dragged the bags out and went through what was left. My Smith and Wesson bullet was boxed up, tossed around in the crash. I tore it open and pocketed the evidence, and then Joe was shouting at me and his hand was on my shoulder.

"We need to go!" he yelled.

So we gathered up the money, one bag each. I heard Joe grunting with the effort but I barely felt it. The officer I'd smacked was stirring as we passed him, and Joe put the bag down for a moment to kick him hard in the stomach.

Chapter Ten

We burned the car in a disused quarry on the outskirts of town. I stood at the edge and watched Joe douse it in gasoline. Inside were the masks and the shotguns. The bullet, too. All of it set ablaze in the falling snow. Even standing thirty yards back, I could feel the heat. Joe stood next to me and we watched it in silence, and when I turned to look at him he had fire in his eyes.

"My gun," I said, holding out my hand. "Shell casing, too."

Joe took a while to respond. Like he was mesmerized by the flames. Eventually he saw me, his face blank and unreadable. Dumbly, he reached into his pocket and pulled out my revolver. Passed it over along with the shell casing. The latter I tossed onto the fire.

"I'm taking my cut," I said, and I did. Counted out five bundles and stuffed them inside my coat. Joe didn't say anything the entire time but I knew he was watching.

I didn't sleep well that night. I think maybe it had been a while since I had.

When I got back it was still early. My entire body seemed to ache with the weight of the last few days. I ran the tub until it was nearly overflowing. Climbed in with a low moan, my muscles tight. The water was warm and when I sank below the surface it sloshed over the sides. I kept my eyes closed for as long as I could bear it; until I thought I felt her hand on my leg. Thin and light, like a child's. Rachel had always hated her tiny hands. Too small to take a selfie without causing the camera to shake. We used to laugh about that.

I'm kind of torn on the whole Rachel thing. How much of her I should tell you. How much I should keep for myself. Is she important to the story? Sure. Do you have to know everything about her? Every little detail? Honestly, who the hell knows.

I guess I already told you how she died. Might as well tell you how she lived.

Rachel was a brunette. Her hair short and choppy. She had her nose pierced; a ring. I didn't like it. We met at a party, some friend of a friend. It was late July and she was wearing a summer dress.

I'm not great at parties. It's not that I'm shy, I don't stand in the corner all night nursing a beer. I just can't be bothered. I'm a bar-and-a-quiet-booth kind of guy. Give me a tiny apartment crammed full of people I don't know and I'll be looking for the earliest opportunity to go home.

At some point I'd decided I'd had enough. Too early to leave, I pushed my way through the crowd of strangers and into the small, deserted backyard. Out here it was warm. A sticky sort of heat. I stood and listened to the muted sounds of the party. I dug around for the joint in my jacket pocket and lit up.

A rustle from behind me. I turned to see her stumbling out from a large bush. She was smoothing her dress down and awkwardly stopped when she saw me staring.

"Hi," she said. "Sorry. I was just taking a piss."

I jerked my thumb toward the house. "There something wrong with the bathroom?"

50

"Yeah, the line. Seriously, it was that or the kitchen sink."

I shrugged. Turned back to the house. She ambled up beside me.

"You know, that thing was practically dying anyway."

I glanced down at her. She was short. Even in heels, she only reached my chin. "What?"

"The cherry laurel. That bush back there? Your friend clearly needs to water his garden more. My piss probably just saved its life."

"He's not my friend."

"Interesting that's the part you have a problem with."

"I'm just saying. I barely know the guy."

She snorted and pointed to my joint. "May I?"

"Sure. You wash your hands first."

"You think I pissed over my hands?"

"I dunno. Maybe. I just don't want to put this back in my mouth if it's covered in your . . . you know."

"My piss?"

"Your whatever. Wash your hands and come back and I'll share."

She glared at me. "I'll go wash my hands, but only because I need to get myself another beer, alright?"

She marched off. I smiled and shook my head. When she returned she held her hands out for inspection, her eyebrows raised. I looked them over and nodded approvingly. They were damp, at least.

"Here you go," I said, and handed over the joint.

"Thanks," she said. "I'm Rachel, by the way."

"Thomas."

"What's the matter?"

"Huh?"

Rachel blew smoke out slow. Handed me back my joint. "How come you're standing out here by yourself?" She narrowed her eyes. "You just like to spy on women pissing?"

I laughed. "I didn't know you were out here, believe me."

"Uh-huh."

"I just needed some fresh air."

"You're not a party guy?"

I shook my head. "Not really. Music's too loud."

"Not enough Sinatra for you?"

"Yeah, yeah. What about you?"

"What about me?"

"You a party girl?"

I passed her back the joint and she took it with a grin. "Sure," she said. "I'm a party girl."

We stayed there for a while, stretched out across the grass. Talking the sort of shit I'd be embarrassed to hear back now. Slow smiles, her fingers on mine each time we passed the joint. The rust sky had gone dark by the time we finished. I'd never tried to make a smoke last so long.

At one point Rachel drew her hair up in one hand and rolled a cool bottle of beer against the back of her neck, and I swear it was just about the sexiest thing I'd ever seen.

At the end of the night we parted. She gave me her number but for whatever reason I never called. Maybe I lost it. I don't really remember. Anyway, a month went by and our paths crossed again in a nightclub. I was in better form—a couple of pills had seen to that. Murky memories of strobe lighting, of packed bodies, of sweat. The music was loud, a bass line that made my teeth shiver. We stood by the bar and shouted in each other's ears. Snatches of her sentences; her lips brushing against my cheek. After a while she smiled and shook her head, took my hand and led me outside. We took a cab back to her apartment. She had some coke in her purse and we shared it on the way. *Now we're equal*, she told me.

At first it was easy. I guess the beginning of a relationship always is. Later—when everything had well and truly turned to shit—I would return to these moments. The lazy morning; the unexpected laugh; the warm embrace. I'd fantasize about them. And I'd wonder about other couples, if it was different for them, if their beginning lasted longer, if they were somehow able to stretch it out. Or if they'd just worked harder at finding their way back when they got lost. I wondered if we would be able to find our way back.

But all that came later.

Rachel worked in a small bookstore. A little independent place down by the river. Stairs off the main street, a basement shop. She took me there once.

"How great is this?" she asked me.

"It's quiet," I said. She gave me a shrug.

It was quaint and badly lit. Shelves stacked haphazardly. Cramped spaces and a musky smell. An actual bell that rang when you pushed open the door. Rachel showed me her desk near the entrance. She was so proud of it.

"I like it," I said afterward. "It's got character."

"Ex*actly*," Rachel said.

But I guess people didn't want character. They didn't want to have to hunt for a book in a dim store, or spend time leafing through hardback classics they'd never heard of. They were looking for internet orders and coffee stands, DVDs and board games. People didn't want a bookstore to just sell books anymore.

The store closed up about four months later. Rachel wasn't prepared, even though the signs had been there for a while. The writing on the wall. Kind of ironic for a bookstore, right?

Rachel was obviously pretty upset. I made the mistake of telling her Barnes and Noble was hiring.

"I don't want to work at Barnes and Noble," she told me. Tearful by this point.

"Then where do you want to work?"

But she didn't know. And no job meant no pay, which meant no rent. She lost her apartment and ended up moving in with me.

And it was a lot of pressure. We'd only been dating a short while. I didn't mind it, not at first. At first it was nice. It was easy, too. No more having to arrange dates to spend time with her, no more having to make our outings special. We saw each other all the time now. I guess we figured we didn't need to try.

By the time Rachel got a job (working the desk at the Georgetown Public Library), the question of her moving back into her own place just never came up.

We were together a few years in that apartment. It was small and cramped, in a rough part of the city. Rachel was home a lot by herself. Alone at night, when I was working.

"I don't like being here by myself," she told me. "The things I hear at night . . ."

I knew the things she was talking about. Gunshots, mainly. The sharp crack echoing around the courtyard. Police sirens, wailing and wopping. High-pitched screams, women's screams. I don't know if she'd always felt like this or if me being a cop made it worse for her. I never bothered to ask. Regardless, it made her nervous. It made us fight.

We'd fight about her job, about my working patterns. She'd see blood on my shirt. Bruising across my knuckles. I never told her what went on. What me and Isaac did. Was I ashamed? Maybe. But I brought home the stuff she liked and that counted for a lot. Weed, pills, booze. What was it she'd told me? *I'm a party girl.*

So we'd argue and then we'd self-medicate and drift off to sleep. Wake up in the morning and move on like the fight never happened. No resolutions to anything. Our lives were like the first episode of a two-parter. Like when Picard got turned into a Borg on *Star Trek*. We just never bothered trying to turn him back.

She wasn't happy. I got that. But I wasn't happy either. Truth was I wasn't always working late. Often I would finish a shift and not want to come home. I'd spend a few hours in my squad car or at a bar. A selfishness I paid for, believe me.

You know what happened next. You've already got my confession. Her eyes open and the water cool. There was nothing I could have done.

And yeah, sometimes I climb into baths to see how long I can hold my breath before I have to break the surface. It's stupid, I know, but there it is. Sometimes, if I've had enough to drink before I do it, I feel her in there with me, under the water. I swear once I even saw her.

Only this time, in Cooper, after what Joe and I did, when I opened my eyes she wasn't waiting for me, she wasn't there with her sad smile and her pale skin. When I finally emerged, gasping for air, I was alone.

It's a long walk from my cell to the room where I tell my story. And I walk it every day now. Me and Rookie. There and back, nice and regular.

At first I kept quiet, but then I got bored. Besides, I got more than one story to tell. I got history of my own. And Rookie seems like a nice kid. Figure he's more deserving than the others.

So one day I started talking, and Rookie just hushed up and listened.

I was born in a prison hospital in Burlington, Vermont, to a woman serving time for murdering her rapist boyfriend. Some opener, I know.

My mother was raped in the front passenger seat of a silver Buick by a man named Robert. It was October fifth in Burlington, and they'd just been to see Clint Eastwood in Two Mules for Sister Sara *at the Strong Theater on Winooski Avenue, and then for dinner at the York Steak House in the Burlington Mall (the film had apparently been excellent, the food decidedly less so).*

They hadn't been going out long, my mother and Robert. A couple weeks, maybe a month. My mother's name is Sandra, by the way. She was found the next morning by her *mother (a great hulking beast of a woman whom I never had the pleasure of meeting) lying in a crumpled heap by the front door. I often wondered about her journey home that night. Cab, probably. Did he see her shuddering and heaving in the back seat? Maybe his mind was more concerned with his newly polished leather seats and whether or not this drunk bitch was going to puke all over them. Maybe that's why he didn't bother making sure she got inside.*

Anyway, we all know where this is going. Mom got raped, Mom got pregnant, Mom went out and bought herself a handgun and blew Robert's brains so far up the wall of his apartment building the cleaners would need a crane to get it all off.

She'd bought the gun from a shop on the corner of Bradley and Hungerford (God bless Vermont's unconditional love of the Second Amendment) and had traveled halfway across town to wait three hours in a playground for Robert to finish work. It was the three hours that got her in the end. Turns out the courts don't like killers waiting that long. Implies premeditation. Plus, you know, they weren't wild about the whole 'hanging out in a playground with a loaded weapon' bit.

Most of this stuff I got from the court records. It's all there, packed in boxes in basements. Files of papers, all held together with staples and elastic bands. I'm sure nowadays they've got it all stored on hard drives and USB sticks. Everything saved up there in the cloud. You ever wonder why they called it that? The cloud. I never really gave it much thought before. Back when my mom shot my dad, clouds meant rain.

I wasn't sure if they'd let me see it. I was a teenager at this point. Nineteen and skinny as all hell. Slicked-back hair and dressed in my best suit, which believe me didn't mean much. But it turns out anyone can read this stuff if they want to. Public records, the lady at the desk told me. How about that? The story of my conception available for everyone to enjoy. I felt a bit like Jesus when I found that out.

I'd rented a motel room next to the courthouse, and I spent two days reading through everything. After I was done, I saw her in a whole new light. My mom. She wasn't some weak-willed object that got used and abused. She was bad-ass. I remember reading and rereading some of the transcripts and she gave as good as she got. Gave it back better. Now, like I said, it was the playground that got her in the end, and the judge sure did make a show about that. Droning on about the children on the swings, about their mothers sitting on benches watching. The innocents, *he kept calling them. Asked her what would have happened if something had gone wrong. Talked about the blood and the gore and how people didn't need to see that sort of thing at four o'clock on a Tuesday afternoon. At the end, when he was passing her sentence, he asked her if she had anything to say, and she said sure, she had something to say.*

And the transcripts—they're good up to a point. They get the words all right, and they're typed up nice and neat, but they don't get the emotion of it all. You understand me? I read those words over and over and I imagined my mom standing there in that court, her voice steady or maybe just cracking a little. I imagined the quiet of the place, the reporters hanging on her every word. The still air in the room near stifling on a warm June day. I imagined her telling the judge exactly why she'd done what she'd done, how Robert had been sweet on her at first—flowers and chocolates and holding the door open for her and all that stuff. Hell, he'd even met her mother for afternoon tea, which had gotten her mother's stamp of approval, and that might not mean a lot to the judge, but it meant a lot to her. She'd never been with anyone else but Robert, and now her first time was probably going to be her last, unless more men like him existed (which they surely did) and they happened to work at the Chittenden Regional Correctional Facility (which she couldn't pass any comment on, but she wouldn't be surprised given the state of the American justice system). She said she was sorry if she'd ruined anyone's day by shooting Robert in the head but she wasn't sorry she'd done it. Said she'd do it again if she had to. Said he might have been her first but she doubted she was his. It was a public service, she said. And if it made all the other Roberts out there think twice, then that was enough for her.

I often wondered if he knew. Just before she pulled the trigger. If he turned to face her, even a little. Or if he was completely oblivious, if his last thought was what to have for dinner, or whether the new Planet of the Apes *movie looked any good, or maybe who he should rape next.*

Apparently his right eye popped clean when it happened. Made an all-or-nothing leap to safety across the sidewalk.

Chapter Eleven

I woke on Thursday morning to the sound of my cell, buzzing on my nightstand. I fumbled for it. Knocked over something that clinked on its way down. Tried to read the screen but my eyes wouldn't focus.

"Hello?"

Silence. Then, "Mr. Levine, did I wake you?"

It was a woman.

"No," I said, rolling onto my back.

The room was cold. The cool morning air tainted with the musk of sweat and the stink of bourbon. I cleared my throat, kicked off the sheets and tried to ignore the beads on my forehead. Maybe I was coming down with something. What time was it?

"Mr. Levine, my name is Debra Mansfield. I'm a State Patrol detective out of Omaha. I was wondering if we could arrange a time to meet." Her voice was professional.

"What?"

"I assure you, it's nothing to be concerned about. Is now a bad time?"

"To meet?"

"I'd like the opportunity to introduce myself properly."

"Whatever you're after, I'm not interested."

"Perhaps I could offer you a ride to work? We could discuss my proposal on the way."

"Listen—"

"I'm parked outside."

"Now hold on. What time is it?"

"Just after eight forty-five."

"Shit," I said, and ended the call.

I got ready fast. Nine minutes, shower included; a new personal best. Stumbled out into an exceptionally bright morning. Even the snow was glaring at me.

I spotted her parked on the other side of the street. Next to a dented lamppost and behind the piece-of-shit pickup that had probably dented it.

A black sedan.

I watched it as I walked to my car. Noted the glossy black paint job and tinted windows and tried to picture Detective Debra Mansfield from Omaha staring back. The thing couldn't have looked more out of place.

When I reached my Impala I heard from behind me the soft click of an expensive door. From across the roof I saw a suited woman clambering out, smile already in place like she'd started it early. She was short, with big shoulders and a little pig face framed by curly black hair. A pair of oversized sunglasses on an upturned nose.

Now Debra, I'm sure they'll give you a copy of this tape, so let me add that I did feel a little mean for thinking this, but only a little. You'd caught me on a bad morning.

"Mr. Levine," she called as she strode awkwardly across the snow-covered street. Her thick heels made deep imprints in the white, and I wondered how much shorter she'd be without them. I popped open my door.

"Don't have the time," I said.

"Running late?"

I grunted and climbed in. Slammed the door and turned the key. The car gave a shudder but refused to start. "Come on," I muttered, holding the key down until I thought I might blow something.

There was a short rap on the passenger window and her face loomed large.

"Engine trouble?" she said loudly, crinkling her pig nose. "I can give you a ride to the station."

I scowled at her. Squeezed the steering wheel. Finally let the key go.

"You giving me a ride home too?"

The woman smiled.

Chapter Twelve

The sedan was a palace. Leather seats, the heated kind. I stretched my legs as we pulled away and glided down the empty street.

After some time had passed I turned and stared at her. She gave me a side-glance but kept quiet.

"What did you say your name was?"

"Debra. Debra Mansfield."

"And you're a detective?"

"From Omaha, that's right."

"Long way for a conversation," I said. "You could have just called."

She turned onto the main street. The only other car in sight was an SUV, dirty red. It coughed and shook as it passed, and I watched mistrustful eyes track us from behind a grubby windshield. I was suddenly thankful for the tinted windows.

Mansfield said, "What I need to discuss, it's better in person."

I grunted and rubbed at my face. Despite the shower, my skin felt hot and grimy.

"How do I turn this off?" I asked.

"Turn what off?"

"This . . . seat."

She pushed a rocker on the dash. Her finger was small and stumpy, her nail neatly cut. I opened the window and cold air washed over me.

"Better?"

"Much," I said, my eyes closed.

For a few moments we were quiet, and I felt myself relax into it.

"How are you finding Cooper so far?" she asked.

I snorted.

"I just checked in this morning," she said. "They had to move me to a different room when they realized it didn't have any running water."

"Sounds about right."

I was starting to gather myself. The cold breeze was helping. I peered at Mansfield through a slitted eye. Ran my gaze over her expensive ride.

"You work Homicide up there in Omaha?"

She paused before she answered, rolling the car smoothly around a tight bend in the road, feeding the wheel from one hand to the other.

"Used to," she said, and there was something about the way she said it.

"What case you working?" I asked. I was paying attention now. "What is it you're so desperate to talk to me about?"

"Your partner."

"Isaac?"

"Your new partner."

"Joe?"

"Now, it's all rather delicate," she started, and at once it became clear.

"Oh hell, stop the car," I said.

"Excuse me?"

"You're IA."

"Well, no. State Patrol Internal Affairs only investigates State Patrol officers. That's the 'internal' part." She chuckled to herself. "I'm looking into this matter on behalf of the state AG's office. They have jurisdiction over—"

"You serious? You go after cops, you might as well be IA. Jesus, I can't believe I let you give me a ride."

"Levine—"

"You know, I always wondered what kind of asshole drove a car with tinted windows."

"It's a company car."

"I know it's a company car," I snapped. "Pull over."

She brought the car to a halt by the side of the road. I was already out of my seatbelt and opening the door.

"It's another mile to the station," she said.

"I'll manage."

"Thomas, please, I just want to talk."

"Well I don't. Now get lost back to Omaha."

"I understand—"

Her words were lost to the slamming of the car door. My tinted reflection glared back and I had to fight the urge to pound my fists on the glass. I turned and walked away, plunging my hands deep into my pockets.

Behind me, tires crunched on fresh snow and then faded into nothing, and I was left with only my anger for company.

As traveling companions went, anger wasn't bad. When it burned, it was all-consuming. Hot and bright, like a firecracker in my chest. Sometimes it felt like it had always been there. A parasite buried deep in the hollows of my bones, and that was fine with me.

As I walked, it ebbed slowly. Seeped out through my pores and sank into the ground beneath my feet. I passed a bearded man in rags, hunched in a doorway, his glazed eyes sliding over me. A block later a dog, thin and wary, chained to a rusted metal fence outside a boarded-up shop. A car with its windshield shattered. I walked on, and with each step my anger drained away, and the town leeched off it and ate hungrily, and it dispersed into the slabs of concrete and then into the soil and then down farther, where it coalesced and flowed like a river. A deluge of filth running just beneath the surface. A sewer system of hate.

By the time I arrived at the station the anger was gone. Instead I was filled with a nervous energy, like my heart was beating off-time. My hands shook. I eased them open in front of me as I stood on the steps outside. They were red and sore and I could feel the blood pounding. Pins and needles danced on my fingertips.

I'd felt it before. Sixteen years old and fooling around with Lisa Simone in the cramped back seat of her dad's extended-cab pickup truck. That rush of adrenaline, so strong it made me shiver. Pills, liquor, sex; I guess I've been chasing that fix my entire life. Kicking down front doors and breaking noses does it too.

I paused at the top of the station steps and stared through the murky window. I'd been in Cooper six days now. Six days of stumbling, of trying to find my feet. I took a breath, pushed inside, and began running through everything in my head.

Kevin Foster. Alcoholic cancer patient, convicted triple murderer, and all-round American schlump. You believe Joe? This guy strangled three women. In the dirt and the cold and the early hours. Strangled them and scooped out their eyes with a spoon. Served his time like a champ and when they finally set him free on appeal he went right back out and strangled a fourth. I guess some guys just don't know when to quit.

If you believe Joe.

You ask me—and I'm going to assume you are, otherwise what's the point in any of this—that whole thing stank. It stank then and after all I've been through since, it stinks twice as bad now. You want to know who killed Kelly Scott? Well, it wasn't Foster, that's for damn sure. The guy just about pissed his pants at the sight of us. Poor bastard was struggling just to survive.

So I finally decided to wise up and play it smart. The killer hadn't left anything on the body because he knew what he was doing. Which meant he'd done it before, which meant he'd do it again. I needed to reconstruct the scene. Follow the evidence and see where it led. Might be it'd take me somewhere interesting.

So, like I said earlier, my mom gave birth to me in a prison hospital. We're skipping ahead a little here—nine months later, hardened inmate, blah blah blah. The only thing to really note at this point is how much of a bitch her own mom was to her. I guess being given the option to either support her sexually assaulted daughter or chastise her for shooting the guy was too much to handle. She chose door number three: skip town and leave a tearful note to your landlord about the rent.

To be honest, I don't know if she was ever aware I existed. I'm sure the state tried to contact her. There's a part of me that hopes they reached her, you know? That they got her on the phone and said, Congratulations, you're a grandma! *Made her tell them she didn't want to look after me. Made her say the actual words out loud.*

'Cause if it hadn't been for her? If she hadn't run off when it all got too much? I might have ended up with a more normal life. Might not have been bundled up and sent to live with Nancy and Eddie.

They were Robert's parents. Catholics, after a fashion. Maybe they thought taking me in was the Lord's work. Apparently they'd asked for me, wrote a letter to social services and everything. I saw a copy of it years later. Important to show that miracles can be born in even the most awful of places. *You believe that crap? I think they got it from a Hallmark card.*

Nancy and Eddie. They lived in a little hick Kansas town called Eudora. Stupid name for a town if you ask me. The sort of place the word dustbowl *was invented for. Warm and sticky, crops and cattle. Old cars with battered suspensions, and Saturday night dances at the juke house before church the next morning.*

Growing up in Eudora, it wasn't exciting. Wasn't fun, wasn't enjoyable—wasn't unpleasant either, don't get me wrong. It just . . . was. You ever watch those crappy made-for-TV movies they used to show on CBS or whatever back in the day? They always sounded so grand. The ABC Movie of the Week! *They were awful, but Nancy used to devour those things. You know, the ones about the smart kid trying to make it to Harvard, only her parents are broke and alcoholic. Or the couple with the strained marriage who move next door to an eighteen-year-old seductress. Or the woman who falls in love with the Benedictine monk. They're all the same, they're all shit, and they're all set in Eudora.*

My memories of that place aren't great. No flashbacks of warm summer days, of a swing set in the backyard, of fields and streams and climbing trees. All of it filmed on Super 8 with the saturation cranked too high. Maybe it's just me, but the visual stuff never bothered to stick around too long.

It's the sensations I remember. The feeling of the air in the evening on my bare arms, the sound of the wind as it rolled through the corn, the smell of the earth after a thunderstorm.

Nancy was old, I remember that. She was probably only in her fifties, but to me back then she might as well have been a hundred. Kids don't have a good grasp of that sort of thing. Aging is something for the old.

But it wasn't just how she looked. It was like she'd given up on being young, like she'd spotted death coming for her a little ways down the road and just thought, Screw it. *You could see it in the way she walked, in the way she dressed, in the way she talked. Like she'd lived a full life already.*

Her hands were near crippled with arthritis, and she'd rub this stinking paste on them every night. God knows what it did, or where she got it from. I'd imagine her fingers curling inward, day by day, until all she had was a pair of fists. I'd imagine her trying to put on that goddamn paste then, and laugh. Or doing up buttons, or tying her shoelaces. Anything that required fine motor skills and unclenched hands set me off.

Looking back, it was probably a relief thing. Maybe I thought she wouldn't be able to slap me with crushed hands. She was a slapper, Nancy. If she'd been a puncher, I'd have been worried. It would have been like a boxer walking around with his goddamn gloves on all the time. But that wasn't Nancy's style, and as time went on she slowly lost her power, retreating more and more into her chair by the television, illuminated by shifting light, watching the doorway with eyes that gleamed.

Chapter Thirteen

Kelly Scott hadn't kept a diary, she'd tweeted instead. Privacy, it seemed, was somewhat outdated.

A Facebook password and an inbox filled with discounted Viagra; she might have been dead but her life lived on. Stored on servers and downloaded onto USB sticks. A person's legacy in my pocket.

I spent the morning at the station, hunched over my computer with a steady stream of shitty coffee and twenty-five grand in the lining of my coat to keep me going. You might not agree with my thinking here—might say carrying that much cash on my person was downright stupid—but frankly I didn't trust Joe not to break into my apartment when I was out, to try to steal it back.

Now Kelly Scott was lying one floor down and everyone I'd spoken to said Kevin Foster did it. I decided I wanted to be sure and put in a request for Foster's original case files to be dug out. Twenty years in a dusty basement; I hoped Cooper PD didn't have damp.

I trawled through Kelly's life while I waited, going backward from her date of death. She'd been planning on going to Austria in the summer with her older sister, a childhood fascination with *The Sound of Music*. She worked as a teller in a local bank. She was good at her job—recently promoted to supervisor. A weekend in

Rapid City to celebrate. I skimmed through the photos, more out of ordinary curiosity than anything else. I doubted I was going to find an obvious stalker hanging around her all night.

Midway through the morning someone banged a metal tin against the side of my desk, making me jump. It was Lloyd, the greasy-faced robbery detective from Kelly Scott's backyard. He cleared his throat noisily, rattled the tin at me.

"Collection," he said.

"For what?"

"Drivers of the transport. Everyone's putting in for a stripper down at the hospital."

It was the first I'd thought of them since yesterday morning. Self-absorbed asshole, but I'm sure I don't need to tell you that. I reckon I could still remember the taste of the officer's blood on my lips, hot and bitter, like burnt coffee. It's not a flavor you forget.

I looked away.

"Don't worry," Lloyd said hastily. "It'll be classy."

"How are they?" I asked.

"They're alright. Not as nice as the ones down in Scottsbluff, but you know. Clean."

"I meant the drivers."

"Oh. Well, they're doing alright. Broken nose, fractured jaw. Concussion."

Fractured jaw. That was mine.

"They talking?"

"Talking? They're *drinking*. Mack is, anyway."

"He the driver?"

"Nah, that's Casey. Casey's still out of it. But the doc says he'll come around when he's ready. I told him Casey's never been ready for anything, so he should be prepared for a long wait." Lloyd let out a watery laugh that quickly descended into a hacking cough. His face turned red with the effort.

I thought about Casey, about how hard I'd smacked him. Remembered Joe kicking him when he was down. I wondered if we maybe hadn't done some permanent damage. What if he'd recognized my eyes through the mask?

Lloyd had finally managed to compose himself. "Anyway, I bet they can't wait to get rid of them. Now, you putting in or not?"

I thought about tossing in one of the bundles of cash. As though that would somehow make it alright. Hell, I'd happily take a busted face for a couple of grand. I'd taken them for a lot less.

In the interest of maintaining a low profile, I fished in my pocket and deposited the best part of two dollars in change. Managed to add a couple more in bills. I wasn't sure how my donation compared to the rest of the station's, but Lloyd gave me a nod and ambled off, shaking the metal tin like a beggar on a busy street.

I watched him waddle away. Told myself that everything would turn out alright in the end. Told myself that neither of them could have seen anything.

Turning back to the computer, I focused on moving through Kelly Scott's feeds, scanning for anything of interest. Cinema trips, broken heels, burnt dinners; snapshots of a life that had ended in the early hours of a cold morning in late November. She'd updated her status the day before her death. *Four weeks until Christmas!!* ☺

I clicked past her posts and into her list of friends. She'd been popular. Opening up another window, I began cross-referencing the people she'd had most contact with against Cooper PD's database. School friends, college roommates, ex-boyfriends. One at a time I ran their names and peeked a little into their lives, too.

Which was how I stumbled upon her past relationship with Gary Hadley. A realtor with a predilection for big houses and beating on people with his bare fists. Prone to outbursts of jealous rage, spent a night here and there in the bullpen to cool off. Kelly had never pressed charges. I slowly went through his Facebook profile pictures, one by one. His grinning face filled my screen.

A cardboard box landed on my desk. A young officer smiled at me. "That's everything we've got on the Foster murders, sir," he said.

"Thanks," I said. "I don't think we've been introduced."

The man nodded. "It's Officer Gordon, sir."

"Levine. Pleasure to meet you."

"Likewise. How you finding your first week?"

"Ask me again once we've caught this guy."

Once Gordon had left, I popped open the lid and peered inside the box. A couple of manila folders and some plastic bags. The box was less than half full. Three murders clearly didn't mean much in Cooper.

I pulled out the files and set them down. Dust fluttered in the air. A woman's blouse was next, wrapped in a clear-plastic evidence bag.

I opened the first folder and found Kevin Foster staring back. A mugshot, bleary-eyed and disheveled. Dated June 1995. Thinning hair. He'd lost weight since then, if his corpse was anything to go by. I spotted his address (lived with his mother), his occupation (cleaner), his nighttime habits (prostitutes). Photographs of him in the early hours, stopped by the side of the road in a beat-up blue Honda Accord, a plump, half-naked woman leaning into the open window. His fingerprints were here too.

The second folder was more gruesome. Dead women lying faceup. Gaping holes where their eyes should be. Three victims, killed over a four-month period in early '95: Natalie Hardy, Mary Lee Smart, Shirley Stevens.

The ties to Kelly Scott were glaring. All three had been strangled to death, their bodies left out in the open. Their eyes taken.

Beyond the surface similarities, I found more. They were successful. They were single. They lived alone.

The evidence against Foster was simple. A thumbprint, found nestled in the cheap plastic of a blouse button. Shirley Stevens's blouse. I glanced back at the evidence bag, lifted out the item of clothing. Ran my thumb over the buttons. Was that how he'd done it? One little motion, one simple mistake. I refilled my coffee and settled back in my chair.

I skimmed the reports. They were short, written in the punchy style of someone who had better things to do with their afternoon. I recognized it well. It was standard operating procedure; post-event justification. The reports weren't lies, they just weren't much of anything else, either. A handful of paragraphs too vague to ever really mean anything. Details were dangerous; they were your rope. Besides, no one bothered to check these things too closely if the evidence was strong. Then I remembered that Foster was released on appeal, and I wondered if maybe that single fingerprint wasn't quite as strong as they'd hoped.

The paperwork was all signed by the same guy—Brian Ackerman. Lead detective, by the looks of things. Joe Finch's name was there too. Twenty years younger. Fresh-faced and eager to please, I had no doubt. I ran Ackerman's name and pulled his last known address. An assisted-living facility, poor bastard.

I held the blouse in my hand again. It still surprised me how something so significant could be so light. I went to write Ackerman's details in my notebook, then caught myself. It wasn't that I didn't want to look into him further. More that I was worried what Joe might say if he spotted the name there. I didn't exactly want to telegraph my intentions. Hell, I didn't even know what my intentions were. I just knew there was more going on here than what Joe had told me. More than what Ackerman had noted in his official reports.

I closed the folders and glanced at my computer screen. Gary Hadley smirked back. I'd nearly forgotten about him. I brought myself back to the present and wondered how a man like Hadley might react if he saw his ex-girlfriend on a night out. Might be she was dancing with another guy. Might be Hadley had had a little too much to drink. I tried to picture him on top of her in the snow, tried to picture him in place of Kevin Foster, and the image came all too quick. Did he know that Foster had been released? Maybe this was all just an exercise in misdirection. It wouldn't have taken much to make her body look like one of Foster's earlier victims. All he would have needed was a spoon.

I flipped open my notepad and scribbled it down. As good a working theory as any.

Chapter Fourteen

I was leaving the station when I spotted Joe by the coffee machine. It was nearly four.

"Afternoon," he said. "I get you a cup?"

"No. Where have you been all day?"

"I've been sleeping, son. I'm not as spritely as I used to be."

"Well, listen. I—"

Joe gave a shake of his head. I clammed up and a moment later Captain Morricone walked past. His head was buried in a file but he stopped when he saw us.

"Gentlemen, hello," he said. He closed up the folder and slid it neatly under one arm. Pushed his rimless glasses up the bridge of his nose with a thin finger. "How are we?"

"Good, sir," Joe said with a smile. "Just refueling."

"Excellent, excellent." Morricone turned to me. "What's the progress on the Foster shooting?"

Joe didn't miss a beat, said, "Right now, we're thinking vigilante killing. Retaliation for Kelly Scott."

"You think Foster killed her?"

"If the shoe fits," Joe said.

Morricone inhaled heavily, nodded. He took the file out from under his arm and tapped Joe with it. "Don't let this one cut any corners, now," he said to me, smiling. "Back when I didn't just sit around behind a desk, my partner used to tell me to follow each lead, no matter how remote it might seem. Always kept me in good stead."

"Yes, sir," I said.

"Excellent. I look forward to reading your report when this is all over."

He left then, opening his file again as he meandered back to his office. I waited until he'd turned the corner before speaking.

"I want to talk about Foster."

"Drop it."

"I don't sleep well, Joe. What we've done, it keeps me awake."

"Relax, kid. It's street justice. It's nature, the animals taking care of themselves. My guess is they all sleep just fine."

He finished his coffee and crushed the Styrofoam cup. Dropped it into the trash and reached for another.

I waited while he got himself another. "You heard what the captain said."

"About following every lead? What a cliché."

"But he's right." I flipped open my notepad. "I want to speak with Gary Hadley."

"Who?"

"Kelly Scott's ex-boyfriend. Got a violent streak, used to knock her around a little when they were together. Now, listen, here's what I'm thinking—"

Joe lowered his coffee. "When did you do all this?"

"This morning. Why?"

A heavy sigh, a hand on my shoulder. "Listen to me carefully. Kevin Foster killed her. Alright?"

"Come on, Joe. You saw the guy. Bob said he was riddled with cancer. He could barely open a can of beans."

"Tommy . . ."

"Hell, Hadley's almost as obvious a suspect as Foster. Christ, it's suspicious if we *don't* talk to him."

Joe glared at me. Went to take a sip but changed his mind, tossed the entire thing in the trash. I could hear his breathing.

"You want to go talk to him? Fine. Lead the way. But once we're done? Once this little box-ticking exercise is over?" He leaned in, his face shiny. "You fall into line, boy."

Chapter Fifteen

We interviewed Gary Hadley on his own turf: a conference room in his fancy office. Walls lined with glossy marketing photos, certificates and framed quotes from the local paper. People with awkward smiles shaking hands with Hadley, holding up the keys to their new homes.

It had been Joe's idea. Strike him off-balance, hit him at his place of work. *Maximum impact*, he called it, like some straight-to-DVD movie. Nothing made a guy sweat more than knowing his colleagues were whispering about him on the other side of a door.

Whether or not it was working I wasn't sure, but Hadley was certainly pissed to see us. Already sat at a table when we entered, hands in fists and a face like he wanted to use them. Blond hair left a little too long; styled to be messy, a poor compensation for the onset of baldness. A prominent brow and the build of a football player. He was a collection of muscles, knotted together under an ill-fitting suit.

He waited until the young receptionist sealed us in, then leaned forward and said, "I didn't kill her."

"Kill who?" Joe said.

"Kelly."

"Okay, you didn't kill her." Joe settled into a chair. "You know who did?"

"Everyone knows who did."

"Come on, Gary, play the game," Joe said, flipping open his notepad. "Say his name."

Hadley paused, scratched the side of his nose with a thick finger. "Kevin Foster," he said.

"Alright, good. Now, tell us what you know about Foster."

"I know he should have gotten the electric chair."

Joe glanced over at me and I squiggled a doodle in my pad. Hadley shifted in his seat.

"When was the last time you saw Kelly?" Joe asked.

"Couple weeks. A month, maybe."

"She was out drinking the night she died," I said. "Didn't get an invite?"

"Why would I?"

"She tell you where she was going?" Joe said.

"Like I said, we hadn't seen each other in a while."

"You talk to her on the phone? Send her a text? What is it the kids do nowadays, Tommy?"

"Facebook," I said.

"Yeah, Facebook. You ever Facebook her, Gary?"

I thought I heard a creak from just outside the door; Hadley must have too because his eyes leaped to it. He looked about ready to topple the table.

"So let me just make sure I have this straight," Joe said, turning a blank page for effect. "You and Kelly broke up a while back, haven't seen or spoken to each other in a month. What happened? She suddenly get tired of you beating her up?"

Hadley half rose from his chair. "I never laid a finger on her," he said loudly. Too loudly, judging by the commotion from the corridor.

"Oh, I doubt that," Joe said coolly. "You've spent a fair few nights in the drunk tank, though. Gotten into a lot of bar fights over the years."

"So?"

"You a jealous guy, Gary?"

"Not particularly."

"You liked it when other men stared at Kelly? When they checked her out?"

"I . . ."

"Don't you lie to me, now. I've seen her, and she's a good-looking girl. I mean, not so much anymore, but—"

"Please, don't—"

"Saw her this morning, in fact," Joe said, leaning in a little. "Wasn't planning to, but the thought of her lying there, all naked under that sheet. I'll be honest, I had a peek. You ever peeked under the sheet, Tommy?"

"I've peeked."

"Great tits," Joe said. "They really perk up after death." He held up his two hands, cupped suggestively.

"Now you wait a minute," Hadley growled. His voice was low but I thought I could hear a nervous crack running through it. "What gives you the right—"

"The right?" Joe said, and laughed nastily. "What gives me the right, son? This *badge* gives me the right. Gives me the right to haul your ass down to the station and charge you with the murder of Kelly Scott, which so help me God I am this close to doing."

I watched him as he spoke. For a guy that didn't think Hadley was a killer, he was certainly putting in the effort.

"Where were you last Sunday?" I said.

"I think I want to speak to a lawyer," Hadley said, reaching for a phone on the desk. "We're done here."

"Hey!" Joe barked, snapping his fingers in the air. It was a habit of his. "Lawyers are for the guilty. Sunday evening, where were you?"

"Sunday . . . I was at the hospital."

"Sure you were. Here's what I think. You were out Sunday night and you saw her, and all those little memories of the two of you just came flooding back. The bruises, the black eyes, all those good times. You see her dancing with another guy, was that it? See him putting his hands all over her? All over those nice tits? How'd that make you feel?"

Hadley's face was white now. His eyes wide, his throat bobbing quickly. He looked like he was about to pass out.

"You still got a key, Gary?" Joe said. "You let yourself in when she was sleeping? Now look, maybe you just wanted to talk. I get that. But maybe you wanted to do more and I get that too. I mean, she's a total bitch, right? Stepping out on you like that? Hell, I'd probably want to drag her from her bed and strangle her in the backyard myself."

Hadley stared at Joe for a moment, then clamped both hands on the edge of the conference table and pushed his chair back. Joe exhaled, and a moment later I saw it too. A white cast, his left leg bound in plaster. All the way up to his balls. I closed my eyes.

"I slipped on some ice on my way to work," Hadley said. His voice was high and fast. "The day before Kelly was killed. That's why I was at the hospital on Sunday. You can ask anyone there, they'll confirm it. I never killed nobody. I can barely piss by myself."

I looked over at Joe. His gaze met mine and I could see it in his eyes. *I told you.*

"Now, please, I want you both to leave," Hadley continued. He picked up his phone. "I'm not answering any more questions without a lawyer."

I stood up and Joe leaned over the table, pressed his finger on the base to cut the call.

"You find it hard to piss now?" he said softly. "You knock any more girls around, you show up in my station again, and I'll break your other leg, understand?"

The office was silent as we left.

We didn't talk on the way back to the station.

I was glad. I'm not sure I could have taken a lecture from him right then. If this was vindication that Foster had killed her, then so be it. I just wanted to go home. I just wanted a drink.

There was a man waiting for us in the station parking lot. Tall and slim, dressed in black. Leaning on a large sedan. He was smoking, but he tossed it aside when he saw us. I tracked the glowing orange on its low, lazy arc into the snow.

"Head on inside," Joe said, and when I glanced over at him his face was ashen.

"You alright?"

The man in black was coming over to the driver's side.

"I'm fine," Joe said, looking pretty far from it. "Just give us a minute."

"Yes, give us a minute," the man in black said, with a smile and an accent I couldn't place. His teeth were dark yellow and one of them was missing. Front row, upper right. I wondered if someone had knocked it out.

"I'll see you later," Joe said.

But of course I didn't. Last time I saw Joe that day was through his windshield as I pushed open the station doors to go inside. The toothless man was in the passenger seat and laughing with his mouth open like Joe was telling him a doozy. Then he was jerking his thumb and they were driving off.

I spent the next few hours catching up on some paperwork and ate an early dinner alone at my desk. Some chicken and noodle dish with too much soy sauce.

Afterward, I opened a new browser window and double-checked Brian Ackerman's address. Placed a phone call with the facility to make sure it was current. The station was quiet, footsteps squeaking on the linoleum and a hobo in the bullpen, sky-high and hustling his reflection in the plastic mirror. I dumped the lukewarm remains of my meal in the trash and grabbed my coat. It was just after six, and visiting hours were starting.

Chapter Sixteen

The Ladybird assisted-living facility sat on the edge of town. Short and squat, a row of windows providing a view of the river and what looked like an abandoned waste-processing plant. Grim viewing without a doubt, but somehow I didn't see anybody in Cooper springing for an upgrade. After all, what was the point? The Ladybird didn't care about making you better.

The woman at the front desk was midway through both her forties and a chunky romance novel. One of those erotic pieces of shit with a woman in riding gear on the front cover. She barely glanced up at me. I reached for my badge, went for a smile instead. Said I was looking for Brian Ackerman.

"You family?" she asked me.

I shook my head. "A friend."

"Uh-huh." She raised an eyebrow. "Brian doesn't have many of those."

"Then I'm sure he'll be pleased to see me."

She pushed the visitors' book across the desk. Handed me a chewed pen and asked me to sign in. I hesitated for a moment, unsure whether to put down a fake name, then figured it was all a little too late for that now.

"Third floor," the woman said as she took the book back. "Room seventeen. But you'll need to take the stairs." And she pointed toward a peeling "out of order" sign that had been stuck to the elevator.

"Room seventeen," I repeated. "Thanks for your help."

She grunted and returned to her novel.

I headed off down the corridor. There was a smell of bleach in the air, nearly overpowering in places. And underneath it the hint of something stronger. A rotten stench, a masked secret.

Glancing in the rooms as I went by, I spotted dark shapes huddled in blankets, on beds next to windows with the curtains drawn. The dim air lit by slices of amber streetlights and pulsing LEDs. Chirps and whirrs and the steady beat of ventilators. A heartbeat of heavy sighs. Every so often I'd spot a nurse, backing out of a room like a parent who'd just gotten their child to sleep. Catching my gaze and sending me a sad smile. Pale faces and dark bags under their eyes. Defeat weighing visibly on their stooped shoulders. A janitor guarded the door to the stairs, mopping a small patch of floor over and over, talking quietly to himself.

The lights on the third floor flickered, and I had to navigate past a row of empty beds to get through to room seventeen. Outside, I took a breath and knocked on the door. No one answered. I twisted the handle and let myself in.

Ackerman was sat across the room. By the window, in a wheelchair with his back to me. His curtains were open, and he gazed out across the dark of the river and the snow that drifted past. A bedside lamp threw his reflection onto the pane, and I saw myself enter the room. His mirrored eyes found mine.

"Brian?" I asked.

He grasped the wheels of his chair with shaking hands and slowly turned himself around.

I knew from Ackerman's file that he was pushing seventy, but he looked a hell of a lot older. Thinning grey hair fell across his discolored scalp in wisps. Yellowed eyes peered out at me from deep within sunken sockets, his skin dry and grey and stretched across cheekbones so sharp they threatened to burst through.

"Brian," I said quietly, stepping fully inside and closing the door behind me. "My name is Thomas Levine. I'm a detective here in Cooper. I wonder if I could ask you a few questions." I paused, then added, "I'm working a case with Joe Finch."

At the mention of Joe's name, the old detective stiffened slightly. Opened his mouth a few times before anything came out, like he wasn't used to working it, and when he finally spoke his voice was soft and rasping.

"Get the hell out of my room," he said.

"I could really use your help."

"You tell Joe . . ." he started, then stopped. He stared at me for a moment, and then swung his chair around and went back to gazing out the window.

I found his face in the reflection and took a step closer. "Brian?"

"What's done is done," he said to the river. "I don't want anything to do with whatever you boys are up to now."

I stopped, glancing around his room. Decided to take a different approach. I sat on the edge of his bed. Let the moment stretch out a little.

"Is it cancer?"

Ackerman let out a long, slow breath. "Lungs," he said finally, and he patted his chest. "Least that's where it started. Damn thing's spread to just about every organ I've got."

"I'm sorry to hear that."

"Don't be. I'm not. Brought this on myself. There's smoking and then there's smoking, you get me?"

"I get you."

He let out a soft laugh. It quickly turned into a hacking cough, powerful enough to twist him forward, hunching over his chair as he retched into his lap. I picked up a box of Kleenex from the nightstand and passed them over. He pulled one out with a trembling hand and wiped at his mouth.

"Thanks," he said, sighing with what seemed like relief as his body relaxed.

"How long have you been in here?" I asked him.

"Just about two years now. But I reckon my stay's nearly over."

I nodded and looked away. Through the window and out over the dark of the river. Past the water, where the land was flat and featureless. I found myself thinking about the Pine Ridge again; that curious swell on the horizon. Canyons and rivers. Cottonwoods that lit up orange in the fall. Mary had made it sound like another world.

We sat in the quiet. There was a comfort to it that I hadn't expected. He had a few personal items scattered about the room. A photograph of a younger woman, a daughter maybe. A small pile of books. A Stetson hanging from the bedpost. I picked it up and looked it over, imagined Ackerman as a cowboy, walking the streets with Joe. The woman at the front desk had said he didn't have many friends. I got the feeling he didn't get many visitors, either. I wondered when he'd last spoken to someone who wasn't here to clean his bedpan or change his sheets. Hook up a fresh bag of morphine. I wondered if they ever thought to give him a little extra, and I felt a flush of guilt for having done so. I didn't mean anything by it. This just wasn't the way I'd want to go, is all.

"What is it you want to talk to me about?" he said suddenly.

Ackerman's initial anger seemed to have faded. Whether from lack of energy or a simple desire to speak to someone new, I didn't know.

I chose my words carefully. "I'm looking into a series of murders," I said. "Took place in ninety-five. Three dead women, all found in their backyards with their eyes missing."

"Sounds familiar," he said, his voice flat and hard to read.

"The first two girls, the killer was smart. Meticulous. Wiped everything down after him. But the third girl, he was sloppy."

"Left a print," he said softly.

"That's right," I said. "On her shirt button."

Ackerman sat up a little at that. I watched his eyes in the reflection of the window and they slid about uneasily.

"You know who I'm talking about?" I asked.

"Course I do." He fumbled in his pockets for something. "You got a smoke?"

I shook my head.

"Damn, I could really go for one right now. You know Joe didn't used to smoke either, not when I first knew him. But that case changed him. Changed a lot of things."

"Brian," I said quietly. "There's been another murder. The killer used the same MO. The same as the first three girls, you understand?"

"Why are you bringing this to me? I don't do that sort of thing anymore."

"I went back through the original case files."

"I told you, not anymore."

This wasn't exactly going the way I'd hoped. My temper started to rise.

"I read your reports, Brian. You hear me? I read them all. And they stink."

His head whipped around sharply. His bony cheeks were flushed, his breathing coming in short, heavy pants. "What?"

"No confession, no evidence he was at the crime scene, no evidence he'd ever killed so much as a fly." I reeled them off, ticking each one with a finger.

"Fingerprint not enough for you?"

"For a triple murder conviction? I'm amazed it took a judge this long to throw it out. It's circumstantial and you know it."

"He killed them."

"Yeah, I read your reports. Nice and brief. Why the hard-on for Foster?"

"Because *he killed them.*"

"Well, I don't know if you've seen the news, but he's out on appeal. Killed a new girl last week, too."

"Sounds like someone screwed up there."

"Oh, come on, Brian. The guy was in worse shape than you are. Weak as a dying kitten. There's more going on here. You planning on taking the truth with you when you go?"

Ackerman fell quiet. I worried I'd pushed him too far. But hell, what else could I do? The guy wanted to lock up on me, fine. Just, *after* he'd told me something.

"Cooper's a small town," he said at last. His voice had taken on a sort of pleading tone. "People spend their whole lives there. Dying in the same house they were born in, across the street from the same neighbors they grew up with. You understand? It's a community." He was becoming more animated now. "Now, I didn't get that. Not at first. But if we weren't careful? If we'd taken too long on a case like this? Folks would get impatient. They'd get restless. They'd start getting concerned about their safety, about their family's safety, about their *neighbors'* safety, and before long we'd have a goddamn mob marching down Main Street and son I'm not joking."

His chest rose and fell in a quick staccato. He looked wiped out. A machine by the bed gave off a short series of chimes. He reached down and grasped an oxygen mask, took in a number of long, deep breaths. I looked away. Stared at the photograph again.

"That your daughter?"

Ackerman followed my gaze, nodded gently. A slight smile appeared from nowhere. "That's Becky. She's a vet, down in San Antonio."

"You sound proud."

"Oh, I am."

"She come visit you much?"

"Not as much as I'd like." His smile dipped a little. "We had a falling out a while back. The usual family bullshit."

"She know how bad you've got it?"

"She knows some. I keep things to myself too much. That's part of the problem, I guess."

"When's the last time you spoke with her?"

"What is this, you a therapist now?"

"I'm just saying, maybe you should give her a call."

Ackerman turned his attention back out the window, his smile gone completely now. He coughed again into his Kleenex. When he took it away I caught a glimpse of red.

"What we did . . ." His voice trailed off. "It wasn't right," he said, barely audible now. I leaned closer to pick it up. "It wasn't."

"What, Brian? What wasn't right?"

"I always said to him, I said, 'Joe, there's a *procedure* to all this. You do it wrong and everything gets thrown out.' You know how many people I've seen walk because some dumb cop tried to jump an arrest too soon? But Joe, he was headstrong, wanted to keep people safe. Wanted to skip ahead a few steps, didn't see the harm . . ."

"What did you do, Brian?"

"I told you, I don't do that sort of thing anymore."

"I don't understand—"

The door swung open. A nurse entered, stopping when she saw me.

"Is everything alright in here?" she asked, her eyes narrowed.

"Everything's fine," I said.

The nurse bent over the various machines next to the bed, scribbled a note on his charts. "I think it's time Mr. Ackerman got some rest," she said, and held my gaze challengingly.

I glanced back at Ackerman but he was out of it. Medication had kicked in. His gaze slid over everything, taking in nothing. I wondered if the nurse had slipped him something extra to get me to leave.

I got to my feet, collected my notebook and said my goodbyes. Retraced my steps through that grim human warehouse and out into the cold. As I walked away I nearly stumbled over something. A dark shape, a cat, lying motionless on the sidewalk. Its glassy eyes stared up at me and I caught the sharp tang of decay. Its stomach was burst. Looked like someone had beaten it to death.

Afterward I drove home, slowly because I needed to mull everything over, and for some reason my headlights seemed to be on the way out. They were working, but just barely. Like a flashlight with its battery winding down. Damn car was falling apart on me.

When I got home I pulled the bundles of cash from my coat. Set them out on the kitchen counter. If you want to know what changed my mind, then you've not been paying attention.

Joe had talked about the Omaha cartel, about the guy who was in charge. It wasn't difficult to work out who the toothless foreigner in the police station parking lot was. Walking around with twenty-five grand in my coat suddenly didn't seem like such a smart idea—last thing I wanted was to get jumped in some dark alley in the dead of night, and it wasn't the beating I was scared of. Bones heal.

So I hid it. Wrapped the bundles in plastic, stuffed them behind a cabinet by the bathroom sink. Temporary, until I had a better plan. I kept a few notes back for myself, and I figured it was about time for that drink.

Chapter Seventeen

Mary was behind the bar. Leaning, like she always did. She was drying a glass with a tattered rag. Gazing at the counter, her pink-streaked hair tied up. When she saw me she smiled. Flipped the glass she was drying right side up and placed it on the counter.

"Didn't think I'd see you back here so soon," she said teasingly, moving on to the next glass. "Not given the state of your tab."

"Yeah, well, I'm paying it off in full," I said, sitting, pulling out a hundred-dollar bill and dropping it onto the bar.

Mary's eyes slid onto it, and she paused her drying. "I see you found the local betting house."

"Poker game at the station."

"That right?"

"That's right."

Mary raised her eyebrows as she picked up the money. Stared at it for a beat, hard to tell what she was thinking. She rang it up in silence and counted my change.

The place was practically empty. "Sultans of Swing" on the jukebox and the steady clack of two big guys playing pool in the back corner. A television set above our heads played silent news footage of the hijacked police van. Text scrolled along the bottom, *daring early-hour heist* in a never-ending loop. I felt sick.

"It always this quiet?" I asked.

"Pretty much," Mary said, her voice clipped, and when she closed the cash drawer she did so with just a little too much force.

"I guess that's nice," I said.

"I guess."

"Don't suppose I can tempt you into joining me for a drink?"

"I don't drink."

I shifted uncomfortably on my barstool. "With me?"

"With anyone."

"What, you got some sort of problem?"

"Says Mr. Johnnie Walker." She stared at me as she placed my change on the bar. "What can I get you?"

"Have I pissed you off?"

"Why would you have pissed me off?"

"Jesus, Mary, I just came for a quiet drink."

"So order it."

"Gimme a beer."

"Coming right up," she said, turning to the fridge before stopping. "You think I haven't seen this before?"

"Seen what?"

"Guys like you."

"Like me?"

"Tough guys, like to throw their weight around."

"Mary—"

"You tell me you got that money from a poker game, and I want it to be true, Thomas."

I forced myself not to glance up at the news footage. Kept my eyes on hers. "It's true."

"I tried to warn you about this place," she said softly. For a moment she lost her hard edge. "It'll pull you under. You've got to push against it."

A rattle from behind me and Johnny Cash started singing. I cocked my head. Kickback rising in my throat. I could never just let things be.

"I'm not some kid, Mary. I can stand up for myself."

"Jesus, how do you not get this?"

"You know, given the state of this bar, I thought you'd appreciate someone spending some money here. I don't get why you're so pissed."

"I don't care where you spend your money." Mary popped the cap off a beer, placed it down hard enough to make it foam. "It's not my bar. And yeah, fine, I guess I am pissed. At you, at me, at every goddamn jackass that steps foot in this town."

"You think I *wanted* to come here?"

"You want my advice?"

"I got a choice?"

"Get the hell out of Cooper," she whispered, leaning in close, her hand still on the bottle. "Get back in your car and drive back to whatever crappy life you had before because it's a hell of a lot better than the life you'll have here."

I blinked. It was suddenly very hard to think of a snappy remark. A long pause and then Mary backed off, withdrew her hand, and wiped it down her apron. I thought I saw it tremble. From behind me there was a thump and the music stopped dead. Mary's eyes rose and focused past my shoulder.

"Hey!" she shouted.

I swiveled in my seat. Watched her march over to a big bald guy by the jukebox. One of the pool players from the back corner. He was wearing a stained wifebeater and when he turned around I saw his hairy stomach hanging out beneath it.

"Touch the machine again and you're done."

"Relax," the guy said. He stepped forward and leered down at Mary. "Not my fault this piece of shit keeps sticking."

"It sticks because people like you keep smacking it."

"Some things like being smacked. People too." He sniggered, took a drink from a bottle wrapped in pudgy fingers. From across the room his large friend let out a guffaw.

"What's the problem here?" I said.

Wifebeater looked over at me. "And who the hell are you?"

"Someone trying to listen to the music. Leave the machine alone."

Mary said, "Thomas, I can handle this."

"You heard the lady, Thomas," the man said, wiping at his wet lips with a dirty thumb. "She can handle this."

His friend hooted again. "I bet she can handle it!"

"I bet she can too," Wifebeater said quietly, his eyes running over her.

I could feel it flickering in my chest. That old familiar sting. I slid off the barstool and onto my feet.

With the music gone, Stingray's was near silent. The only sound was that of heavy breathing—Wifebeater's, not mine. His paunchy stomach rose and fell, the thick bundle of exposed hair shimmering in the light.

I held his gaze. Dared him to start something. If I'd been smart I'd have pulled my gun already. Or my badge. Only that would've wrapped things up too quick. I wanted to draw this out.

"Why don't you mind your own business," String Vest said. "I don't remember this having anything to do with you."

"Want me to jog your memory?" I said.

Footsteps from across the room as his friend moved closer.

Mary said, "Okay everyone, let's just take a moment."

"Tell you what," Wifebeater said to me. "You go home, and Jimmy and me won't kick your ass. How does that sound?"

"When was the last time you kicked anything, you fat fuck."

"What did you say?"

96

"You look like you're one stuffed crust away from keeling over. What's going on with that thing anyway? You've got more hair growing out your stomach than you do on your head."

Mary put her hands up. "Alright. Enough. I want you guys out."

"You heard her," I said. "You and your buddy Jimmy better leave before I beat the shit out of you."

"I want *all* of you out," Mary said.

I stared at her. Then at Wifebeater. And suddenly it wasn't Wifebeater anymore at all. It was Joe. Brass knuckles glinting. I thought of Kelly, and of Rachel, and of every other woman that was hurt or dead because of me. Because of what I'd done. Because of what I hadn't done.

Wifebeater was saying something but I didn't catch it. Fire in my chest and rocks in my fists; I closed the distance in a few quick strides and drilled him in his large stomach.

He dropped his beer and stumbled back. Crashed into the jukebox. A mechanical squeal and "Gimme Shelter" started up.

Movement from my left. Jimmy closing in with a pool cue in his hand. Mick Jagger started wailing over the guitar intro as Wifebeater came to life and threw himself at me.

We fell across the room. Somehow I managed to turn him as we collided with those fixed barstools. We flew apart. I stayed on my feet but he went tumbling to the floor. I ducked just as Jimmy swung his pool cue. It cracked in two on the bar, shattering glass. Mary shouted as Mick threatened to fade away.

I scrabbled for my beer bottle and swung wildly. By some miracle it connected with Jimmy's face. He howled and staggered back. I leaped at him, landed a couple of blows. Blood sprayed and an audible crack. I pushed him away and he collided with the door, half stumbling out into the cold street.

Then thick, pudgy hands were on me. Clutching at my neck and chest. I struggled but he was too strong. Reaching back, I went for his eyes, my fingers inching across his cheekbones. With a yell he threw me across the room and into a small table. Wood splintered around me as I crashed through it. Rolled onto my back just in time to see him reaching down to grab my shirt. I braced myself as he started punching. The back of my head bounced off the floor.

Then from behind the bar, the unmistakable ratchet of a shell sliding into a chamber. Wifebeater froze. I focused my gaze and saw Mary, standing across the room with a pump-action shotgun in her hands.

"You," she said, pointing the barrel at him. "Out. Now."

Afterward I sat at the bar with a shot of Jim Beam and a damp cloth. Mary swept up the fragments of broken table as I picked at glass shards. The back of my head was pounding and someone else's blood was dotted down my front. I was starting to make a habit of that.

"Sorry about the mess," I said.

Mary stared at me as she emptied the dustpan. She still looked pissed.

I started to explain. "I was just trying to—"

"I know," she said.

"I'll pay for the damage."

"You can certainly afford it."

I ventured a smile; tentative, unsure. Fleetwood Mac played on the jukebox, one of my favorites. A soft beat, slow and steady. Mary smiled at me and I felt relief expand in my chest.

"About before," I said, and Mary shook her head.

"Forget about it," she said. "I shouldn't have said what I did."

"What are you doing here?" I asked her.

"I work here."

"You know what I mean."

"I know what you mean."

It was the second time she'd dodged the question. She didn't want to give me an answer and that was fine with me. We all had our shit to deal with.

Mary stood up straight and stretched her back. I heard it pop. She tossed the dustpan on a shelf below the bar and wiped her hands. She stopped there, on the other side, looking at me, leaning on her broom, sweeping her dark hair out of her eyes.

"It's late," I said. "You got a ride home?"

She gave me a look. "You sober enough to drive?"

"Hey, I never did get that beer."

Mary laughed and put the broom to one side. "You eaten dinner yet?"

"Not really."

"You like Chinese?"

"Sure, I like Chinese."

"You drive me home, I'll let you pay for takeout."

"That make me even for the table?"

She grinned. "Not even close."

Chapter Eighteen

Turned out Mary didn't live far away. Drive only took a couple of minutes. We didn't talk but it wasn't awkward. It was nice.

"That's me," she said as we approached an apartment building.

It was a rundown-looking place. Dirty brick, the kind that's gone black from exposure. It wasn't late but, even so, most of the windows were unlit. White garbage bags were piled on the sidewalk outside, and one of them had split open across the front steps.

"It's not much," Mary said, and gave what sounded like an embarrassed laugh.

"Hey," I said, "it looks a hell of a lot better than my place."

Mary led me through her narrow entryway and into the front room. Turned on a couple of lamps along the way. A soft glow fell about us. I stood by a large window and looked out onto the building's backyard but all I saw was myself and Mary and the rest of her living room. It was a barrier. The lamplight shielding us from the snow. From the darkness, from the cold, from whatever else lurked out there in the night. I thought back to Brian Ackerman and his view of the river. I wondered if he was sitting at his window, looking out, same as me. What was it he'd said? *What we did.* What did you do, Brian? You and Joe, all those years ago?

"You alright?"

Mary was standing behind me. I focused and saw her in the window.

"Sorry," I said. "Long day."

She held up two takeout menus. "You got a preference?"

"Whatever's good."

"Not sure I'd call either of them 'good' . . ."

"What is it with this town and bad Chinese food?" I said. "I swear that's all I've seemed to eat since I got here."

"There used to be a pretty nice pizza place on the east side," Mary said. "Someone tossed a couple firebombs through the front window."

"Why does that not surprise me?"

Mary grinned and held up a menu. "I'll be right back."

She left to make the phone call. I ran my gaze around the place. Looked for the things that others might not. A detective's eye; a habit that's hard to shake.

Artwork on the walls. Framed prints, mostly. Abstract stuff. All I could see were the brushstrokes, the thick lines of paint. I didn't get it, I never had. Modern art always went over my head.

Rachel knew about stuff like that. Art. Nature. She was the cultured one. I hadn't even set foot in a gallery until we started dating. She dragged me to a whole bunch of them at the start. Museums, too. Stood me in front of statues and photographs and weird sculptures made of welded metal. Asked me what I saw. What I thought it meant. Hidden meanings, all that crap. And look, I'm a surface guy. I told her. Straight up, no surprises. Symbolism was always wasted on me.

Only now I'm not so sure. Maybe I got it wrong. Maybe she saw something in me after all, a part I'd tried to keep under wraps. A hollow space, filled with secrets.

Maybe she thought I just needed the exposure. That baring my soul might be a good thing. See, I got depths. I got that hollow space. It's what it's filled with that scares me.

And then—stay with me—you let that thought spark and burrow through the messed-up tunnels in my brain and now I'm wondering whether Rachel *did* see inside it. Whether the exposure *worked*. You want to know what really keeps me up at night?

What if the shit I've got inside of me was so bad it drove her insane?

A clatter from the kitchen brought me back. I stepped away from the print and moved through the rest of the room.

No photos—of Mary, of anyone. Flowers on the coffee table and not the romantic kind. It was cozy, sure, but it was bland. A rented life. A catalog life, lifted wholesale. It wasn't hers. It wasn't anyone's. And there was something sad about that.

The one piece of Mary I recognized sat in the corner of the room. An expensive-looking record player with two floorstanding speakers either side and a set of shelves with more albums than most music stores I'd been to. I was thumbing through them when Mary came back. Two glasses of what might have been gin and tonic. The back of my throat went slick.

"Don't be getting any marks on my collection," she said, handing me a glass.

"I've never seen so much music," I said. "The jukebox at Stingray's must be like nails on a chalkboard."

She shrugged. "It's not so bad. It fits the place."

"Bowie, Prince, Dylan. Frankie Valli? You've got eclectic taste."

"What can I say, good music is good music. What about you?"

"Anything but jazz." I took a sip of my drink. "This is lemonade."

"I can see why they made you a detective."

Mary went to her record player and flicked it on. Spun a knob on an amplifier, moved some sliders. Changing settings only she could hear. Music faded in, filling the room. Something mellow. Guitar and sax. Roxy Music, maybe. She sat on an armchair by the window. I took the sofa.

"You're working that murder, aren't you?" she asked me.

"Which one?"

"The girl."

"Yeah."

Mary nodded. Took a drink and drew her legs up under her. "You want to talk about it?"

"Do you?"

"Not really."

"Fine with me."

"You want to talk about what happened back there?"

"Look, I really am sorry about that table."

Mary shook her head. Lowered her lemonade onto her lap. "Forget the table, Thomas." A pause. "Those guys could have really hurt you."

"I guess I wasn't thinking about me."

"I don't need protecting."

"I never said you—"

"All I'm saying is I've been trying to keep my head down here . . ."

"You're saying I made things worse?"

"Of course not. I mean, I *do* keep a shotgun—"

"How was I to know?"

"You think that's the first drunk guy I've had try to put his hands on me?"

"Well, excuse—"

"You think I wasn't able to manage until you came here?"

"Jesus, Mary, I wasn't asking for a thank you, I was just trying to help."

103

"And it was nice, alright? It was nice. And I never said thanks back there because I guess I *was* scared. I mean, that shotgun looks good, but I've never fired a gun in my life, not that most of those drunk assholes would ever know. But *I* know, alright? I know. And you think I don't feel shitty when guys like them come in? Like I don't feel their eyes all over me? Like I don't know they're going to do something the first step they take? But you know I've been managing just fine by myself and no one's ever done that sort of thing for me before and I didn't know how to take it, so yeah I never said thanks back there and now I feel shitty for that, too."

I stared at her.

"Well, you know, don't mention it," I said quietly.

Mary looked over at me. Her face was flushed. "I do appreciate you trying to help, Thomas. Like I said, it's been a while."

"Been a while for me too."

Something heavy in my throat. I took a large gulp, hid it with a swallow.

"You've got a lot of anger inside you," Mary said.

"Is it that obvious?"

"You don't have to talk about it if you don't want to."

"I don't want to."

It came out sharper than I'd intended. I saw her flinch slightly.

"Look, I get it," I said, struggling to keep my voice level. "You want me to open up. See who I really am. Only you don't, not really. You think you do. But this?" I beat my closed fist against my chest. "It's better off staying inside. You're better off. You wouldn't much like the real me, I don't think."

"Thomas . . ."

"What was it you said? That whatever happened before didn't matter? Well you were wrong, Mary, you were so wrong. It matters a hell of a lot. I'll never escape it, and maybe that's how it should be. This is my punishment."

"Then start over. What do you want?"

"I want to be better."

"Then be better."

"I'm trying, Mary."

"It was a woman, wasn't it?"

I started a little. "What?"

"You think protecting me makes up for whatever happened to her."

"Stop."

Mary held up her hands. "I'm sorry. I shouldn't have pried. You're right. God knows we've all got our shit to carry."

"You want to talk about yours?"

She fell silent.

I sniffed, drained the last of my lemonade. "Sometimes I wonder, I've been living with this so long I'm not so sure I know how to live without it. It's a part of me now. Like a kidney, I need it. How pathetic is that?"

Mary fixed me with a smile. "Plenty of people give up a kidney just fine."

I laughed at that. Rubbed at my face.

"Look," Mary said. "Let's just have a normal evening, alright? Let's forget everything else that's going on in our lives for a few hours, eat some shitty takeout, and watch a dumb movie. How does that sound?"

I started to speak just as my cell buzzed. I pulled it out but the number was withheld.

"Hello?"

There was a brief silence before a man spoke. He had a soft voice. "I'm looking for Detective Thomas Levine."

"Speaking."

"I saw what you did."

"Excuse me?"

"On the highway, Detective. And in the quarry. I watched you burning your car."

I sat up a little when he said that.

"Who is this?"

"I want to meet, Thomas, you and me. Let's do lunch."

"How did you get this number?"

I turned away, but I could feel Mary watching me. The man on the other end of the phone groaned theatrically. "Oh do we *really* have to do the usual dance? It's so *boring*. You don't believe *me*, I don't know if I can trust *you* . . ." He made an *eurgh* sound. "How about we skip straight to the part where I stick a photograph under your windshield wiper and call it a day, hmm? What do you say?"

I rose from the sofa, clutching for my firearm, said, "What photograph?"

The line went dead.

I glanced back at Mary. She was leaning forward, staring at me. "Is everything alright?" she asked.

I was already moving for the door. "It's fine."

"Who was that?"

"No one. Thanks for the talk. Sorry about dinner."

I stumbled out into the cold evening. The street was empty and my car was a hundred yards away. Lit up under the harsh yellow of an aging streetlight. I half ran toward it, scanning the area for any sign of movement. As I neared I saw something white under the wipers. An envelope, and inside a photograph of me and Joe standing next to a burning car. I felt my stomach flip.

On the back of the photo was a phone number, and as I dialed I tried to remember if he'd given his name. He answered on the first ring.

"What the hell do you want?" I growled.

"I already told you, Detective," the man said, and I could practically hear him smiling down the line. "Now tell me, how do you feel about Italian?"

Eddie and Nancy's backyard looked out onto a forest, and I'd wander it, running my fingers along the rough bark of the trees and jumping back and forth across the little winding stream that snaked through it. Nancy would ask what I got up to in there. She'd be watching from the living room when I got home and she'd call me in and ask why I was covered in dirt, or water, or blood.

The blood . . . she only saw that the once, and she beat me something fierce because of it. It wasn't my blood, I know that. This was later, after Eddie had taught me how to hunt. Gave me an air rifle for my tenth birthday. I guess I got pretty good at it. Rabbits, mainly. And I was curious, what can I say. What ten-year-old boy doesn't want to see what's underneath the skin?

I'd emerge from those woods, blinking from the sudden light with crimson coating my fingers, or smeared up to my elbows, or splashed across the front of my shirt. I quickly learned to wash it off in the lake, to bury my clothes in the soft earth. Getting a slap for tracking mud into the house or losing my sweater I could handle.

It all probably sounds worse than it was. I wasn't some psycho, I was just bored.

Grandpa Eddie was big. But I guess everyone's big when you're little. He was fat, with a red nose and patchy stubble over his double chins. He had some sort of liver problem, most likely on account of the fact that he'd drunk a half-rack a day since he was seventeen, and his eyes bulged a little because of it. It gave him a constant expression of surprise. A lot of people called him names behind his back; a couple said them to his face. I once saw him arguing with some guy at a barbecue in our front yard. Eddie was breathing heavy and his face was red, I thought he was going to have a heart attack. I was hoping he'd have a heart attack.

The hunting I enjoyed fine. The quiet, the creeping, the stillness of it all. The half hour of tension and the split second of release. We'd camp for the weekend. Come back with a collection of rabbits and squirrels, all trussed up and hung over our shoulders.

Only we didn't just hunt, me and Eddie. I don't remember much of it. Bits and pieces. The silence as we walked home together. The way he'd give me a piece of candy from his pocket, bubblegum or licorice or a Snickers, like I'd done a good job, like it was our little secret. I threw it away once, and he beat me for it. After that he made sure I ate it in front of him.

Nancy would skin what we brought home, and she'd let me watch. I tried it a couple times and at first I wasn't any good at it. I'd slice the meat, or my fingers, and Nancy would yell and slap me across the back of the head. But I kept at it, and before long I could skin a squirrel just as fast as her. Faster, even, on account of her twisted-up hands.

Eventually Eddie let me go out on my own. Maybe he figured he was getting too old to be spending the weekend outdoors, sleeping on a tarp and shitting in a dirt hole. Or maybe I was getting too old for him. I didn't really care.

There was one evening, after a particularly successful hunt, when I asked Nancy if I could keep one of the rabbits for myself. She looked at me for a minute, and I'm not sure what was going on inside her withered skull, but she said if I was going to start stuffing animals I'd do it properly or I wouldn't do it at all, and that if I didn't the smell would bring rats, and I said okay.

The local library turned out to have a pretty decent how-to book on taxidermy. Did you know taxidermists don't use the body? I'd figured I'd need to slice open their little bellies and scoop out their insides, pack it with cotton or whatever, but turns out all you need is the skin. And I had the skinning part down pat.

It still took me a while to get the hang of it, mind you. Took me a bunch of rabbits, too. But by the time I went back to school at the end of that summer I had a small army of the things dotted around my room. I turned them all so when I'd wake they were facing me. I liked the idea of them watching me sleep.

There was only one thing I could never get right, and that was the eyes. The how-to book said I had to use glass, which would have been fine if it hadn't been for Nancy. Oh she indulged me well enough— bought me ammo and helped me sharpen my knife—but for whatever reason she refused to buy me the eyes. She said she couldn't afford it, but that was bullshit. She could afford her dirty cigarettes and her stinking hand-paste, and when I told her that she slapped me so hard she made my gums bleed.

I still don't know for sure why she refused. They freaked her out a little, I know that. I was so pissed off that afterwards I moved them into their bedroom when they were sleeping. Set them up all over the room, their blank faces and empty sockets pointed right at the bed. I still remember the scream when she woke up. Remember the beating, too.

She threw them out after that. I came back from school to find their remains in the bottom of the fire. My how-to book, too, and that wasn't even mine to burn.

Chapter Nineteen

The restaurant was called Marco's and it didn't look like much. Hidden away from the main drag, down a snowy side street. An old woman was standing there, out of the cold wind, stooped over and sucking on a cigarette. She watched me pass, her face wrinkles and suspicion, her skin so pale it was nearly translucent. I nodded a hello and she shuffled away. It was early Friday afternoon but it was dark; clouds and cramped buildings on either side saw to that.

When I finally found the entrance, I looked it over. Dirty windows and a mechanical whine from the laundromat next door. Before I went in I spent a couple of minutes with my notebook. Took down the license plates of every car that was parked outside. It was a long shot, sure, but I figured it couldn't hurt to try. When I was done, I squeezed the photograph in my pocket and walked inside to a world of checkered tablecloths and Dean Martin.

The place was small, maybe ten or so little tables. Most of them half set, all of them empty apart from one. He was sitting against the back wall, where the light was dimmest, and he looked up at the tinkling of the door. Hooded eyes regarded me from across the room.

I made my way to him, weaving through the tight spaces. With each step I felt the familiar presence growing from within. That bundle of nervous energy; anticipation with a dopamine twist.

Suddenly I was sixteen years old and Lisa Simone was unclasping her bra, straddling me in the cramped back seat while country music played on the radio. Then it was fourteen years later and I was holding down a screaming skinny junkie while Isaac tossed his filthy apartment for pills.

It was all the same. That fevered rush, that edgy buzz. A precursor to something bigger. Flooding my system and overloading my senses until my temples pounded with the pressure of it. I was tense—too tense for a meeting such as this—and liable to take it out on whatever was close to hand. Upending a table, maybe, or snapping a man's finger. I could feel the reassuring weight of my switchblade in my pocket.

Movement on my left and a plump waitress in a turquoise uniform emerged from the kitchen. I just about slit her throat. She was carrying a plastic tub of silverware and a bored expression. Her nametag read *Suzanne*, and *Buongiorno!* underneath. She asked if she could take my coat, and I told her no. She shrugged and wandered off.

The man at the table was watching. This close, I could finally make him out.

He was big; high-angled cheekbones and blond, floppy hair that fell across his eyes. His nose looked like it had been broken at least once and never quite healed right. Arms that filled the sleeves of a plain white T-shirt stretched tight across a broad, powerful chest. I wondered what he could bench. Two hundred, two-fifty. His hands were clasped in front of him, fingers interlocked. A couple of glasses of something dark on the table.

I folded my jacket over the back of a nearby seat. Sat down opposite him.

He said, "Morning, Detective."

"Morning."

"I took the liberty of ordering you a drink. Figured you were a liquor man. Got you a rum."

"It's a little early for me."

"I thought all you hardened detectives were borderline alcoholics. Or is that just a cliché?"

He smiled at me, bouncing the ice around in his glass playfully. He didn't look like I'd expected him to. His voice was soft, a little high-pitched. I'd imagined someone scrawny. A pervert with a little pot belly and a zoom lens. Not a big guy like him, who looked like he'd been in a few fights and probably enjoyed them.

"What's your name?" I asked.

"Simon," the man replied. "My name is Simon."

"Simon what?"

"Just Simon."

"Well then, Simon," I said, leaning back slightly in my seat. "Let's get one thing clear. I'm not here to drink with you."

"Sure you are. Why do you think we're in a restaurant?"

"Now listen—"

"If I just wanted to talk, I'd have asked you for a stroll along the river. You been down to the river yet? It's shit. Now, you're new in town and I'm guessing you've been surviving on takeout. You've got that look about you."

"What look?"

"You need to get more sleep, Thomas. And get some fish in you. But not from here. Christ, last time I was here I tried the catch of the day. That was me for the rest of the night. Ass like the Japanese flag." He ran a large finger down a laminated page. "Where'd they catch the thing from? That's what I'd like to know. Probably from that damn river. The veal, on the other hand, is particularly good. It's the only reason I come here. Despite the godawful music they play."

"You don't like Louis Prima?"

"Who?"

I pulled the crumpled photo out of my pocket and dropped it on the table. Tapped the corner.

"Never mind. You got more of these?"

"A few," he said, shrugging. "Heavy-handed, I know."

"What do you want?"

"Right now? Lunch." He grinned. "I think this is going to be fun."

I'd started to tell him exactly what *I* thought when Suzanne the plump waitress appeared at the table's edge. I rested my hand over the photo.

"Are we ready to order?" she asked, digging out a pad.

"I'm not hungry," I said, staring at Simon.

He turned to the waitress with a smile. "You'll have to excuse my friend," he said, leaning in close to her. "He'll have the veal."

"I will?"

"Yes," he said. "And so will I."

Simon snapped the menu shut and handed it over. The waitress smiled at him, sent me a dirty look. As she walked away, Simon raised his glass to me.

"Cheers," he said, and clinked it against mine. When I didn't join him, he rolled his eyes. "If you're not going to drink that, then at least let me have it."

I lifted my glass. Went to take a drink and then paused.

Simon bellowed with laughter. "Oh come on, Detective. Do you really think I've poisoned it? Hmm? Me and Suzanne over there are going to roll you up in a carpet and drag you out back? I mean, just look at her. I doubt she'd be much help."

I drained half the glass in one shot. Felt like I was making a point. Simon motioned for another round.

"Before we get down to business," he said, "what do you think of Cooper?"

"I think it's a cancer. I think it's rotten and should be torn down, brick by brick."

Simon swept blond hair out of his eyes. "It's a shithole, isn't it? I used to wonder if it wasn't some front for something more exciting. A secret, maybe, if only I could shift my perspective." He paused for a moment. "I suppose I must sound a little nuts."

"You do this kind of thing a lot?"

"What's that?"

"This. Us, speaking here, in this place. The photograph under my wiper. That how you spend your time?"

"You think I'm playing with you."

"What else would you call this?"

"Getting to know each other."

"Oh yeah? What's your last name?"

"It's Jacobs. I did two stints in Nebraska State for arson and petty theft. I'm a size-twelve shoe and I can bench two-sixty-five." He gave one of his thigh-sized biceps a loving squeeze. "I saw you looking."

I downed the rest of my drink.

There was a clatter from the kitchen and a moment later the door swung open. Suzanne reappeared and placed two large plates down in front of us along with another couple of rums. The booze must have been working because the food looked incredible. Thinly sliced breaded veal topped with tomato sauce and melted cheese, small boiled potatoes and green beans on the side. The smell of it reminded me I'd skipped last night's dinner. When I looked up, Simon was watching me.

"What did I tell you?" he said.

"Jack shit, so far," I said. I nudged the photo. "You take this yourself?"

Simon nodded as he cut into his food, suddenly serious as he began chewing. "I did."

"Tell me what you saw."

"I saw you," he said. "Saw you and your partner burning that car."

"So we burned a car. So what."

"Not *a* car. *That* car. And *that* car was used to rob a police transport."

"You saw that too?"

"I did. Interesting choice of masks, I must say. And those bags, Thomas. Or do you prefer Tom? Tommy?"

"Detective Levine is fine."

"Well, Tommy Boy, judging by the weight of them, I'd say those bags were quite full."

My empty stomach was fluttering, a heaviness behind my eyes. I popped a potato into my mouth and it melted into a warm, garlicky mess. I was suddenly very glad to have decided to stop carrying the money around in my pocket.

"I'm supposed to believe you just happened to be there?" I said. "Nice early-morning drive out by the reservoir?"

"Of course not. I've been watching you for a while now. Getting a feel for you." He nudged the photo with a large knuckle. "Imagine my surprise when I saw that."

"And at last we reach the point of this conversation," I said. "You think blackmailing a cop is a smart move?"

"Actually, yes."

"I'll ask again. How many of these do you have? They saved on a hard drive somewhere?"

"I'm old-school, Detective. Been using the same Leica for twenty years."

"You're an artist. I got it." I leaned in close. "Simon, I want those photos, you understand me? The negatives, everything. My patience is evaporating."

"Tell me about the girl," he said.

I fell silent, his question catching me off guard. "What girl?"

"You *are* investigating a murder, aren't you?"

"I don't see the connection."

"They say Kevin Foster killed her."

"I'm not at liberty to—"

"Discuss an ongoing investigation, yes yes yes I understand all that. But have you seen the poor guy? Course you have. You found him. Anyway, they had his picture in the paper. I'll be honest, Thomas. That man does not look like a killer."

"You know what a killer looks like?"

"I understand you've yet to release everything to the press."

"That's right."

"She's missing a watch, isn't she."

I took a deep breath and let it out slow. Picked up a green bean with my fingers and chewed on it. "You talk to one of my men at the station? That it? Late-night chat with your drinking buddy who says something he shouldn't and you think you'll have a little fun?" I moved my glass to one side so I could plant my elbows on the table. "Let me tell you something. This whole charade you've got going on? This . . . lunch, this forced air-of-mystery bullshit you're peddling? I'm not interested. I don't have time to be interested. You want to mess around with a cop? Run a red light and tell your story to the highway patrol. Don't waste my lunch break with this Hollywood crap. Now, you give me those photos before I really start to get pissed off."

Simon grinned. "You're lecturing *me* about Hollywood crap? Seriously? After that?"

He was devouring his lunch now. Laughing as he swirled large chunks of meat in thick, red sauce.

"Alright, alright," he said. "Let's make a deal."

"I don't break that nose again," I said. "That's the deal."

Simon picked up the photo. "Remember who holds the leverage." He glanced beyond me, catching the eye of the waitress and motioning for the check.

"Where you going?" I said. "We're not done here yet."

"You know, I read a book recently," Simon said. "I'm a voracious reader. I'll read anything. I once read every ingredient on the back of a shampoo bottle while taking a shit. Anyway, this was about an illness known as Capgras delusion. Fascinating condition. It's most commonly found in those suffering from paranoid schizophrenia, and it manifests itself as . . . now I have to make sure I get this right . . . *one's belief that someone close to them has been replaced by an imposter.* Ah, thank you my dear."

That last part was aimed at Suzanne, who had briefly returned with the check in a little silver dish. Simon began counting out cash.

"One of the cases they talked about was a woman from North Dakota, I forget her name. She was young—late twenties—and had recently given birth to a child. A boy. Now, they don't know what triggers the condition, but believe me, this woman had a laundry list of mental problems. A hotel laundry list, you get me?

"So her husband was a traveling salesman, and after a long trip selling cleaning supplies to single mothers he returned to the family home to find his wife curled up on the bedroom floor, covered in blood and repeating over and over to anyone that would listen that her darling son, her infant boy no older than six months, was a fake, an imposter, a carbon copy replaced some nights previous while she'd slept, and after living with it for three days she hadn't been able to stand the notion of doing so for a second longer, and so she'd bludgeoned the poor thing to death with a rolling pin just before noon."

He dropped the cash into the dish and reached for his coat.

"I'm not sure I can imagine anything worse," he said. "Losing my grasp on reality like that. You know, ever since reading about it I've had this recurring dream, where I'm staring into a mirror and the person staring back is a stranger. I wonder what that means."

Simon paused, perhaps waiting in case I said something, and then flashed me a strange, slightly sorrowful parting smile when I didn't. He got to his feet and I made to do the same and he gave me this look, his features all at once different, his eyes narrow and his jaw set. "Don't follow me, Thomas," he said. "I see you in my rearview, I get stopped by some traffic cop a half mile down the road, these photos reach your captain's inbox before my engine's cool."

And so I waited until he'd left, until Suzanne had returned to clear the table and take the money and I told her to keep the change. That nervous buzz I'd felt when I'd arrived had left. The anger that usually rode alongside it nowhere to be seen. In its place I felt dejected and melancholic, and I just wanted to go home.

When I went outside the street was darker still. The old woman I'd passed on my way in was gone now, a little pile of matches and a half-smoked cigarette in the spot where she'd stood. As though she'd vanished into thin air before she'd had a chance to finish. It was frosty, and I hurried back onto the main street and into my Impala, where I turned the heater up to full and held my hands over the vents. My fingers trembled with the cold, or at least that's what I told myself.

Rookie never speaks to me. Keeps that mouth zipped up tight. He's more of a listener, Rookie. Might be he just zones out while I talk, but I doubt it. Either way, it's good getting some of this stuff off my chest.

As we walk to my cell, I take him back. Back to Eudora. To the dustbowl and the cornfields and the warm summer nights, and the house where I grew up.

There was a room in that house that was always locked. Through the front door, straight past the kitchen and on your right. Grandpa Eddie kept the key to it on a chain around his neck, and there were only two occasions when he'd take it off: when he was showering and when he was screwing. Seeing as how he didn't like showering all that much—and judging by the mood Nancy was always in—I reckon it's safe to say he pretty much wore it around his neck twenty-four-seven.

When I turned five, just before I started school, Eddie took me by the hand to that door (straight past the kitchen and on your right), removed the key from under his shirt and ushered me inside.

I don't remember what happened next all that well, and that was perhaps on account of the fact I was only five, and who the hell remembers much from when they were five.

All I knew was that I had wet myself, and Eddie had started screaming at me. There was a cross on a mantel and a bible on a desk, a hook in the ceiling and a chain on the floor, and the walls were red and I'd wet myself.

But that was then and this is now, and I'm sure we've all seen enough Hollywood movies to get the subtext. If you've been paying attention you might have already worked it out.

I mean, it actually makes a whole lot of sense. Eddie's son—my dad—was a rapist, right? And who do you think he picked up that little trick from? I bet that Eddie did the same to him as he did to me. Right down to the goddamn candy when he was finished. Smarter folks than me talk about it all the time. The abused becoming abusers. Countless generations of screwups; one big, happy, sexually abused family.

And I know what you're thinking. What about me? What did I become? Well let me set that record clear once and for all. I never touched no girl, not like that. I want that written down. Type it up, Tubby. In bold, you hear me? In bold.

So, after that day, if I was ever laughing too loud, or making too much noise, or I dropped a plate or forgot to do my homework or didn't take the dog out for its morning walk, or if Eddie had just been drinking, out would come the key from under his shirt on the chain around his neck and I would go to that room with the red walls, straight past the kitchen and on your right, and I would pray to the man on the cross that this time I wouldn't wet myself.

Chapter Twenty

I'm not sure why I didn't tell Joe about my meeting with Simon Jacobs. Maybe on some level I couldn't shake the notion that he was somehow involved. It would certainly be a convoluted way to get back my cut of the money, but for all I knew this had been his plan from the start. I kept thinking back to the foreigner from the parking lot. Kept wondering when he would show his face again.

So, regardless of the reasons, I shut my mouth about Simon. You can ask me if it was a mistake or not, but looking back I don't think telling Joe would have made any difference. Not to what happened in the end.

Anyway, let's keep going. We've got a lot of ground to cover still.

I headed to the station after my meeting with Simon. I had research to do.

First off, I ran his name through the system. Pulled his file. There wasn't much, but what little I could find matched what he'd told me. Two stretches in Nebraska State Penitentiary for arson and petty theft. A soft spot for robbing gas stations and setting people's cars on fire. Hardly a stand-up guy, but no evidence that he'd murdered anyone. Least not the three girls back in '95. His second stint lasted just over seven months. Covered the killing period nicely.

I tried to look into his prison record, find out what he was like inside. A pop-up window asked me for my credentials and I clicked it away. Last thing I wanted was a paper trail.

Digging out my notepad, I fired up a new tab. There had been three cars parked outside the restaurant. I ran each of their plates. First one belonged to Suzanne the waitress. I discounted that. The second was registered to an insurance company. Their office was located across the street from Marco's. I discounted that, too.

Scoring through each failed hit in my notepad, I tried the last one. A red Nissan Sentra. Plate number 248 UGN. Owned by a senior citizen named James Catterson. No parking violations, no speeding tickets. Lived in a small house near the edge of town. I leaned back in my chair. Couldn't hurt to check it out.

It didn't take me long to reach the Catterson house. I parked on the opposite side of the street. Got out and leaned against the door of my Impala.

Late afternoon and the day was beginning to darken. The snow had let up a little, but it was still in the air. Flakes drifted around me on a breeze too light to feel, swelling and falling on eddies so rhythmic it was like the very town itself was breathing. The sky was a dirty, depressing shade of grey and I counted six homes before the encroaching darkness ate them up. I imagined a great Nothing creeping closer. A massive beast hungry for dilapidated property.

The house was a mess. A rusted gate and an overgrown front yard gave way to a rundown two-story building. Gutters that hadn't been cleared for years. Wooden shutters that hung at angles. And the red Nissan, too. Parked in the driveway. 248 UGN. I pulled my collar tighter around my neck and trudged over.

I hit the car first. Glanced around before trying the doors. Locked. Peering inside, I saw discarded candy wrappers and a half-empty bottle of soda propped up in the cup holder. Turning, I stared up at the house. Part of me said to leave. The rest said what was the point in coming if I didn't check.

I rapped on the front door. Popped the leather clasp on my holster before I did. When there wasn't any answer, I tried again.

"I help you with anything?"

The voice came from down the street. A neighbor, leaning over the front of his porch and staring at me with suspicion. I let my jacket fall across my revolver and hit him up with my best smile.

"Morning," I said. "I'm just looking to speak with Mr. Catterson. Have you seen him recently?"

"You got any ID, pal?"

I reached into my pocket and—somewhat reluctantly—pulled out my badge. So much for the low profile. "Detective Carson," I said.

The neighbor's eyes widened slightly. "Is James in any sort of trouble?"

"Not at all. Just following up some routine investigations. Simple traffic violation, that's all."

The man nodded. "Well you won't find him here."

"That right?"

"Yessir. Lucky guy's off on a cruise. First vacation I think he's taken in years."

"When did he leave?"

"Oh, 'bout a week ago or so."

I ran that through my head. "You seen anyone else here since he left? Tall guy, blond hair? Well-built?"

"What, you think I just sit here watching this place? Like I got nothing better to do?"

I was pretty sure he didn't. I smiled. "Thanks for your time."

"You want me to let James know you're looking to speak with him when he gets back?"

"I wouldn't bother." I closed my pad and waved my hand through the air. "I don't even need to speak to Mr. Catterson that badly anyhow. Just dotting some Ts. I can finish up my report just fine without him."

The neighbor shrugged and turned away. I padded down the steps toward the street. Glanced over my shoulder when I reached my car but the house was just as still as before. I wondered if Simon was inside, hidden behind the slanted shutters, staring back.

Chapter Twenty-One

I ran through it all on my way back to the station. I had a lot to consider. I drove slow.

I figured there was a decent chance Simon was staying there. The problem was what to do next.

The neighbor was an issue. I'd been sloppy—should've gone for the back door. And showing him my badge under a fake name might come back to haunt me. It wouldn't take much. A phone call to the station would do the trick.

The other issue was Simon himself. I couldn't take the chance that he hadn't seen me. Whatever I was going to do, it would have to be fast.

I figured the best move would be to go back at night. Break in through a window, maybe. He'd had me on the back foot at the restaurant this afternoon. It'd be nice to even the score. Worst-case scenario, he wasn't there; I could check the place for the photographs instead.

When I arrived I found Joe stretched out in his seat, flicking through a file, his legs up on his desk. He grunted when he saw me.

"I been waiting on you," he said, climbing to his feet.

"Any particular reason?"

"We've got a visitor."

"Who?"

"Gary Hadley."

"Kelly's ex-boyfriend?" I frowned. "I thought he didn't check out."

"Maybe," Joe said. He scratched at his grey stubble. "You're not the only detective around here."

"You find something on him?"

Joe grinned.

◆　◆　◆

Gary Hadley had worry in his eyes. It pressed against the mirrored glass. He didn't say anything as Joe entered the room and sat down at the table.

The guy had come back with a lawyer. Just the sort you'd expect from a successful realtor. A heavyweight bruiser, all hawkeyed and hungry. Wearing a made-to-measure suit and a suntan in December.

I watched through the one-way glass from the adjoining room as Joe produced a thin folder and a little plastic cup of water. I watched as Hadley's gaze fell to them.

"Sorry to keep you waiting," Joe said. "Got you some water, they told me you were thirsty."

"My client's not under arrest," the lawyer said. "He's come in to answer some questions on a voluntary basis. I want that noted."

"Sure, let me just find a pen."

"Detective—"

Joe smiled and held up a finger. He switched on the recorder.

"This is an informal interview with Gary Hadley. Present is Detective Finch and . . . what did you say your name was?"

I saw the lawyer bristle slightly. "Christopher Moreno."

"Moreno? What is that, German?"

"Can we please get on with this?"

"The time is ten past five on the afternoon of December second." Joe paused. "How's the leg, Gary?"

Hadley glanced at his lawyer before speaking. "Uh, it aches a little. You know, on account of the cold and all."

"Bad time to break a bone, winter," Joe said, and gave a chuckle I thought was a little forced. He leaned back and crossed his legs. "Wouldn't you say?"

"It's always a bad time to break a bone."

"Yeah, but there's bad times and then there's *bad times*," Joe said. "Although I guess it can be useful too."

Hadley frowned. "I don't follow."

"Neither do I," Moreno said, clasping his hands together.

"Well." Joe took a thoughtful breath. "Maybe you want to get out of something, you know? Pretty good excuse to take some time off work, right?"

"I like my work."

"Yeah, but those clients, always on the phone. All that pressure. You know I saw a billboard for some real-estate guy over on Maple. How come you don't have a billboard, Gary?"

Moreno cleared his throat. "Is there a point to this, Detective?"

"All I'm saying is maybe your client wanted a little break. Figured now would be a good time to hurt himself. The best time, in fact." Joe smiled thinly. "I mean, what's better than ruling himself out of a murder charge?"

Hadley's eyes popped. Moreno barely flinched.

"Is this all you have?" the lawyer said. "Because if it is, I'll have to insist that we end this questioning now."

"Easy there, counselor. I just want to run one thing past your client. You'll make that evening pedicure."

Joe reached down and opened the folder. A stack of photographs; he'd shown them to me already. A nightclub, grainy and shot from above. Kelly Scott was laughing.

"These are stills from CCTV the night Kelly died," Joe said. "She looks like she's having a good time, wouldn't you say?"

Hadley was pale, his eyes locked on the top photo. "Yeah."

"She looks good, too. Looks better with her clothes on, in fact. Funny how some women are just like that. Like it's the *idea* of what's underneath that gets you going."

Joe peeled the top photograph away. Kelly was dancing now.

"When we spoke yesterday, Mr. Hadley, you told my partner and I that you'd broken your leg the day before Kelly was killed. Said you'd slipped on some ice on your way to work." He paused to consider his notebook. "On a Saturday," he added.

"I often work weekends," Hadley said. "It's real estate, you know?"

"Not really, but I'll take your word for it."

"Detective . . ." Moreno said, stretching the word out.

"Now I put in a call to your office landlord," Joe said. "So imagine my surprise when he told me the place was closed last weekend. Something about a busted heating pipe. Sound familiar?"

"I . . . yeah, I didn't find out until later."

Something about the way he said it. Moreno must have noticed, was smart enough not to react. Kept his gaze leveled across the table.

I watched as Joe turned to the next photograph. And the one after that. And the one after that. Kelly Scott relived her final hours once more; drinking, dancing, laughing.

"Then of course we found this," Joe said as he reached the final picture. Now Hadley was in the club, at the bar, and standing on two feet. Kelly was next to him, her face turned away, one hand up and pushing out. Her intention clear.

"I can explain," Hadley started.

"Don't," Moreno warned.

"You know, I'm not sure what I find more offensive," Joe said. "That you didn't think we'd check the cameras from the club, or that you didn't think we'd check your goddamn hospital records. You broke your leg three days ago, shit-for-brains."

"Fine," Hadley said. "I was at the club the night she died, alright?"

Moreno touched his arm. "My client has no comment."

"Oh come on, your client was caught on CCTV. What I want to know is why he was there."

Hadley spoke again before his lawyer could interrupt. "Because I wanted to say congratulations on her promotion is all. I was happy for her."

"Looks to me like she wasn't happy to see you."

"She wasn't," Hadley said. He seemed miserable.

Moreno leaned in and whispered something in his ear.

Joe pushed on. "Let me see if I've got this straight," he said. "You weren't pleased about the breakup. She dumped your ass, and you thought your little heart was going to burst because you loved her so damn much. Am I right so far?"

"No comment," Hadley said.

"Then you found out about her night out. Thought you'd try and convince her to take you back."

"No comment."

"Maybe you thought you could buy her a drink, beg a little. Maybe double-check there weren't any other guys on the scene you'd need to teach a lesson. You know, remind her of the good times."

"She said she never wanted to see me again," Hadley said. His eyes shimmered with tears. "She told me I made her sick, that I was a bully and a thug and—"

"Alright that's enough," Moreno said. "Either charge my client or we're leaving."

"She make you angry, Gary?"

Hadley leaned forward. "Don't you get it? I was *there* the night she died. I was right there, man, and I went home and she was killed by that monster. By Kevin Foster. I wasn't there to protect her. Because of me, she was murdered. Because of me."

He started crying. I stepped forward until I was inches away from the glass, until my reflection was so close it was almost in the room. Standing on the other side, staring back.

It had been a solid lead—it still was. An easy motive. But my gut wasn't on board. A dirty feeling that Joe was playing him as well as he was playing me. Gary Hadley had been my discovery, and now I was resigned to watching it unfold behind mirrored glass in a soundproofed room. I'd never felt more uninvolved.

Joe didn't say anything for a while. Just let the guy blubber until he'd managed to compose himself. Then, "You blame Kevin Foster for Kelly's death?"

Hadley nodded. "Course. I mean, he did it, right? Everyone knows he did it. Just like before."

"How'd you feel when you found out?"

Moreno must have realized where this was headed. He started to speak but his client got there first.

"How do you think I felt?"

"Pissed off? Angry?"

"You're damn right I felt angry."

Moreno pointed to the recorder. "Switch that off, we're done here."

"You glad he's dead?" Joe asked.

Hadley pounded the table. "Yeah, I'm glad he's dead! I only wish he'd suffered more."

"Did you shoot him, Gary?"

Hadley suddenly stopped talking. Wisest move he'd made all day.

Moreno was on his feet, livid. "This circumstantial circle-jerk is done. You want to talk to my client again? You come to me." He dropped his card on the table, hauled a mute Hadley out of his chair. "I'll drive you home."

"I understand why you did it, son," Joe said. "Not a jury out there that won't."

Moreno flashed him an angry look from the doorway. Joe shrugged and turned off the recorder, closed the file. Turned to the glass and looked straight at me.

Chapter Twenty-Two

By the time I left work I was antsy. An irritation under my skin. I knew I had to deal with Simon but I couldn't concentrate, couldn't focus. A feeling like I was missing something. A nagging fear that breaking into the Catterson house was just what Simon wanted me to do. I was hungry and I needed a drink.

I went to Stingray's. I hadn't spoken to Mary since last night. It all seemed so long ago now.

We'd ended the night on uncertain terms. Maybe that wasn't surprising. She'd given me the opportunity to open up and I'd shut her down. Left in a panic, left things hanging and unsaid. I figured I'd ask her if we could talk. Maybe offer to buy her a drink. Non-alcoholic, of course.

But when I pushed open the door and entered the bar I knew she wasn't working. It was the music that did it. Heavy metal, a thudding bass and a man screaming

I turned and left.

Which isn't to say I didn't buy that drink. A bottle of rum with a name I didn't recognize from the liquor store on the corner. It was cheap, which meant it was nasty, which meant I'd probably

be throwing up half the night and popping painkillers half the morning.

I thought about driving over to her apartment. Having it out on her front step. Decided against it, unsure what I'd do if she told me to get lost. Besides, ambushing her at home just so I could get some peace felt wrong.

The money was playing on my mind. Had been, ever since I'd stuffed those bundles into my pocket. It wasn't just Simon's photographs that tied me to the heist. Every one of those hundred-dollar bills was like a finger pointing right at me. It had been stupid to spend one. I needed to start playing it smarter.

When I got back I went to the bathroom cabinet. Pulled out the plastic bag, the sight of the money making my stomach cramp. For a moment I thought about burning it. Just dropping the bag into a metal drum and setting it all ablaze.

Then that little part of my brain kicked in. It was evidence, sure, but that went both ways. I didn't know what Joe's next move would be, and this stuff might come in handy in a pinch. Look, I wasn't planning on ratting anyone out, but shit. It wouldn't be the first time I'd thrown my partner under the bus.

I took the money outside. A shared yard behind my apartment building. Hard topsoil and weeds; clearly nobody spent much time here.

It took me almost twenty minutes to dig a big-enough hole. Just about ruined my switchblade and most of my fingers by the end. Packing the bundles inside, I filled it in and smoothed it over. Marked it with a couple of rocks.

The slam of a car door cut through the still night. I turned toward it as my cell buzzed, that same number I'd been dodging. Debra Mansfield from Omaha. Woman sure had a knack for timing.

I killed the call. Had just started for the gravel path that ran along the building down to the street when I heard footsteps crunching toward me. Too dark to tell if it was her or someone worse. One way to find out: I dialed her number. Her cell lit her up like a flashlight.

"Mansfield?" I said. "I was just returning your call."

Pocketing the phone, she moved into the backyard, curling her pig nose at me. "What are you doing out here, Levine? Gardening?"

I shrugged. "Just checking out the place. I never had a yard back in DC."

"Looking at this, I'd say that was a blessing."

"Can I help you with something?"

"I hope so," she said, and pulled out a notepad. "I'm looking into the attack on the police transport."

"They sure do keep you State Patrol officers busy."

"Where were you Wednesday morning?"

"When it happened? I was in bed, asleep."

"Anyone with you?"

"This is starting to get a bit personal."

Mansfield ran the torch from her cell down her notebook, reading.

I jerked my thumb up at my apartment. "You want to continue this with a coffee? It's freezing out here."

"I'm just about done."

"You know, I hear the officers in the van are going to be just fine."

"That right?" She was still reading her notes. "Mack's certainly awake."

"What about his partner?"

"Casey?"

"Yeah, Casey."

"Still out of it."

"You spoke to Mack?"

"Uh-huh."

"What'd he say?"

She looked at me. "Said they were attacked by two men armed with shotguns and wearing masks. Clown masks, if you can believe that."

"Clown masks, is that right."

"Found them half melted in the remains of the car they used."

"Forensics get anything off them?" I said, and Mansfield paused just long enough to let me know I was asking too many questions.

"Nothing yet," she said.

"Well, if that's everything," I said. Gave her a parting smile as I turned to leave.

"They took the bullet that killed Foster," she said.

I stopped at the doorway. Turned back. "What's that?"

"The bullet that killed Foster. They stole it from the evidence van along with the money. I can't get my head around that part."

"'Fraid I can't help you there."

Mansfield moved closer. "Now, when you found him—Foster, I mean—when you found him, he was already dead."

"That's what it says in our report."

"I've read the report."

"Then I don't have anything to add."

"Why do you think somebody would steal the bullet?"

"I don't know."

"Come on, hypothetically. A bullet on its way to be tested."

I blew air out the side of my mouth. "To cover their tracks."

"Right," she said, taking another step toward me. "That's what I was thinking too. Which means whoever shot Foster stole the bullet."

"Sure."

"And the money."

"Okay."

"So I find the money, I find the shooter."

I paused. "Makes sense."

"Makes sense," she repeated. She cocked her head slightly, her eyes thoughtful. "You should really invest in some winter mulch."

"Excuse me?"

"For the garden." Mansfield ran her gaze over the dark yard. "You want to trap the air, try and provide the soil with some insulation."

"You sound like an expert."

"It's basic stuff, Levine. If you're serious about sorting this shit heap, it wouldn't hurt to read a book."

I smiled thinly as I opened the back door. "Thanks for the tip. Goodnight, Detective."

Mansfield nodded and walked off. I went up to my apartment. Got there in time to watch her black sedan drive away.

I waited another couple of minutes, then went back down to the yard and moved the money.

Chapter Twenty-Three

Saturday morning was quiet. Not just the station, but the whole town.

I woke early. My clock blinking five. My brain too wired to let me sleep. Outside it was dark, and when I went to the window it was still, and I stared across the street at the drawn curtains and wondered if anyone was standing there staring back. In those moments—before the birdsong, before the dawn light—it felt like time had stopped. Like I could've walked out my door and down my street and into the homes of my neighbors and stood over their beds as they slept.

I ate breakfast in a diner just outside town. Fried eggs and bacon and black coffee. Here it was busy; people huddled under strip lights, a brightness so harsh it made me squint.

It was still dark out, and in the inky black the diner was like a beacon. I imagined us all weary travelers, drawn to its welcoming flame. Its protection from the darkness and from what creatures lurked out there.

I sat at the counter because I didn't want to take up a booth but I still felt out of place. Sitting there, eating my runny eggs and watching the morning news on a small TV, next to truckers with checked shirts and extra chins and three-plate breakfasts.

I didn't belong here. This was just a rest stop for those passing through. For whom Cooper didn't hold any sway or exert any control. I could see it in the way they looked at me; the big men who spooned whipped butter onto their toast, who drowned pancakes in syrup and fed powdered eggs into open mouths that hadn't yet finished what was already inside. Those guys, they knew this wasn't a place to stay and enjoy a meal. Lest they end up like the skinny waitress behind the counter, her ginger hair thin and falling about her lifeless face in dry strands; or the kitchen boy standing by the cookers, wiping sweat from his forehead with a rag tied around his hand, only it wasn't a rag at all, it was a bloodied bandage.

Lest they end up like me.

When I was finished I dropped a twenty next to my plate and left. I could feel the eyes of the truckers on me, the cool breeze from the opened door reminding them of the road, of doggie bags and sliding their trucks into gear and getting the hell out of there. I was swallowed up by the charcoal night, just another lost soul.

The station wasn't much different. Quiet. I was the only detective there; a guy on the front desk and some bored woman I'd never seen before speaking on a phone as she flicked through a magazine. I sat down heavily in my chair and unclipped my holster, set it down next to my coffee. If I'd had a hat I'd have pulled it over my face and slept. It was early still, just before eight, and I was tired. I still don't know why I hadn't just stayed in bed.

I guess he was watching the station. Either that or he was following me. But I hadn't been there more than a minute before my cell buzzed. The number was blocked.

I answered it. "Levine."

"Early riser, Detective?"

It was Simon.

"I'm not in the mood," I warned him. "So speak fast."

"Alright," he said. "I want to cash in that favor."

"Finally thought of something you want?"

"Oh I always knew what I wanted," he said. "I just needed to know you had it."

I thought briefly of putting up a fight. Decided to hear him out. "You give me those photos and we'll talk."

"I want Kevin Foster to officially take the blame for Kelly Scott's murder," he said. "And I want the case closed."

"Why are you so interested in who killed Kelly Scott?"

"Because I was the one who did it."

"And you've just decided to confess."

Simon laughed lightly down the line. "I didn't expect you to take my word, Detective."

Sudden footsteps as two uniformed officers walked through the doorway, heads bent in discussion. They sat down at a nearby desk. I turned away from them, dropped my voice.

"Spit it out, Simon," I said. "Some of us have actual police work to do."

"There's a package on your desk."

I glanced down at the mess of paperwork. Pinned the cell between head and shoulder as I rifled through my in-tray until I came to a small brown envelope, padded and with my name handwritten in thick black pen. One more glance at the officers as I ripped it open and shook out the contents.

It was a silver watch.

Small, with a thin strap.

A woman's watch.

"Is this a joke?" I said.

"The punchline, maybe."

"This could be anyone's."

"Thomas, please. It's engraved."

I spun the watch around and sure enough there it was. *To Kelly, Happy Birthday, Love Gary.* I closed my hand around it and squeezed tight.

"Where did you get this?"

"From her wrist."

"No you didn't, you understand me? Did someone slip you this? One of my men? Tell me the truth."

"You know what your problem is? You want everything to be simple. Mr. Foster, I'm sure, makes for a far better suspect than I do. Or Mr. Hadley, maybe. Domestic abuse, neat and tidy, hmm? Rather that than some drifter, just picking up girls at random. But the world doesn't work that way, Thomas. It doesn't want to be put in a box."

"I'll put you in a box," I spat. Too loud, drawing glances from the men nearby. I took a breath, hissed, "Nebraska still has the death penalty, asshole, so stop messing me around and tell me where you got this watch."

"I'm getting tired of this," Simon said, sighing theatrically. "Do you want the photographs or not?"

"Let's *assume* that I believe you," I said. "Why'd you kill her? You got a thing for young women? Mommy never show you enough attention as a kid?"

"Why don't we settle for simple inspiration from Mr. Foster's example."

"So you're a copycat now? How many other girls you killed? And what'd you do with the eyes, anyway? You one of those sickos that likes to take trophies? You wear them on a necklace and howl at the moon?"

"Do I strike you as a crazed psychopath running around wearing my victims' skin as a suit, Thomas?"

One of the officers slapped the other on the back and walked away. He looked over at me as he left, and I sent him a friendly nod.

139

"You strike me as a goddamn queer," I said, smiling like I was talking to my grandmother. "You hear me? You're a liar. You're a stain, you're nothing. Screw you and screw your watch. I'll find you and take back those photos myself."

Simon fell silent. When he spoke again, his voice was quiet, measured.

"Thomas, I need you to think of this as an exchange. Kevin Foster is a killer. His death affects no one. His passing will be mourned by no one."

"You say he's an innocent man."

"Three dead women say otherwise."

"He served his time for them. This is different."

"Oh, Detective, suddenly we're a man of principle? Now you're going to make sure Foster takes the fall. You do that, and all these photos disappear. We both get away clean."

"No one gets away clean, asshole," I said. "That's the whole point of this place."

"You're finally getting the idea."

"I'll find you."

"Like hell you will," Simon snorted. "You've got until the end of the day, Thomas. After that, I'd start packing."

The line went dead.

Chapter Twenty-Four

I sat for a long while after he hung up. Cleaned up my coffee and got myself another, turned the watch over and over in my hands, studying every inch of it as though it might contain some hidden secret.

To Kelly, Happy Birthday, Love Gary.

I felt sick to my stomach.

If I'm honest, I'm not sure why. Was it a surprise that Simon had killed Kelly Scott? Despite what he'd said on the phone, Simon was the better suspect. Better than Kevin Foster, better than Gary Hadley. Maybe not on paper, but one conversation with him—one look in his eyes—and anyone would be convinced.

He hadn't mentioned anything about my turning up at the Catterson place. Might be he didn't know. I had until the end of the day, he'd said. That didn't leave me much time if I was going to break in and get those photos. I thought back to yesterday, to the exposed street. To the neighbor. I pulled up a map online; an alley ran alongside the houses.

I still didn't like doing it in the daylight, though. Easy prey for prying eyes. I leaned back in my chair and worked it through. If I waited until it was dark, it might be too late. I stared at the watch, at the envelope it had arrived in.

I thought back to the Foster files. To what Brian Ackerman had told me at the Ladybird. *What we did.* I hadn't confronted Joe about it yet, but I was starting to put the pieces together.

Three dead women in the spring of '95. Foster had been their man, the surveillance photos in his file made that clear. When Joe had come around to my apartment he'd told me they'd found Foster's print on Kelly Scott's belt. *Partial thumb*, he'd said. *Good enough for any judge.*

Only now I wasn't so sure. From Bob's autopsy report, Foster had been just about pushing up daisies when we'd busted down his front door. My bullet had simply helped him along. No way did he pin down a struggling girl and strangle her to death.

But if I was right, that meant his print on her belt had been planted. Joe's handiwork, I was sure of it. Probable cause to get us to the scene. To knock me out, to take my gun. A dead suspect and leverage to force your partner into helping you rob a police transport. Hell of a plan.

Now I knew Foster's prints were still in his file. Worse, the partial print from Kelly Scott's belt was from the same thumb as the one found on Shirley Stevens's blouse button back in '95.

Was that what Brian Ackerman had been talking about? *What we did.* Three dead women, a town about to explode. Did Brian and Joe plant Foster's print back then? Was this just history repeating itself?

I hadn't spent enough time with Foster's file. I knew the guy never confessed. Didn't mean he hadn't done it. I wasn't questioning whether Foster had killed those three women. I just didn't think he'd killed the fourth. Either way, it all gave me a pretty awful idea.

I snatched the envelope the watch had come in off the table. Stuffed the watch into my pocket. I didn't dwell on it as I took the stairs. Knew if I did I might change my mind. Last thing I wanted was my conscience kicking in. I could already feel it, scrabbling to life in the back of my brain like a startled dog. *What they did was wrong*, it said. *Do this and you're no better.*

I wasn't surprised to find Cooper PD didn't lock down their evidence room—that would be going against type. Temptation within arm's reach; this place was nothing if not consistent.

A small forensics kit hung on the wall. I grabbed it, popped it open, and smoothed out the envelope on the desk. I knew it was a gamble, but I was running out of options. Simon was smart, and I tried not to overthink it as I dusted the corner of the envelope. Told myself that even smart people make mistakes.

It took less than a minute to lift the print. A perfect thumb impression, left right at the top as he'd sealed the envelope.

I peeled the print onto a plastic label. Course, I still didn't know for sure if it was his. For all I knew, he'd asked some poor postal worker to take care of it for him. I checked my watch. Still early. Pushing on, I propelled the chair across the floor. Fired up the monitor and scanned the print into the computer. Normally this thing would take an age to run. I helped it along. Clicked through the dropdown menus.

Nebraska State Penitentiary. 1990–2000.

It took less than a minute for his face to pop up. I allowed myself a smile of relief. I had him. All I had to do next was roll it onto Kelly Scott's belt. If Simon wanted it wiped clean, he knew what to do.

I quickly scanned the shelves of the room, looking for Kelly's belongings. They weren't here. I swore in frustration—Bob hadn't filed them away yet. They were still in the morgue.

I slipped the plastic label into my pocket. Packed everything away and turned off the computer. Headed for the morgue stairs.

I was halfway down when Mansfield emerged through the PVC strips at the bottom like a ship from fog. I froze.

"Detective Levine," she said, and she wrinkled her nose.

"Mansfield," I said. "You're in early."

"So are you." She smiled thinly. "Thought you might be at home nursing a hangover."

"Powering through it. What are you doing here?"

"I was looking for Bob. Does anybody here bother to turn up when they're supposed to?"

I shrugged. She began climbing the stairs. I could feel the plastic label in my inside pocket. Its sharp corner pressing into my chest. I rubbed at it.

"I know you don't want to talk to me," she said, "and that's fine."

I stayed quiet.

"The way I see it, there's a scale to all of this," she said. "From good to bad to downright shitty. Most people, I suppose they live somewhere near the middle. Maybe just beneath. Just enough brightness in their lives to keep them going through the dark. But you, Thomas, you're down at the other end, you understand me? God knows what must go through your mind at the end of a day here. You spend your nights getting loaded and, hand on heart, I don't blame you."

She took another step toward me. Took hold of the railing.

"But you listen to me now. You let this seep inside that skull of yours, past the booze and whatever else, and you listen to me. That partner of yours? He's a user, Thomas. He's playing you, has been since you got here. Whatever he's doing—whatever he's done? It'll come to light, it always does. Lit up like a bare bulb. You carry on down this path and you'll answer for your part. I'll break down your goddamn door myself if I have to. So you go on keeping your mouth shut, and you go on pretending I'm not here. But I don't know how to make this any more obvious, so I'll just say it out loud. I'm coming for you, Detective. And you best make whatever peace you can before I do."

I stared at her. Above us I could suddenly hear the sound of footsteps, of people moving about the cramped office. Mansfield held my gaze, her expression blank. She tried to act cool but when she unwrapped her fat little fist from the railing I could see her palm was red from holding on so tight. I could see her nails, too.

She had dirt under them.

After she left, I stayed behind. Sat and watched the fluorescent light of the morgue as it flickered and danced on the bottom steps, warping and shifting through PVC strips caught in the eddies of an air conditioner set too high. I took the label out of my pocket, ran my thumb over the print sealed inside. The noise above seemed to fade, and in the quiet stairwell I could hear the faint sound of a neon bulb, popping and singing to itself beyond the swaying strips of plastic where the light was cold, and where the body of a man and a woman lay in temperatures even colder.

Chapter Twenty-Five

In case you're wondering, I didn't go through with planting the print. Maybe I was tired of committing crimes to cover my tracks. Maybe part of Mansfield's speech got through. More likely my conscience just finally kicked in, a few years too late.

In some ways DC had been simpler. I'd known where I stood there. Worse than that, I'd enjoyed it. I recognized a lot of myself in Joe—a lot of who I had once been. I reckon he probably saw something similar in me. But how could I confront him about Foster—about whatever it was he was involved in—if I was just as dirty?

I'd told Mary I wanted to be better. *Then be better*, she'd said. I thought of those words as I tossed Simon's print into the trash. *I'm trying, Mary. I'm really trying.*

I still had options. Cards I hadn't yet played. I tossed them around a little, saw what was left. Mansfield had dirt under her nails and it wasn't hard to guess whose yard it was from. If she had the money, then what was she waiting for? That feeling like I was being played came back hard.

Some things were becoming clear. Joe, Simon, Mansfield; I knew the time was coming where I'd have to pick a side. Turn on others if I wanted to save my own skin. I'd done it before and it'd hurt like hell, but like most things I figured it'd be easier second time around. I was a scrapper, a survivor. I'd get by. Besides, I still had until the end of the day.

Walking into the main office, it was clear I'd missed something. A gathering of some kind. Officers were standing about. Raised voices and hands being clapped on backs. Took me a couple of minutes to work it out, but when I did I felt that net closing in a little tighter.

The driver of the evidence van had woken up.

I went to my desk and flipped open a file. Held it up like I was reading. Told myself that he didn't know anything. That his partner certainly hadn't. And that even if he did, his broken jaw would keep him from talking a while longer. For a few moments I even entertained the idea of paying him a visit to make sure.

"Hang on, give me a second."

It was Mansfield. Striding past my desk, cell pressed tight to her ear in a pudgy hand. I watched her over the top of my file as she snapped her fingers at a young officer. I think it was Gordon. Same kid who'd brought me the Foster files earlier in the week.

"You," she barked. "I need you to run a license plate for me."

Gordon scrambled to log into the nearest computer and fire up the search.

"Ready," he said.

"Okay, give it to me again," she said into her cell. Then to Gordon, "Two-four-eight UGN."

My stomach flipped.

"License plate is registered to a red Nissan Sentra," Gordon was saying. "Owner is a James Catterson."

"You got his address?"

"Right here in town."

"Good. Note it down. Get a judge on the phone. I want a warrant in the next five minutes."

Mansfield turned to leave and caught me looking. I thought I saw the beginnings of a smirk. I lowered my file.

"Break in the case, Detective?" I asked, a little surprised at how level my voice sounded.

"Officer Casey finally decided to join us," she said.

"So I hear. He must have had some good news for you."

"Maybe." She paused. Tried to read my expression. "Said he saw a red Nissan pull up by the reservoir just before they were ambushed. Sat there the whole time."

"Possible witness?"

"Or a lookout. Casey said the car headed off after the hijackers when they were done. Even managed to memorize the license plate."

"Casey said a lot for a guy with a broken jaw."

Mansfield smiled. "He writes just fine."

Gordon piped up from across the floor. "Detective? I'm on hold with the judge now."

She gave me a final glance, then turned back to the young officer. I swung my chair away and dropped the file on my desk. I still didn't know for sure that Simon was at the Catterson place, but I was soon going to find out. There was always a chance Mansfield's excavation was a bust, the money still buried in the frozen earth. But if she got her hands on Simon—or worse, on the photographs—then I was finished.

I had to get to him first.

Chapter Twenty-Six

It didn't take long for the main office to become crowded. I guess nothing brings over-eager idiots together like the thought of breaking down someone's front door. In the mess, I slipped away. Through the bodies and down the main steps, out into the freezing morning air. I'd left my overcoat on the back of my chair. I didn't mind getting cold if no one realized I'd gone.

I slid behind the wheel of my Impala and started her up. Gunned it out of the parking lot and down the icy streets. Back to the row of houses on the outskirts of town. The snow had stayed away, the thick mist no longer present. That was good. I'd need to be able to see them coming.

It took less than ten minutes to get there. I parked in the alley I'd spotted online. Two attempts to grab hold of my door handle, I was shitting myself so badly. I spent a moment telling myself to wise up and then I was off. Running before my feet touched dirt.

The alley was narrow and I sped through it, jumping a pile of burst garbage bags and sliding out into the patch behind the Catterson house. I paused for a second to listen—nothing—then climbed the tall, wooden fence that surrounded his yard. Grabbed the top, the soles of my shoes sliding on the wet planks. Straining as I pulled myself up and over, falling in a heap at the bottom. Brushing snow from my legs as I scrambled to my feet.

The house had a back door and this time I didn't pause to knock. Threw my shoulder against it. Felt the lock snap.

I crashed into the kitchen, the door nearly bursting off its hinges. With the blinds drawn and the lights off it was dark, and I stumbled forward, groping for a light switch. It was only after I'd flicked it on that I thought about fingerprints. I scrubbed at the wall with the sleeve of my jacket. Grabbed a dish towel and wrapped my fingers in it.

"Simon!" I roared. "Simon if you're in here, you need to come with me!"

There was only silence. I moved from the kitchen into the living room, turning on lights as I went. The house was fairly large; most of the downstairs was open-plan. No sign of life that I could see.

I took the stairs two at a time. Clutching at the handrail with my covered hand, propelling myself upward. When I got to the top I paused. A handful of rooms ahead of me, their doors closed. If Simon was here I couldn't hear him. Couldn't hear anything else either, though. Might be they hadn't left the station yet. I still had time.

First door was a bathroom. Empty. Second was the main bedroom. I pushed the door open, but it was dark inside and as I reached for the switch I recognized the sharp tang of blood.

James Catterson's body lay on the bed. The sheets were stained crimson. His eyes were red and bulging, his tongue blue. Hanging over his icy lips. Someone had slit his throat, a while ago by the look of him. Seemed like the poor bastard never made his cruise after all.

I took a step back into the hall.

I heard them then, in the distance.

Sirens.

It was history repeating itself. Only this time I didn't have anyone else to blame.

There was a sudden clatter from below. Whirling, I ran for the stairs. I could feel my gun tight against my chest. I wasn't going to fire it, not in here. I didn't want to make the same mistake twice.

"Simon!" I yelled. The back door swung on its hinges. I headed across the living room.

Something crashed into the back of my head. I pitched forward, just about losing my balance before catching myself on a coffee table. I whirled around and Simon was standing there, blond hair flapping about his eyes, arms up like he was boxing. A smile stretched wide across his face.

"Detective!" he cried out. "If I'd known you were coming I'd have made some coffee."

I growled and lunged for him. He batted me away, laughing. Bouncing on the balls of his feet.

"Dammit Simon, we don't have time for this," I said.

He responded with a right hook, hard across my face. I took it standing and stepped back.

"Impressive," Simon said. "You've got more fight in you than I thought."

I wiped at my mouth. Last time I'd been in a brawl I'd had my ass kicked. This was going to be different.

When he jabbed again I snapped my head back. Ducked under his next swing and when he was off-balance I slugged him hard in the solar plexus. An uppercut that left him gasping. Followed it up with a light left hook and a stronger right. Simon stumbled, tripped over the edge of a rug and went down hard.

"Now listen to me," I said, panting. "They saw your vehicle when you were taking your photos. That piece-of-shit Nissan parked out front. And trust me, it wasn't that difficult. Christ, you murdered the old guy just to get his car? They're on their way, Simon. Are you hearing me? They're on their way now."

Simon sat up. Used the table to help him stand. "That would be very bad for you, Tommy."

"Not just me. Or have you forgotten who's helping you avoid a murder charge? No more messing around, Simon. I need you to tell me where the photos are. If they find them, it's game over for both of us."

The silence between us was punctured by the screech of tires. The slamming of doors. Slices of red and blue washed over us through dirty blinds. We were out of time.

I grabbed his shirt and pulled him toward me. I was frantic now. "Simon, where the hell are those photos?"

"Relax, Tommy, they're not in the house."

A pounding on the front door. A man's voice yelling. I glared at Simon.

"Back door," I said firmly. "Now!"

A loud crack as someone's foot connected with cheap wood. The front door flexed in its frame. We flew from the room, falling together through the doorway into the backyard. Behind us the front door exploded and my feet skidded out from under me. We tumbled to the wet ground. Dirty snow smeared across my white shirt. The sound of raised voices, of footsteps thundering through the house. Simon was up and running for the tall fence.

"No!" I hissed, motioning with my thumb. They'd have cars there already. "Between the houses, get out at the end of the street."

I led the way. Up and over the smaller fences that separated each yard from its neighbor. Glancing at the windows to make sure we were alone. The last one dropped us back out into the small alleyway. Up ahead was the main street.

I turned toward Simon and he wasn't there. Then his meaty arm was around my throat. I choked out a cry as he dragged me to the ground. His biceps flexed against my neck and I started to feel dizzy. Stars prickled at the edges of my vision.

"I saw you here before," Simon snarled into my ear. "Tell me you didn't tip them off."

I couldn't speak, my fingers scrabbling uselessly at his arm. Then he eased off a little, and I breathed in deep lungfuls as I struggled to my feet.

"I just saved you," I wheezed. "Why the hell would I tip them off?"

He released me fully and I stumbled forward, coughing. I rubbed at my throat. Turning angrily to him, I said, "Tell me where those photos are, Simon. If they find them I can't help you anymore."

Simon laughed. "I'm not so sure you've been helping me that much so far, Thomas."

"Why did you have to kill him?"

"Who?"

"Catterson. The old man in his bed. Jesus, Simon, what's wrong with you?"

Simon stepped forward and grabbed at me. I swatted him away and scrambled back. My shoes kicking a pile of broken bottles. I reached down and picked one up.

"You know what?" he said. "I'm starting to think we've reached the end of our association."

He lunged for me again but I was ready. Stabbing forward, slicing the jagged glass across his hands as he recoiled. I used the space to pull my gun.

"Here's what's going to happen, asshole," I said quietly. "You're leaving Cooper right now, alright? Tonight. No excuses."

"Or what," he spat, his chest shuddering as he clamped his bleeding hands together. "You'll kill me? You're a liar. I can see it in your eyes. You're weak. Murder's messy, and you don't have the guts for it."

"Maybe not," I said. "Maybe I'll just take your eyes instead, how's that sound?"

The sound of more squad cars pulling up at the end of the alley. A short blast of sirens. I turned to look and Simon took off, vanishing down the narrow space.

I tossed the bottle and holstered my gun. Composed myself as best I could. Once I was ready, I walked to the opposite end of the alleyway and onto the street.

"Detective!"

I turned. Officer Gordon was standing there. He waved a hello. I moved toward him and he smiled as I approached, his breath misting in the cold air. He frowned as I got close.

"Damn, Detective. You're blue. You forget your coat?"

Chapter Twenty-Seven

I followed Gordon back to the house. Squad cars were scattered outside, their lights twirling silently. I made sure I was collected. A borrowed overcoat, pulled tight over my dirtied clothes. No signs of my earlier scuffle. My anger had abated, slunk back into my bones. I could feel it sitting there. Weighing me down like a physical presence. Like a tumor.

Mansfield was leaning against the hood of a squad car. She was watching the house with narrowed eyes. They swiveled onto me as we approached.

"Didn't expect to see you here, Detective," she called.

I shrugged. "Figured you could use the help."

She stayed quiet. Her eyes did the talking.

I walked past her. Waited by a squad car until her gaze wandered, her attention shifting to a trio of officers emerging from the house. "You're going to want to see this, Detectives," one of them shouted.

She pushed herself off the car and started toward the front door. Paused as she passed me, snapping on a pair of latex gloves.

"Well?" she said. "You coming?"

Mansfield led, and I followed.

We wore latex gloves on our hands, our shoes bound in plastic sheaths. Technically I should have entered the house first. Cooper was my jurisdiction; Mansfield was from out of town. A guest of the department.

But that didn't matter to her. She didn't care about whether or not my pride was wounded, my feelings hurt. She cared about the truth. Finding it, preserving it. More than I did, I'm ashamed to say. And so we wore latex gloves and plastic shoes, and Mansfield led and I followed.

The officers before us had turned on most of the lights already. A necessity, thanks to the blinds. Drawn across every window, every point where the sun's rays could enter. Every point where someone could have spotted who was really staying there.

We were the only officers here. The others had been told to clear the house until Bob and his forensic team arrived. The place was quiet, and we picked our way through the living room. Mansfield pointed to a fallen lamp, its shade buckled and its frame cracked. Simon's opening attack.

"Thoughts?" she asked me.

I'm amazed it didn't break. "Whoever was staying here knocked it over in their hurry to get out."

"Maybe."

"Maybe?"

"It's not just the lamp. The rug's been pulled up at one end and the coffee table's been knocked aside." She gestured to a collection of enamel elephants, scattered on their sides. I'd not noticed them first time around. "And here," she said, kneeling by the dining-room table, "there's imprints in the rug where the legs normally sit. It's been recently moved."

"What, you think there was a fight?"

"Don't you?"

I made a show of scanning the room. Let out a noncommittal noise.

She turned back to the house. Pointed at the kitchen. "Whoever was staying here must have left through the back door."

"You put officers in the alleyway out back?"

"There's backyards on either side of the property, they could have jumped the fence."

I was barely listening to her by then. My eyes running over every inch of the place. Where would Simon have hidden those photos? I had to get to them before someone else found them. Bob and his boys. Or worse, Mansfield herself.

She ran her gloved fingers over the lock, then, apparently satisfied, stepped away. "Let's go upstairs," she said.

We both knew what was waiting for us. The officers outside had already filled us in. *Dead body, male, late seventies.* Clinical. A safety barrier to keep emotions at bay.

Hey, it worked for me.

At the top of the stairs, we paused at the doorway to the master bedroom. I could smell it from farther out now. Metal in the air. That strong scent of rust. Even though I knew it was coming, the gruesome sight still caught me off-guard. Pale skin on red sheets. His throat sliced open like a gaping mouth.

Mansfield shook her head. "Christ," she said.

There was the sound of footsteps downstairs. A moment later Bob appeared at the top of the stairs. He was dressed in his white hazmat suit and carried a small, plastic case. The same getup he'd worn the first time I saw him.

He frowned at us both. His face half hidden by the plastic hood and safety glasses.

"You two," he ordered. "Out."

Mansfield nodded and gave me a look. We headed down the stairs and back into the frosty morning. I cast one last glance around the house as we passed through it. As though I would suddenly spot a strip of negatives sitting next to a potted plant.

I didn't realize how humid it had been in the house until we were outside. I took in a deep lungful of icy air. Felt it rattle its way into my chest. I still had the smell of it in my nose. The blood. An irrational fear that it would stay with me forever.

The street had been cordoned off. A couple more squad cars were parked at either end, their lights rolling lazily. Bile burned in my chest. A hot, stabbing pain that nearly made my legs buckle.

They were going to find the photographs. It was only a matter of time now. For a few fleeting moments this morning, I'd entertained the idea of coming clean. Of owning up to everything that had happened since I got here. Would it be liberating? For a short while, maybe. Only now the moment had come and I couldn't face it.

How long did I have until they found the photographs? I figured that unless Simon had scrawled *Thomas Levine Blackmail* on the side of an envelope I probably had some time. Even if they were picked up today, they might not get checked straightaway.

I needed to intercept the evidence somehow. Maybe I could go back into the evidence room, grab the photos before they were logged. I ran through a hundred scenarios in seconds, each more outlandish than the last. At one point I even considered stealing a white forensics jumpsuit to get back in the house.

Then Mansfield was on the street beside me.

"You alright, Thomas?" she asked. "You're looking a little pale."

I stared at her. "I'm fine," I said. "Dead bodies, you know?"

She harrumphed. "You really want to be of use, you're welcome to help me take some statements from the neighbors. They're still living, so I expect you'll be able to manage it."

Turning, she marched to the next-door property. The same guy I'd spoken to yesterday. I decided it was probably best I wasn't there when he answered, and I slipped away to my car.

Chapter Twenty-Eight

So, let's skip through the remainder of that Saturday. Trust me, it's not very interesting.

I spent the afternoon at my desk, surrounded by a growing number of empty coffee cups and enough paperwork to put anyone off approaching me.

I wondered how it would happen. A knock on my door one evening, maybe. Shadows and streetlights. The amber glow just starting to work its magic. If it was anywhere else they'd send a friendly face to soothe the pain, only Cooper didn't have any. At least not for me. More likely it'd be a uniformed stranger, a little embarrassed at having to do this to a fellow officer. He'd spare the handcuffs. Tell me it's the least he could do.

Best guess, however, it would be at the station. I'd look up from my desk and see Captain Morricone standing there. His face crumpled. That hope he'd held for me now gone. In some ways I'd rather it was Mansfield. See, I could get angry at Mansfield. I could let the disappointment and the despair turn sour for her, let it build and spark into something more. Into rage. I could hide behind rage. Draw strength from it. I've been doing it my entire life.

I sat at my desk and I felt sick. A sourness that made me sweat. It's difficult, keeping this stuff to yourself. I was getting so tired of carrying it around. If Joe had turned up that afternoon I'm honestly not sure I wouldn't have spilled my guts to him.

But he didn't, and that was good. I didn't want to give him any more ammunition. Mansfield was right. He *was* playing me. Just as she was.

The clock hit three and I headed out.

It was snowing again, but lightly. Like the sky was getting tired. Tufts of white that seemed to hang in the air, near suspended and unmoving, and I imagined them parting as I pushed through.

It wasn't cold, I remember that. It wasn't cold.

It wasn't anything.

Stingray's was quiet. No sign of Mary but that was alright. Maybe that was best. I sat at the bar and ordered the cheapest Scotch they had and knocked back two of them in a couple of minutes. Asked for a third and a beer to go with it. The guy gave me a funny look but my money cleared that right up.

I was halfway through my beer and really getting into that buzz when Mary sat down next to me. She ordered a lemonade and unwound a scarf from her neck. She looked over at me and smiled, and that same urge to spill my guts hit me hard.

"You want to go for a walk?" I asked.

We walked down the same narrow alley we'd gone down before, only this time we kept going. Past the dead grass and along the rickety fence. Following the path of the river as it curved around the edge of town.

"Listen, I just want to say something," I started, but the words caught in my throat. Mary put her hand on my arm.

"It's okay," she said. "We can just walk."

We came out into an open expanse. A construction site, long abandoned. Cracked concrete and weeds. Bookended by water and a quiet road, the fading red of a drifting taillight. Not quite dark enough for the streetlights, too bright for the wanderers and night stalkers. We'd caught Cooper by surprise, and as we strolled across the empty lot I could feel the town shift around us.

Anywhere else, this might have been a basketball court. A football field. It might have been kids yelling, calling out to each other as they scrambled over frozen turf, a ball arcing against the night sky. Here it was forlorn and forgotten. Just another piece of the American Dream left behind to rot. A car's headlights swept ahead of us and across the street something glittered; the sparkling scarf of a whore, drifting low by a driver's window and trailing in the dirt.

The streetlights blinked on and I felt Cooper relax. The scene change complete.

I turned to Mary. "Tell me what it's like," I said. "Living in a place like this."

"It's not so bad." Her head was bowed slightly, her pink streak swaying with each step. "There's worse out there."

"There's better, too."

Mary looked at me and tucked a strand of neon behind one ear. "Not for people like us, Thomas."

We rejoined the sidewalk. "You know, everyone I meet tells me what this place is," I said. "And everyone says something different."

"Maybe it's different for everyone."

"How do you stand it?" I asked.

Mary paused and shook her head. Standing there, in the lull between streetlights, her pink streak near black, I felt a great depression settle itself in my chest.

"How do you not go crazy?" I said, and Mary smiled at me.

"I listen to music," she said.

She stepped closer, her green eyes on mine. She slid her hands into her pockets and nudged me with her elbow. "Walk me home," she said, "and I'll tell you a story."

Chapter Twenty-Nine

And so she did.

"You asked me once why I came to Cooper," she began. "And I said it didn't matter."

"I remember."

We were back on the main street now. Cooper was alive around us. A jumble of half-naked women, of parked cars with their running lights on and their windows down, of doors slamming and voices shouting, of brief blasts of music and fluorescent lights reflecting off frozen brick.

"When I was nineteen I got pregnant," Mary said. "By some guy who used to go to my school. He was a few years older than me . . . hell, he was like ten years older than me. He used to hang around with my brother—I have a brother, by the way—and one summer he was around, like all the time. He'd be there when I got home from work. He used to say hi, and his eyes would just roll over every inch of me. It was so intimate, and when I look back, in*sane*ly creepy. But I never saw it like that then. I was young and stupid, and I thought having an older guy check me out was hot."

She took a breath.

"So there was this house party one night, and he was there and somehow we ended up in the bedroom of this poor kid's parents, and of course afterwards he didn't really want anything to do with me, and a few weeks later I found out I was pregnant. I caught him eventually, you know, cornered him in my folks' kitchen with the goddamn doctor's note and I was screaming at him because I was pissed at myself for having been so stupid and he was getting angrier and angrier probably for the same reason and he didn't *hit* me, it was nothing like that, he just left and said I would never see him again and I was a slut and the baby wasn't his. So having already done one stupid thing, I figured two couldn't make much difference and I drank about a quarter-bottle of vodka, which maybe isn't much for most people but was more than enough for me, and I got in a car and decided to drive over to his house in the rain and ended up wrapping my parents' Honda round an oak tree about a hundred yards from my house and . . . and losing the baby, or whatever you want to call it. I mean, it was just cells at that point, you know? But they said I'd broken a bunch of bones and punctured my uterus and so they . . . they had to take it out. They just took it all out while I slept."

I'm not sure when it happened, but we'd stopped walking at some point. Mary lifted her eyes to look at me and forced a smile. I could hear laughter coming from somewhere, and the sound of car horns and yelling. A man pushed past us, his head down.

"Well," she said.

"Jesus, I'm—"

"Don't," she said, shaking her head. "I haven't told anyone that story since I got here, precisely because I don't want anyone to feel sorry for me."

"No, sure, it's just—"

"Something that happened," Mary said. She started walking again, and I fell into step beside her. "It was a long, long time ago and I've come to terms with it. I was the talk of the town back home and I couldn't stand it and so I left as soon as I was able to.

Said my goodbyes to those that really mattered and hit the bus station with a backpack and a roll of twenties my dad had given me."

"You didn't even know where you were going?"

Mary shrugged. "Didn't matter. Just had to be somewhere else. Honestly, I don't even remember choosing the bus. It feels like I just walked onto one at random, and . . . and I was so tired, I fell asleep and woke up as we were pulling in. Figured this was as good a place as any to start again."

We fell silent for a few moments. I wasn't sure what to say, so I didn't say anything. The snow had turned to rain—not much, not then, just little droplets here and there. We turned off the main street and wandered along smaller roads past little apartment buildings. At last I looked over at her and she looked over at me.

"That's some story," I said.

"I know."

"Next you'll be telling me that pink streak in your hair isn't real."

Mary smiled at that, and I guess I did too.

"I'm actually thinking of getting rid of it," she said. "It's killing my ends."

"I like it."

Mary slowed and I realized we were nearly at her building. I sniffed and stuck my hands in my pockets. I thought about her warm living room. Thought about it in soft focus. All light and smooth edges and filled with music. She'd carved herself out a nice spot here, maybe as nice as it got in Cooper. Maybe nicer than what she'd had before. I didn't want to ruin that for her. Knew if I stayed around too long, that's what would happen. It always did.

I hadn't ended up in this town by accident. I'd come here by choice. Here, I got to run away from my problems and punish myself for them at the same time. Mary talked like there was some point to it all. Like I could find peace here, if I wanted to.

She looked up at me. "You want to talk about it?"

"Every day," I said, smiling a little. "You have no idea how bad." I wiped at my nose. At the rain that ran down the side of my cheek. "The stuff I've got in me . . . I just don't know how to let it out."

"Sometimes when you keep things locked up inside," Mary said gently, "you forget how to live without them."

I took a breath, nodded.

"I killed my girlfriend," I said. "I think that's why I'm here."

Mary was quiet as I told her my story. I told her everything. More than I'd told my old captain. More than I've told you. Maybe more than I've told myself.

We rounded a corner. Up ahead I could see Mary's apartment building.

"Rachel and I, we were unhappy," I said. "Not at first, but . . ."

"At first you were in love," Mary said.

"I don't know if I've ever been in love."

It's true. I mean, I've felt it, sure. Felt it hard, felt it in the pit of my stomach. That chemical rush, that endorphin high. Pulsing through the capillaries of my brain. Oh, I've felt love. Crushed into white powder and pressed into yellow pills. A smiling face stamped on the coating. What woman could compete with that?

"But you were happy," Mary said.

"Sure," I said. "We were happy."

We paused to cross the street, the wake of a passing car a shimmering haze. Moonlight glinted on the frozen sidewalk. Mary slipped her hand through the crook of my arm.

"I told people I was out when it happened. I said I got home and found her."

"But you were there," Mary said.

"I was there," I said softly. "I was in the next room. I was three feet away. You think you'd hear it, the sound of a life ending. You'd think it would be louder, but it's not. It's barely a whisper."

We were nearly at Mary's apartment. The streets here were restless, a wind that shifted the rain back and forth. Cooper's heart was racing. I could feel it in my chest.

"I was high," I said. "I was three feet and a hundred miles away." And I told her about the junkie woman, about the yellow spoon she'd used to kill her old man and the bag of pills I'd lifted from the scene. "I brought them home. Into our house, Mary. Carried them around in my pocket. Nestled in a little plastic bag."

"Just pills, though," she said. "You didn't kill her."

I could feel it stirring inside me. Protective, maybe.

"Rachel was in the bathroom. I thought she'd only taken a couple of them, same as me. She got cold all the time. Her hands, her feet . . ." I let out a liquid laugh. "God I'd forgotten all about that. She used to lie on the sofa at night when we watched TV, and I'd hold her feet. I'd warm them under my shirt, against my skin."

I fell silent for a moment.

"She was running a bath," I said. "She always liked them hot. Like, scalding hot. Way hotter than I could stand. And she'd been in there a while, but I couldn't tell you how long. Jesus, I was so high I could barely recognize what a number was, never mind tell the time."

I took a breath, felt myself tensing up at the memory. Mary squeezed my arm tight.

"So she's in there and it must have been a while because I remember banging on the door. Starting shouting at her to hurry up. I needed a piss from all that cheap shit I was drinking. Budweiser, whatever. I was banging on the door and she didn't answer and—and listen to this Mary—I get *angry* at her. Like she's ignoring me, you know? So I kick the door down and she's still in

166

the bath and of course she's dead, she's been dead for hours. The water is freezing.

"And the bag of pills? It was empty. She'd taken them all, one after the other without stopping. They ruled it an *accidental drowning* in the end, but that's bullshit. Rachel wasn't some dumb teenager, she knew what she was doing. And it was my fault, you understand me? She saw the real me, she saw who I really was, and she just couldn't bear it for a minute longer."

"Thomas, I—"

"And I panicked, Mary, okay? I started cleaning the apartment. Flushing pills and God knows what else down the toilet. Down the toilet that's right next to her. And I even think about putting her in bed and making it look like she died in her sleep. Or, or maybe I take her outside, you know? *Outside*. And do what? Dump her body in the street? What the hell is wrong with me, Mary?"

I'm staring at her. I let go of a breath I barely realized I was holding. I was hunched up. My back arched, towering over her. My hands were shaking. Fingers curled into my palms.

Mary stood there, unmoving. She kept my gaze, didn't back down. Her arm still looped around mine. Still holding on tight.

Slowly I let the tension ebb away. Took in a cold breath, a lightness in my chest.

The rain was coming down hard now. Large droplets collecting in my hair and running down the side of my face.

"It wasn't your fault, Thomas."

I closed my eyes when she said that. I guess I just wasn't ready to hear it yet. Inside I could feel it starting to build. The heaviness, oozing from my bones.

"It wasn't your fault," she said again, and then her hand was on my shoulder, squeezing, and even in the rain I could feel her heat, she was so close.

"Don't touch me," I said quietly. "You don't know what you're talking about."

"Thomas, I just meant—"

"I know what you meant." I took in another breath, balled up my fists. "And I know you mean well. But you *don't know* what it was like, and you *don't know* the things that I did. So don't *tell* me it wasn't my fault." I stepped toward her and she stepped back. The defiance in her eyes flickered. "I'm not a nice guy, Mary, you understand me? You were right to tell me to get lost before. This . . . swapping-stories shit, this *talking*, I can't do it. I thought I could. Thought it might be a relief or whatever, but it's just more pain and I can't stand it anymore. So please, go back to your apartment and just leave me the hell alone."

I turned around and walked away then. Quickly, while the blood thumping in my ears was loud enough to drown out everything else. When I got home I went into the yard and even though I knew what I would find I had to look all the same.

The money was gone.

It was a late one last night. I can smell it in the air.

Rookie seems pretty fresh, though; he obviously wasn't invited to Boys' Night Out. I wonder where they went. Tubby doesn't look like he's shaved this morning, so I'm guessing he slept in. Either that, or the guy never learned how to do it properly. Cumstain's the worst, though. Asshole's got a black eye.

"What happened to you?" I ask him.

He glowers at me over his coffee, says he'll ask the questions. Out the corner of my eye I see Rookie smile as he exits the room. It bolsters me a little, and I lean forward across the table and give an exaggerated sniff, then tell him he smells like dick so I'm guessing he ended up pulling some cock in a skirt who liked it rough, and Cumstain bangs his coffee down so hard on the table it slops over the sides and the bastard goes and burns himself and I squeal with laughter.

Then Cumstain ups and leaves and I get to enjoy my morning coffee in peace. When he returns he's got a damp dishcloth wrapped around his hand and a look in his black eye that says, Try it. *So I say nothing and he starts up the recorder then reaches for his coffee but the cup's already empty because I drank it when he was out of the room.*

Afterwards Rookie takes me back down to my cell. I wonder if he's going to stay and chat.

They've stopped giving me the special treatment now. No more takeout, no more radio. No more natural light, even—someone has bolted a sheet of metal over the window and I bet I can guess who. They must think I'm dragging my feet. Must think I'm keeping some of the good bits back, which of course I am. I'd have to be a Grade A moron to give up what I've got without that signed agreement in my hands. It's on its way, they say, whenever I ask. Has the FBI never heard of a scanner? *I say back.* Is the Director walking it down here himself?

Rookie uncuffs me—small silver key, but there's a bunch on his chain. Kid even keeps his car keys on there too. He slips them into his pocket. He looks like he's going to say something, like he's finally going to strike up a conversation, but then doesn't. The door opens at the top of the stairs and I recognize the shoes as they pad down.

"Smells like dick!" *I yell through the bars and Cumstain's face is dark when it finally comes into view.*

He jerks his thumb at Rookie. Poor kid is too scared to even glance at me as he leaves, takes the stairs three at a time. Few seconds later it's just me and him and the bars between us. I bounce back and forth on the balls of my feet for a bit as he glares at me, then I walk over to the window and point at the metal grate.

"Was this you?" *I ask.* "'Cause"—*and I stick my nose right up against the metal and sniff*—"'cause you know what it smells like?"

Cumstain says nothing, just reaches into his pocket and pulls out a set of keys. I know what's coming next. Spotted the baton in his right hand when he came in. He says I've had this coming a while now, and I tell him I'm surprised it's taken this long.

The bars roll back and Cumstain steps into the cell with wide eyes and I don't even try and stop him.

Chapter Thirty

Needless to say, I woke up Sunday morning feeling pretty shitty.

The rain had continued throughout the night. Lying in bed I could hear it. The metal gutters sang. Drops of the stuff collecting on my window. I rolled onto my side and stared at the grey light. Its anemic glow filling the room.

I couldn't stop thinking about what I'd said to Mary the night before. How I'd lost it. She was the first person who had genuinely tried to help me—who'd been prepared to wait until I was ready to talk and then listen when I was—and I'd pushed her away. I didn't know how to fix that.

Not that it would matter for much longer anyhow. It was coming up on a full day now since Bob and his team had started combing the Catterson residence. They were going to find those photographs. Now that Mansfield had the money, maybe it didn't matter anymore.

I rolled out of bed and saw the picture of Rachel propped up on my nightstand. I reached over and flipped her facedown. I couldn't look at her. Not today. Not after last night.

I showered in lukewarm water. The water heater was on the fritz and I hadn't got around to dealing with it yet.

I didn't want to think about Mary. So I focused on Simon instead. As I dressed, I wondered whether Morricone would be waiting for me when I got to work. I didn't need to go in today, but what else was I going to do? Pulling the collar of my raincoat around me as I dashed to the car, I tried to think if there was any way I could get out from under the pile of shit I was building around myself. Confessing was an option, sure, only I'd given that a shot last night and woken up feeling even worse than usual—and I usually drank a half-bottle of something before going to sleep.

I thought back to what Simon had said, and that's when it hit me. So hard it made me stop. In the street, in the rain, standing staring at my Impala. The photos aren't in the house, he'd said, and suddenly all I could see was the red Nissan parked outside.

I sped down the wet roads. My wipers working double time to keep the windshield clear. My raincoat on the back seat; a sodden mess. The heater was on full blast but I barely felt it. If Bob had been working on the house, he might not have gotten to the car yet. I ran through the preliminary forensic process in my head. Tried to work out whether I could still make it.

They would have taped off the driveway at the same time as the house. Nobody would be allowed near the vehicle. Preservation of evidence was always the first step.

Photographs would come next. Exterior and interior.

Finally, they would have moved to detection. DNA, fingerprints, other trace evidence. Exterior surfaces would be checked for latent prints. Side mirrors, door handles, hood, trunk, roof-support posts, gas-tank cover—everything. Inside they'd focus on the steering wheel, rearview mirror, the windows and window handles, the handbrake, the glovebox, the seatbelt buckles. Any place a person might be reasonably expected to touch. They'd collect hair and fiber evidence with a vacuum system.

By my guess, that process would take the best part of a day. I doubted Bob would do it himself; he'd be too busy coordinating the house. A car was easier, more self-contained. One of his team would do it. They might be slower. Regardless, if they'd started yesterday morning, then they'd probably finished with the preliminary investigation.

Once that was done they'd move on to stage two. Towing the vehicle to the station. Well-covered and secure, safe from the weather. This would be where they'd really go to town on it. A systematic search of every inch of the vehicle. Taking the interior apart, piece by piece. Anything of interest would get a numbered placard. More photographs. All things considered, I figured they'd start on that today.

I arrived at the station and parked in my usual spot. Pulling my coat on, I ran through the rain to the secure garage. It wasn't that early, but it was Cooper. I was banking on whoever was due to look over the car running late.

I slid open the large steel doors and slipped inside. I glanced around. The place wasn't big, maybe large enough to fit a couple cars. A small office at the far end that led into the station. The window thankfully dark.

Without the overhead lights on, the garage was nearly pitch-black. I turned on a penlight I carry and scanned the room. There, in the corner, stood the Nissan. 248-UGN. I breathed out a sigh of relief.

I hung my raincoat on a chair, traded it for the white lab variety, and snapped on a pair of latex gloves. Wrapped my shoes in plastic, too. Last thing I needed was to leave a fresh trace.

I hurried over to the car. It was unlocked. Pulling open the door, I climbed into the driver's seat.

Glovebox.

Cup holders.

Door storage.

Nothing.

I glanced at my watch. I'd been there for nearly ten minutes and it was already after nine. I glanced at the office window. Someone could turn up at any moment. Thinking, I ran my hands over the dashboard and around the sides of the seats. I checked for rips in the fabric, front and back. I popped the trunk and lifted the spare tire.

Nothing.

It was nine fifteen.

I was sweating. I wiped at my forehead with a gloved hand. There was a noise and when I looked up I saw a light flickering on in the office. I clicked off my little flashlight.

"Shit," I hissed quietly. "Alright, Simon. Where did you put it?"

I slid back into the driver's seat. One eye on the shadows moving around behind the mottled glass.

"Come on, come on," I whispered to myself. "Somewhere you could reach fast if you needed to. Somewhere you could hide it in a hurry."

In desperation, I leaned forward to feel the carpet by my feet. Patted my palm around until I felt it.

A slight lip in the material.

I dug my fingers underneath it and gently prized it up.

The office door opening. I could hear voices now. Male. A conversation, someone laughing. The garage was still in darkness but any second that would change.

My fingers were on the hard floor of the chassis. I scrabbled around frantically. And there, nestled in between, was a small envelope. I pulled it out and ripped it open. Spilled a stack of negatives into my palm.

Rolling back the carpet, I clambered out. Clicked the door shut softly. Reached my raincoat just as the overhead halogen bulbs started to ping, slid through the main doors as they burst to life.

Back outside, I hurried through the parking lot. I snapped off the gloves and shoe covers as I pushed through the station's entrance. Threw the plastic into the trash. Reached my chair and collapsed into it. Time to see what he really had.

I pulled out the negatives and started checking each one.

There were over a dozen photographs. All of them of the van heist. All of them of me and Joe. In our ridiculous masks, our shotguns raised. I saw myself smacking Casey square in the jaw. Watched us burning the car, masks off. My face lit up in the flames as I collected my bundles of cash. My stomach flipped a little as I went through them all. Our entire adventure, captured for anyone to see.

I leaned back in my chair just in time to see Morricone striding toward me. I stuffed the negatives back into the envelope. As he got close, I could tell he was pissed. I tried a smile.

"Morning, sir."

"My office," he said. "Now."

I stood up so fast I nearly flipped the chair. Slid the envelope into my pocket and followed him up the stairs. By the time we reached his office, my palms were slick with sweat.

Mansfield was waiting inside.

"Oh," I said.

"Morning, Detective," she said.

She was sitting on a chair at the side of the room. Didn't bother getting up to greet me.

I hadn't been in Morricone's office before. It was nice; looked out over the main area. Big bay window that let in the light.

The captain closed the door behind us and took a seat at his desk. I didn't want to be the only one standing so I pulled out a chair and fell into it.

"What's this about?" I asked. Disdain masking my nerves.

Morricone looked at me and folded his long arms. "I understand you're somewhat acquainted with Detective Mansfield."

"Somewhat."

"I want to make it clear that she's here at my request."

"Alright."

"She's been assisting me on a rather . . . sensitive investigation."

I blinked. "You're building a case against Joe, aren't you."

Morricone nodded. "That's right. And Thomas, we need your help."

"I don't understand. What is it you think he's done?"

Mansfield explained.

It had begun in the east. Omaha, six months previous. A DEA bust that nabbed seventeen drug dealers and nearly five million in narcotics and cash combined. The kind of operation that makes the main page of the local papers, maybe even plays lead in the nightly news. KFAB talk radio, frontline reporting on the war on drugs. Photographs of some bald guy in a flak jacket standing in front of a table creaking with white powder.

Of the seventeen arrests, one was twenty-three-year-old Connor Feltman. Mansfield had a picture of him, and she slid it across Morricone's desk. A pimple-faced kid who looked like he was about to shit himself. Feltman ended up informing on just about everyone he knew to save his own skin. If his own grandmother had inhaled back at Woodstock, she'd have been right up there with the crack addicts and gangbangers.

But Feltman happened to be a pretty well-connected little shit, and two of the names he gave rubbed the right people the wrong way. The first was Demyan Marchenko, a Ukrainian national who moved over to the US a few years earlier. Hooked in with a drug cartel operating out of Omaha, started running drugs and guns from Eastern Europe throughout the state. Used a handful of farms outside Cooper to store product.

I'd heard some of this already. Watched Mansfield as she reached into her folder for a second photograph, laid it out next to Connor Feltman's. Recognition must have been on my face, because she leaned in just enough to let me know she'd seen it. Poker had never been my strong suit.

"You know him," she told me.

"Yeah," I said. "What did you say his name was?"

"Marchenko. Demyan Marchenko. How do you know him, Thomas?"

"Well, I don't *know* him."

"But you've seen him."

I'd seen him. I reached over and tugged the photograph toward me.

"This is out of date," I said. "His hair is shorter now, and black."

"You sure it's him?"

"I'm sure," I said, and stared at the same eyes that had tracked me through a haze of cigarette smoke. Cold and grey like a February morning. I spun the picture around and tapped at the man's half-smirk. "He was missing the same tooth. Front row, upper right."

"When did you see him?"

"Couple days ago. He was in the parking lot outside."

Mansfield and Morricone shared a look. The captain loomed across his desk.

"What was he doing here?" he asked me.

"He was meeting Joe," I said.

Morricone fell silent, his face dark. Mansfield opened her folder, pulled out a third photograph and a smile to go with it.

"Detective Joe Finch," she said, and placed his picture next to the two already laid out. "The second name that Feltman gave up, and the man you're going to help us catch."

177

Chapter Thirty-One

Mansfield laid it out for me, nice and clear. *Wear a wire. Get him on tape.* I interrupted her before she asked me to *do the right thing.*

"Save me the pitch," I said. "We all know I've heard it before."

Mansfield clammed up. Leaned back and crossed her short legs.

Morricone cleared his throat, said, "Thomas, the Nebraska State Police have been working this for the last four months. Believe me, no one in this room wants to set officers against each other. But Joe Finch is a dirty cop, and I will not have a dirty cop working in my station, do you understand?"

"Yes, sir."

"Good. Now Detective Mansfield's remit is the Omaha cartel. Internal makeup, future deals, location of product. If Demyan Marchenko is in Cooper then there's a reason for it. Joe is our way into all of this."

"And I'm your way to Joe."

"Exactly."

"Is this an order?"

The captain sighed. "If it has to be."

Mansfield leaned forward. "We think Joe was involved in the attack on the police transport."

"I didn't come to Cooper so I could set up another one of my colleagues."

"You think DC is the only place with dirty cops?"

I got to my feet. "Do you have any idea what happens to informers? You expect me to have any sort of career here when this is done?"

"I'm not here to make friends, Detective."

I turned and headed for the door. Mansfield called after me.

"Where are you going, Thomas?"

"To do my job."

I was three steps into the corridor when I heard the door open behind me and the sound of heels clicking. I stopped at the top of the stairs and turned. Mansfield was glaring at me.

"You know you're damn lucky I didn't drop you in it back there," she said.

"What stopped you?"

"I'm not interested in you, Thomas. I never have been. As far as I'm concerned, you're a spineless waste of my time. I want your partner and I want Marchenko."

"You burn me now, you lose your shot."

"So our interests are aligned. *Briefly.*"

"Where's the money?"

"Somewhere safe."

"And if I help you? What happens then? You drop the cash onto Morricone's desk on your way out the door?"

"You want to talk about immunity, we can talk about immunity."

"I figure you didn't want to risk putting my name out on the wire. You have a warrant to search my yard?"

Mansfield rolled her eyes. "You trying to argue the twenty-five grand I pulled out of the ground is inadmissible?"

"You counted it."

"You're short. Spent some already, pretty sure I can guess where." She smiled thinly. "And I won't need your name for *that* search warrant."

"This is bullshit."

"This is how I can end you, understand? You think packing up and heading to another shithole town is the worst of your problems? You wear the wire or you go to prison. Grand larceny, armed robbery, aggravated assault. I tie you to Foster and that's murder one."

We stared at each other. Mansfield's face was flushed, her breathing fast. I thought about the photographs in my pocket. Thought about the choices people kept asking me to make. Seemed like I kept making the wrong one.

My mother was released from prison when I was fifteen.

She'd had a rough go of it inside. Being sent away for cold-blooded murder didn't exactly make you popular. Least not with the inmates you wanted to get friendly with. The women in for fraud or tax evasion. White-collar criminals who just wanted to serve their time quietly and get the hell out. Exactly the sort of people who tended to keep their distance once they found out my mom had shot a guy in broad daylight.

And look, I don't know for sure what it was like. But I know my mom wasn't a psychopath. Wasn't some jilted lover who had tortured her ex for three days before mailing his fingers through his new girl's letterbox. Seriously, some of these women were nuts. Sure, my mom was a murderer. But what she'd done? It had been a public service.

Nancy and Eddie never took me to visit her. Never let me speak to her on the phone. Did their best not to mention her if they could, like I was some sort of Immaculate Conception. Looking back now though, maybe I'm glad. You've already heard about my messed-up childhood. I'm not sure driving twenty hours west to sit in a room full of jittery wackos would have done me any favors.

Anyway, I was fifteen when she got released. Nancy and Eddie weren't happy to see her, that was for sure. Happier less to see her take me away. I sat upfront in a faded red SUV and we drove for hours across a flat, uninteresting land. Dusty town and shimmering horizon; we were the last people alive in all the barren world.

She didn't talk much as she drove. At one point we had to pull over so she could cry. I wondered if she'd always been like that or if being in prison had changed her. I wondered if being in prison was like the red room.

But I didn't care about any of that. I would have taken a lifetime of silence in that passenger seat over one more day with Nancy and Eddie. We drove north for nearly ten hours straight, through Des Moines, through Minneapolis. For a while I thought we were going to keep on driving until we reached Canada. Ended up in a place called Duluth, on the shore of Lake Superior. It was the first proper city I'd ever seen. Compared to Eudora, it might as well have been another planet.

Now my mom, she was damaged goods. Whether I realized it at the time or not doesn't matter. She was off-kilter, but then I was maybe off-kilter too, and in the stories when two off-kilter people find each other it's a happy ending, cue the lights and don't leave behind your popcorn for the cleaners. But in reality it's a little different.

Rookie comes to collect me. Cuffs my good arm to my belt buckle. Silver key with the black trim. I talk as he leads me back to the others. About my life in Duluth. Was it better? Sure it was. I didn't get hit, for starters. My mom was many things, but she wasn't violent. Matter of fact, the only violence I remember from that time was some guy at school.

Little Jesse Kane. That was his name. People called him a nerd or a geek. Labeled him a weirdo because he wore glasses and read books at lunchtime instead of making out with girls or getting stoned. Jesse was a sensitive kind of guy, the sort you knew just by looking at that they weren't going to make it in this world. He got upset with the little things, which was just no good. You can't get upset with the little things, because then what do you do with the big things?

Well, everyone found out what it was you did *do with the big things when Jesse's parents got divorced and Jesse hung himself in his room with his belt. I think his little sister found him, or at least that's what they used to say. I always thought it was a pretty shitty thing to do to someone—leave yourself there for them to find. His sister was, like, ten years old. Can you imagine walking in and seeing that sort of shit at ten years old? That kind of thing stays with you. I tell Rookie I have no problem with people killing themselves, I just wish they'd go do it in private.*

Chapter Thirty-Two

It was late, and I was tired. It was just after midnight and I was sitting in my Impala with the engine off, so I guess I was cold, too. A thermos of coffee only goes so far.

Snow drifted lazily through the empty streets, not slowing for stop signs or speed bumps. Every now and then it would catch on my windshield.

Just after midnight meant I'd been here nearly three hours. Another hour and I'd head home. Same as last night, and the night before that. I poured myself a cup of lukewarm coffee and stared up at Joe's apartment and watched his shadow glide across the glass.

Come on, I thought to myself. Give me *something*.

Three nights I'd been sitting there. Three nights I'd gone without sleep, three days without stamina. Avoiding Joe when I could. Burying myself in paperwork and long lunches, snatches of shut-eye in my back seat. I'd stayed away from Stingray's, too. I couldn't face Mary, not right now. I needed something to focus on. Something I could control.

I took a sip of coffee and winced. Even the brew at the station was better than this, and that stuff was pure liquid shit. I'd been drinking so much of it lately it was probably giving me cancer. I stretched across to the glove compartment and rummaged around for the bottle of whiskey I kept for special occasions. It wasn't fancy, just a cheap blend. But I guess that was the point. Anything nicer and it'd be long gone.

I could feel it now, and not the bottle. Ice-cold and making the hairs on my chest rise.

Mansfield's wire.

It was running into a hard drive strapped to my belt. Thing was so old it was like wearing a '90s Walkman. A cassette player in my pocket; the height of espionage.

Pulling out the bottle, I went to add a couple of spoonfuls when the light in Joe's apartment went out. I sat up. Last two nights he'd gone to bed about one. Could be tonight he was just tired.

Then the main door opened and he emerged onto the street, a black duffel bag in each hand. Our haul from last week's robbery. I slid down, watched him scan the area as a car swung around the corner. Headlights washed over me. It pulled in across the street and the trunk popped. Joe dumped the bags inside, then climbed in the back.

I waited a full ten seconds after they'd passed me before starting up my Impala. Debated downing the coffee in one, decided to toss it on the sidewalk. I kept my lights dimmed as I swung a U-turn.

Up ahead I could see Joe, taillights glinting red in the worsening snow. I squeezed the wheel and turned the heater up to full.

We drove for twenty, maybe twenty-five minutes. After the first ten I didn't recognize where I was anymore. I tried to read the signs but my headlights were too dim and the only streetlights that worked flickered like strobes. Cooper wasn't on my side tonight.

Then we were heading out of town. The buildings were shrinking, the gaps between them growing larger. I ignored the unease mounting steadily in my stomach as we drove farther and farther into the wider expanse. The snow had let up, a sudden glint of reflected moonlight on my right; a river, maybe. I wished I'd brought a map.

Now I'm sure all you listening to this don't need me to keep talking about the land around here. You've seen it. Some of you have seen it all your days. A bareness, like what was there before had been stripped away. Shallow fields of broken corn flanked both sides, and every so often the scattered light of a farmstead. An all-too-scarce reminder that even out here, life existed.

Ahead of me the red lights blinked out. I slowed. Headlights raked scrubland to my left. Joe's car had turned off the road. A dirt track through the corn stalks. Past a deserted-looking farmhouse, toward a couple of large barns by the edge of the fields.

I let my Impala roll quietly off the road after them and pulled up snug behind the farmhouse. Killed my engine and climbed out into the cold air. Wrapped my coat around me. Peered around the edge of the house and tracked Joe's car as it continued over uneven ground.

Lights from the farthest barn—a second vehicle starting up. I crouched down by the side of the house. Watched through the shaky zoom of my cellphone camera as three men climbed out. The driver, the muscle, and a man in the front passenger seat I recognized as Demyan Marchenko. Same guy from the police station parking lot. The head of the Omaha cartel.

I tried to snap a couple of photos, my cellphone barely able to make out the details this far away. Figures framed in the headlights' crossfire. Marchenko, his arms open wide, pulling Joe into an embrace. Leading him to the trunk of the car. To the money.

There was a faint yapping sound in the air. A dog's bark, high-pitched and rapid. Marchenko turned behind him, shouted something I couldn't quite catch. Movement by his legs. A small shape running around his feet.

Then Joe was hauling the bags out. Marchenko rifling through them. Saying something, shaking his head like he was pissed. Was this why he was here? Making sure his money was safe? I thought back to what Joe had told me before the heist. How the cartel used Cooper to hold its product. I wondered what was being stored in those barns.

Next: more hugging, more raised voices. Everyone retreating to their cars. I slid my cellphone into my pocket and got to my feet. They were leaving. Both cars heading out the way Joe had come in. They stuck to that route, they'd never spot me.

I moved to my Impala. One hand on the door handle and a hard click from behind my right ear.

"Easy there, boy," came a male voice. Deep, gruff. "Now, you better have a damn good reason to be creeping around my house this time of night."

I guess it'd only *looked* deserted.

"I was just leaving," I said, standing up straight, but slow. "Relax, I'm a cop."

"That don't mean shit. Not out here. Not anymore."

Thinking fast. One eye on the departing cars. "Not anymore? Since when? Since the cartel moved in?"

"Thought you said you were a cop."

"I just transferred in. Let me guess. Local law looks the other way, lets these guys run roughshod out here."

"You're a fast learner."

"Way I heard it, you all were happy enough to take their money."

A pause. "You got any identification on you, boy?"

"Inside pocket."

"Just keep it slow."

I reached into my jacket and pulled out my badge. Held it up. A rough, calloused hand snatched it from me. The brush of a shotgun barrel against the back of my neck.

"What's the deal anyway?" I said. "They pay you to store drugs and guns in those barns?"

"Toss your weapon."

I did as he asked. Up ahead I could see taillights bouncing onto the main road. Both cars headed back to Cooper.

"I think I better call this in," the man said.

"You think that's a fake? Ask the cop on the front desk, he'll tell you who I am."

"I ain't calling your station."

It took me a beat to get his meaning. Must have looked like I was about to jump him, because he jabbed the barrel into my back. I kept still. Listened to the flat tones of a cellphone as he dialed a number.

The cars were on the road now. Growing fainter in the dark.

"I'm not after you or whatever's in your barn," I said quickly. "I don't care how you make your money."

"Shut up."

"You make that call and I'm a dead man."

"I'm a dead man if I don't." Then, into his cell, "It's Noah Johnson. Listen, you fellas know you had a tail on you tonight?"

I closed my eyes.

"Don't worry," the man continued, "I got him here. Reckon you might want a look at him though. Badge says his name is Thomas Levine. *Detective*."

He said the last word like it was dirty. I watched those faint taillights. Saw them brighten as the cars slowed. Headlights slicing across the cornfields as they turned back.

I thought about the wire running under my shirt. Whether Joe would check for it. I had to dump it somehow.

"You think they'll be happy you called this in?" I said. "You can scratch your barn off their storage list. How much is that worth to you?"

"I told you to shut up."

"Or did they sell this as a partnership? You know they'll burn you in a heartbeat if they have to."

The shotgun barrel pressed harder into my back. "Don't start pretending like you understand what it's like out here. People make the deals they have to."

The cars were moving through the fields now. I was out of time.

"You better hope Marchenko shoots me," I said quickly. "Because otherwise I'll be back tomorrow morning with a goddamn warrant, you hear me? I'll tear every inch of this place apart if I have to. Whatever you're hiding, I'll find it. I'll *ruin* you."

"Listen here—"

"You got a wife? She ever been in a federal prison? Shit, I hope she's not a looker. Not that it matters. You spend thirty years inside, you take what you can. They're going to be all over her like a—"

The butt of the shotgun cracked against the back of my head. Pain exploded, running down my jawline. I fell to the dirt, momentarily hidden behind my Impala from the oncoming cars.

"I told you to shut up," the man said.

Bent over on my knees, I reached up under my shirt and yanked the wire out. A button popped, the tape on my bare chest taking a patch of hair with it. I let it all drop into the darkness. If he noticed any of this, he didn't let on. I guessed he was watching the approaching headlights. When I got to my feet, the cars were pulling up.

Doors opened and Marchenko emerged. His eyes found mine and he broke out into a nasty smile, his lips curling back to show off his missing tooth.

"Detective," he purred in that stupid accent of his, "what a surprise to see you again."

Chapter Thirty-Three

I found Joe among the men. Stance lit up red in the scattered glow of brake lights. His face hidden in darkness.

"You really need to be more careful," I said. "It wasn't hard to find you."

Marchenko let out a bark of laughter. "Almost as hard as it was finding you," he said. He turned to the farmer behind me. "You did good to call me, Noah. I will not forget this."

Joe caught Marchenko's eye and put a finger to his lips. Walked over without saying a word and pressed his palm flat against my chest. I felt his index finger on my skin, slipping through the gap in my shirt from the missing button. His gaze went to it.

"You think I'm wearing a wire?" I said to him.

"Not now I don't," he said, finally looking at me straight on. Fury danced behind his eyes.

"Aren't you going to introduce me to your friend?"

Joe stepped back as Marchenko considered me for a moment.

"You follow your partner here from Cooper?" he said.

I kept quiet.

"Clearly I need to have a word with my men," he murmured. "Tell me, do you have backup, Detective? Or are you out here all alone?"

"If you're going to kill me, just do it," I said.

Marchenko fell silent. He took in a deep breath, clasping his hands together in front of his chest as he breathed out slowly. Then he opened his jacket and I braced myself but all he pulled out was a pack of cigarettes and a lighter. He tilted the pack toward me and I shook my head. He lit up.

There was the patter of light footsteps and the small dog appeared once more. Its fur was jet black, with streaks of brown and white. It trotted up to Marchenko's feet and stood there, staring up at me. The thing was tiny, barely reaching the top of his boots. Its large eyes bulged from its face somewhat, its little ears perked up high. There was a snarl and it pulled its lips back to reveal rows of miniature, jagged teeth.

Marchenko ignored it. His attention was trained on me. "Do you know who I am?"

"You're Demyan Marchenko," I said. "You head up a cartel working out of Omaha."

"That's right. And you are Detective Thomas Levine." He bent down and picked up the small dog. "And this is Rocket."

Right on cue, Rocket fired out a series of rapid barks, twisting and writhing in his owner's hands. Marchenko laughed and ran his hand roughly over the dog's head, dancing his fingers between Rocket's snapping jaws.

"He's a Jackhuahua," he said. "His Mexican blood keeps him fiery." He placed the dog on the ground and watched him affectionately as Rocket ran over to the driver's loafer and started gnawing on it. The driver barely flinched.

Marchenko turned to me. "He belongs to my daughter," he said, sighing. "I don't see her as much as I would like. Me and her mother . . . it is a long story." He almost looked sad for a moment. "I bought her the dog for her birthday. To bond over, father and daughter. But her mother, she says my daughter hates dogs. A lie, yes? A lie to keep me from her. Her own father. So now I have

Rocket, and I see him more than my daughter. Rocket, he is like a son to me."

He shook his head. Took a breath and brought himself back to the present. A snap of his fingers and the driver picked up the yapping dog. Rocket fell silent as he was carted off. His bulging eyes on me all the way to the car.

"You know, it has been a while since I was back here," Marchenko said. "I try to stay away from Cooper, if I can."

"Can't say I blame you."

"Coming here, it is dangerous. I feel exposed." He smiled. "How many Ukrainians do you think are here beside me, hmm? Not many, I think."

"Smart move keeping your product this far west. How many of these farms do you own?"

"Own? I don't own. I am no farmer. But I do help some farmers remain farmers."

"Must be difficult, running things from Omaha."

"It becomes easier. Once you have the police, everything becomes easier."

"Oh yeah? How much does it cost to make a cop look the other way?"

"Less than you think." He tapped at his cigarette. Orange embers drifted between us. "Not everything is measured in money, Detective."

"What does that mean?"

"It means you point a gun at a man's wife, and maybe that man now works for you."

His voice was cold. The smiles and laughs gone.

"So why are you here?" I asked him. "I heard you had a money problem."

"I heard you helped me solve it."

I glared at him. He sniffed and wiped at his nose. He almost looked bored.

"These farms," he said, "they are very important to me. Any problem with them, any disruption, that is bad for business." He took a long inhale on his cigarette, blew it out slow. "You being here, Detective. I think you are bad for business too."

I scanned the brush where I'd tossed my gun, but it was too dark to see anything. Behind me, I could hear the farmer shifting his weight uncomfortably. I looked over at Joe. "You going to let this guy do all the talking?"

"You're in serious trouble, son," Joe said.

"Stop calling me son," I said. "You sound like an idiot."

Marchenko let out a dry laugh and took a step closer.

"This quipping you are doing," he said. "I do not think you do it because you are brave."

"No?"

"No. I think you do it because you are scared. You do it to hide your fear from me." He leaned toward me. "You think anyone would find you out here, Detective? Hmm? Buried in an unmarked grave?"

I swallowed. "You think you can kill a police officer and get away with it? You're crazy."

"You spy on your partner and you call me crazy," Marchenko said, standing up straight and shrugging. "That is an interesting viewpoint."

He was just about finished with his cigarette, and something told me we weren't going to stand around chatting long enough for him to light up another.

"People will come for me," I said. I could feel my legs beginning to wobble, the adrenaline buzz starting to fade. "They will, Marchenko, and you know it."

"Why would they come for you," he said, "when they have never come for those before you? You think you would be the first police officer I have killed? My friend, this is not some big deal. This is just good business."

He took one last, final draw and then flicked his cigarette away. It soared through the air and faded into nothing. I never saw it hit the ground. Marchenko reached into his jacket and pulled out a large silver semiautomatic. Thing looked like a goddamn hand cannon.

"Now Thomas, please. Into the field."

I turned to run, but the farmer drove his shotgun into my spine so hard I pitched forward over my Impala. Marchenko's men grabbed my arms, dragged me away. I caught a glimpse of Joe's face as I was led deeper into the ravaged cornfield. He looked resigned.

It was dark in the field. Away from the cars, moments of moonlight where the scudding clouds allowed. The earlier snow shaking free as we pushed across the rattling rows of broken cornstalks. When they forced me to my knees I felt it darken my trousers. Felt it trickle into my shoes.

It was going to end here. In the snow and the corn and the low grass. I heard a hammer being pulled back and Marchenko was there. He pressed the barrel against the side of my head. I closed my eyes and was surprised by who I saw. Her eyes open and the bathwater warm.

"Wait," Joe said.

The pressure against my skull faded slightly. I looked up to see Marchenko staring at Joe, irritation scrawled on his face.

"Wait," Joe repeated quietly.

Marchenko let the gun fall away completely. "Why should I wait? This is your mess I am cleaning up." He turned and spat into the darkness. "Always your mess I am cleaning up."

"Then let me take care of him."

"You want to kill him? Here, take it."

"I said I'll take care of him."

"That is not the same."

"He's more valuable to us alive, Demyan."

The Ukrainian thought it over for a while. He tapped the barrel of the gun against his thigh as he did so. Then he motioned to his men, jerking his head toward the cars.

"You want to clean up your mess? Fine. But if he is not with us, then you kill him. You do it proper."

He started to leave and then stopped, turned, and gave me a blank look before stepping right up inside Joe's space.

"You do it proper, understand?" he repeated, and sniffed noisily. "You do it proper or you don't come back to Cooper."

Chapter Thirty-Four

They left us by the side of the road.

We stood in silence and watched them drive away. Stood in silence until their taillights had danced off into the dark, and then stood in silence for a little bit longer after that. Eventually Joe sat down heavily against the side of my Impala.

"I guess we need to talk," he said.

"I guess so."

He nodded, patting himself down for his smokes. I waited for him to light up. Used the time to steady my nerves. Although I'd never admit it to him, I was shaken up pretty bad. I was suddenly grateful for the shroud of inky black.

"Morricone got you spying on me?" he asked.

I nodded.

"A wire?"

"Yeah."

"How much do they know?"

"They know you work for Marchenko. Drugs, whatever. They seem pretty sure you were involved in the van heist, too. Maybe more, but that's all they told me."

Joe grunted as he inhaled. Glittering lights in the distance. Cooper was watching.

"This has to stop," I said.

"Tommy, look—"

"You shot a man. Shot him in cold blood. You murdered him. And for what? Money?"

"And who was he? This man that I shot, hmm? Who was he?"

"Joe—"

"No, son, let's not pretend he was some saint, alright? Or some down-on-his-luck poor son of a bitch. Or even some piece-of-shit petty criminal—twenty years ago he killed three women, Tommy. Three. Last week he killed a fourth. Scooped out their eyes with a goddamn teaspoon."

"Wrong!" I barked at him. So ferociously that he actually jerked backward a little. I advanced on him. "Foster didn't kill Kelly Scott. Simon Jacobs did."

"Who's Simon Jacobs?"

"And Christ, I nearly helped him get away with it."

"Tommy, *who's Simon Jacobs?*"

I blinked. Joe was staring at me, eyes wide and on his feet now. I wanted to drive my fist into his stomach. Grind his face into the dirt until he begged me to stop. I felt my fingers curl into my palms. Felt that old familiar anger boiling inside, filling me from the ground up. Overspill from the town beyond, seeping through the dirt and the muck and floating in the air between us.

I dug in my pocket. "Simon Jacobs is the guy who took these," I said, and threw the crumpled photograph at him. It bounced off his chest and landed by his feet. He picked it up and examined it wordlessly.

"And there's a hell of a lot more where that came from, too," I said. "You know what I've spent the last week doing? I've been *saving* your ass." I pulled out the negatives. "Jacobs followed us the entire time we were robbing that transport. Took a whole bunch of nice pictures to remember it by."

Joe's face was drawn. With fury or fear I couldn't tell.

"He wanted me to frame Foster for her murder," I said. "Wanted me to help him get away with it. Know why I didn't? Because I didn't want to end up like you."

"And you believed him?"

"He took her watch, Joe. Took it from her wrist after he was done. He killed her."

A horrible silence after I said that. Joe gazed at the photograph for nearly a minute. I wondered what was running through his mind. Images of Kevin Foster ran through mine. The red wall, his eyes rolling away.

"Why the hell didn't you tell me this earlier?" Joe said finally.

"I was just trying to keep my head above water."

"That's why you tell me these things!"

"No more lies," I said. "You planted Foster's print, didn't you? You and Bob. Or were you just going to doctor the records afterwards?"

"Tommy—"

"I pulled Foster's file from storage, Joe. You've had his prints in a box this whole time." I stared at him. "I spoke with Brian Ackerman."

"You what?"

"He's pretty far gone, but he just about shit himself when I mentioned your name."

"He's an old man, Tommy!"

"And twenty years ago he helped you frame Foster. Don't deny it. Was it his idea? That where you got all your tricks from? Tell me I'm wrong. You figured you had your man and so you set him up for an easy arrest. Only what if it wasn't him, Joe? What if it was *never* him?"

"You want the truth? Fine. Let's start with your personnel record."

My heart dropped, and my voice along with it. Joe pushed forward.

"Turns out you were quite the dealer back in DC."

"Those files were sealed."

"And worth every penny extra, believe me. Remind me, did they rule it an accidental drowning in the end? Or was it a suicide? Which one do you tell yourself to help you sleep at night?"

For a moment I saw her again. Floating just beneath the surface, her eyes open and staring endlessly upward.

Joe was close now. I could smell tobacco and sweat. "You're a hypocrite," he sneered. "You want to know how I could work with someone like Marchenko? Because people like him keep this town safe."

He took another step toward me.

"I don't expect you to get it, you little shit, but I've sacrificed everything for this town. I've bled for it. You sneer at dirty money but you take it, same as we all do. Because deep down you know you need it. People out here have been left behind for a long time, Tommy. You think that farmer back there wouldn't love to tell us all to go to hell? He swallows it down, takes his share so he can keep his family going. What I do, I do for the greater good. But you? You beat up junkies and sell out your friends. And for what, a bag of pills? A line of coke? Or maybe just so you can feel like a man. Just for those few seconds."

I stayed quiet. Scared to look too hard at what he was saying. Scared in case I found some truth. I could hear him panting. A long sigh and then he was next to me, the two of us looking out across the silent fields and the shimmering lights in the distance.

"So what happens next?" I said. "What's your great plan for all this?"

"You drive me home," Joe said. He reached into his jacket and pulled out his cigarettes.

I pushed off the car and leaned close. Flicked the photograph he was still holding. "What about Jacobs?"

"Screw Jacobs," Joe growled. "We'll deal with him personally. You and me. Far as anyone is concerned, Foster killed Kelly Scott. We get rid of Jacobs, that's the only story that matters."

"You forgetting someone shot Foster in the head?"

Joe lit up, nodded. Breathed it in deep. Blew it out the side of his mouth. "I think our real-estate friend makes a good suspect, don't you?"

I stared at him. "Well, you've got this all figured out."

"Don't worry, Tommy, I'll take care of you."

I pushed off the car and walked around to the driver's side. "You want to deal with Simon Jacobs? You want to arrest Gary Hadley? You do it yourself."

"You fight me on this, I might not be able to protect you next time."

I turned the key. A meaty roar in the still air. Snow scattered as I bounced onto the road, and by the time I looked back Joe was nothing but the fading glow of a cigarette against the dark of the night.

Most of my life up in Duluth was pretty uneventful. School was school, which meant it was shitty and less shitty in equal measure. I never really fitted in. Always felt like I was the odd one out. Didn't have that many friends, didn't want any. I wasn't unhappy or anything. I just . . . was.

I've told Rookie about little Jesse Kane already. The kid in my class who hung himself because his parents got divorced. That kind of defined my time at high school. Kind of defined everyone's. Jesse had never been popular, but his name was on all our lips after he strung himself up. People said he shit himself after he died. Imagine being found swinging from a light fixture with shit in your pants. I always figured if you're going out, go out with some goddamn dignity.

See, on some level I respected Jesse. He ended it on his own terms. He messed up the execution—no pun intended—but at least the guy tried. He didn't waste away in some hospital bed or get clipped by a pizza delivery boy on his way to the library or whatever. He looked death straight in the eye and said, Fuck you. *Then he shit his pants and kind of ruined the moment, but he was nearly there. He was like, ninety percent there. Take-home message from this story? Take a dump before you step off the chair. Take a goddamn laxative if you have to.*

When I was in my final year of high school, my mom got diagnosed with breast cancer. Docs said she had it bad. Both barrels, if you get my drift. She was given six months at best, maybe a bit more if she had chemo. We'd never really had any sort of meaningful relationship, me and my mom. I reckon too much time had passed. I was too messed up and she was completely insane so the whole thing was probably doomed from the start.

She worked two and a half days a week for a hardware store that paid lousy to begin with, and when she was diagnosed the chemo wasn't even an option. I mean, the store wasn't exactly handing out free health-care along with their ten percent staff discount. But I don't think she would have taken it anyway. What was the point in living those extra few months so you could sit on a bathroom floor puking your guts up? Screw that. We might not have been as close as I'd hoped, but I always respected her for that decision.

By the time I left school it had gotten pretty bad. She didn't have much of an appetite and spent most of each day feeling tired. Sometimes I could hear her struggling for breath. Her eyes took on this hollow look, like they were sinking farther and farther into her sockets. It made her seem like she was sad all the time, which maybe she was. Then after a while it wasn't just her eyes, it was everything. Her whole body just dropping away, like a skin-suit deflating right back to her bones.

I started working part-time at a chicken factory. Stacking boxes onto the back of loaders for eight hours a day, three days a week, then going home and helping my mom go to the toilet.

I think it happened about four months after she was diagnosed. She'd started taking these vitamin pills because that's all she could keep down. I was buying boxes of the stuff for her, she couldn't take them fast enough. Popping them like candy as she wasted away. I came back from work one night and she had fallen out of bed trying to get her pills from the dresser. God knows how long she'd been lying there for.

I told you already about how she was when she was younger. Before prison broke her. She was strong back then. Stood up for what she believed in, for what she thought was right. I wish I'd known her when she was like that.

Most of my mom's life was dictated by others. By her mother. By Robert. By the Chittenden Regional Correctional Facility. By cancer.

I wondered at the time if I'd look back on it differently later. But now it is later and I look back on it the same. Some things in this life are timeless, and mercy is one of them. When it comes down to it, I guess there's not much we can control in this life, but how we go out is one of them. And I know—I just know—if my kid had walked in on me lying there like Skeletor with a busted hip, I'd have begged him to stick a pillow over my face and hold it there until I could escape this shitty world.

Rookie looks a little pale at this point. I don't think he was expecting the story to go where it did. Way I see it, I was doing her a favor. She didn't struggle, I tell him. Didn't try and fight me off or tell me to stop. You ask me, she was smiling under that pillow.

Chapter Thirty-Five

What little was left of that night, I didn't sleep it.

Outside there was more rain. Standing at my bedroom window I could see the last of the snow was melting. If the weather didn't let up, everything would soon be rinsed clear. I padded through to the kitchen and there was a bottle in the back of the cabinet and a glass on the counter. Sleep wasn't going to come tonight. I didn't think I wanted it to.

I sat at my kitchen table and watched the rain trickle down the window. Placed the bottle in front of me and for a while I watched that, too. It was cold in there. When I checked my cell it was nearly 4 a.m., and when I called her she didn't answer. I put the phone to one side and rubbed at my face.

I waited as long as I could before pouring, which to be honest probably wasn't that long at all. The heady scent hit me the second I twisted the top off the bottle. Warm and heavy, like a thick blanket. My mouth was already wet, my lips parted. I turned the glass around and around and when I called her again she still didn't answer.

Maybe I'd just have the one. Settle my stomach, get me going. There were eggs in the fridge and I was pretty sure they were still good. One to get me on my feet and I could make myself an omelet for breakfast. I could have coffee too, strong and black, that would help me power through till sunrise. Then I could go for a run; I hadn't done that in months.

I always felt good after a run. Clearheaded. That's what I needed to be right now: clearheaded. I'd know what to do then, I'd have an answer to all this. I turned the glass around and around. Just one to get me going.

I lifted the glass to my lips and my cell buzzed.

I let Mansfield in and we went to the kitchen. The glass was still sitting on the table, untouched. She shot me a look and poured it all down the sink. Told me to go shower. When I got back she'd made coffee.

"Feeling better?" she asked.

"Much," I said, taking a seat. "I didn't wake you, did I?"

She gave a grunt. "I don't sleep much when I'm working a case."

We sat quietly. All of a sudden I was tired.

"Did you grow up in Omaha?" I said.

"It's late, Thomas."

"Just making conversation."

"It's been three days now. What have you got for me?"

"Jesus, do you ever relax?"

"I'll relax when this is over."

"Somehow I doubt that."

I glared at her over the top of my mug. She looked away. An icy silence.

"I was born on the West Coast," she said. "Santa Cruz. Studied business in college to keep my father happy, moved to Omaha as soon as I was done to get away from him. Applied to join the FBI and flunked pretty much every entrance exam they gave me. Settled for a studio apartment and a place at the State Patrol Training Academy instead. Ten years later and here I am."

She took a drink, shifted in her seat.

"Santa Cruz," I said. "I went surfing there once."

Mansfield sighed and looked away. "Is that Rachel?" she said.

I flinched a little. Her gaze must have fallen on the photograph on my windowsill. I couldn't remember placing it there.

"You know about her?"

"Just what's in your file."

"Oh. I didn't realize you had a file on me."

"I have a file on everyone."

I made a disapproving sound. Took a drink and a deep breath, suddenly wishing I'd had that glass of whiskey after all. "That's Rachel," I said.

Mansfield's eyes lingered on the picture. "Pretty girl," she said.

"Yes she was."

I wondered about that file.

"Do you blame yourself for her death?" Her eyes on me.

"I blame myself for a lot of things."

"That's a copout of an answer."

"Can we talk about something else?"

"Some people might say you did some good back in DC."

"Some good?"

"Well, you did put a dirty cop away."

"Dirty cop." I shook my head. "I was a dirty cop too."

"You think you should be in prison?"

I shrugged. "I've . . . done things."

"I know." Her tone was ice.

"Since I got here, I mean. Bad things."

"Considering you only got here less than two weeks ago, that's kind of impressive."

I drained my coffee. "I really should get some sleep."

206

"Oh don't do that."

"Do what?"

"*That*. Run away."

"I'm tired."

"Hey, you called me."

I sighed heavily, pressed fingers into weary eyes.

"I get it, you know," she said. "You've got guilt, deep down and riding around with you. Your captain sends you to Cooper for a fresh start and you think maybe you can complete your path of self-destruction. Get yourself tossed in a jail cell, or catch a bullet in the line of duty. Or maybe you just want to drink yourself to death. Spend three weeks rotting on your bed with your dead girlfriend's photo until your neighbor investigates about the smell. And maybe that's what you deserve."

I lifted my head and stared at her.

"Now Morricone's offered you something different," she continued. "A reason to be here, a way to do some good. And the only thing stopping you from taking it is you. I have no time for self-pitying pricks who enjoy wallowing in their own filth when there's a perfectly good alternative being waved in front of their face. You say you've done bad things? I can offer you immunity. But you either take the help that's being offered, or you go and eat that bullet. I really don't care which, I just wish you'd choose."

I got to my feet. "That's a great speech. Real inspiring stuff."

"Thomas, did something happen last night?" she asked.

"Marchenko happened. Guy just about shot me in the head."

Mansfield stared at me for a moment without speaking. Then she gingerly placed her mug on the table and stood up. "Did you record it?"

"Did you hear what I said? The only reason he didn't pull the trigger was Joe."

"So what, you owe him now or something?"

207

I gave a wry smile. "I actually don't care anymore. I'm done. This place, everyone's got an angle. Everyone wants something."

"If you try and leave town, I'll have you arrested. Don't test me, Thomas."

It wasn't the first time I'd thought about it. Just sliding behind the wheel of my Impala and driving that long road out of town. Maybe I'd head north, to the Pine Ridge. Watch Cooper dwindle in my rearview until it was gone forever. Mary sure had made it sound nice, and maybe there I could finally find some peace.

Chapter Thirty-Six

Once Mansfield had left, I slept.

When I woke I was facedown in my bed, the sheets tangled around me like we'd done battle, and outside it was dark. My stomach lurched with that nasty overslept feeling. I was warm, too warm; I'd sweated into my shirt. I wondered if I was coming down with a fever.

I sat up and fumbled for my cell. It was just after 5 p.m., which meant I'd slept for almost twelve hours straight. I groaned and got to my feet. My head was fuzzy, and my hands shook like I'd spent the day drinking. Guess sleep was just as potent. It all felt a little unfair.

I showered, and that helped. Took a couple of aspirin with water so cold I could feel it all the way down. Mansfield's empty coffee mug was still on the kitchen table. I'd told her I was leaving, and I'd meant every word.

I packed light. Strapped my revolver to my chest. Slid my switchblade into my pocket. Spotted Rachel's photo on the windowsill, and after a moment's hesitation stuffed that in along with it. Propped my badge in its place.

There wasn't anything else. I'd arrived with nothing and I was leaving with less.

The snow was almost gone; transformed into piles of dark sludge, its color drained. Even the air itself was wet; I could feel it brush against my skin, like a spider's web.

I was on edge. Couldn't shake the feeling that I'd screwed up. That I shouldn't have gone back to sleep. That my window of escape had closed. A million scenarios turned over in my mind as I hurried to my car. The engine dying, maybe, a stone's throw from the town limits. Or maybe a collision with another vehicle. A carjacking, a roadblock, an invisible barrier, a twist in the fabric of the universe and an infinite road that forever looped back to Cooper.

My Impala started on the first attempt. I patted the wheel affectionately. Breathed out and told myself to man up. I swung her around in a U-turn, flicked the heating up to full, and bombed down the quiet street.

It had been snowing in Cooper when I'd arrived. I remembered standing outside Kelly Scott's front door waiting on Joe, staring at a row of houses that seemed to just vanish into the sky. It wasn't quite as bad as that now, but it was going to be. It was going to be worse.

You'll call me crazy for thinking it and that's fine. Hell, I'd have called me crazy for thinking it, but that didn't make it any less true: Cooper was going to be smothered from above. Shrouded in mist until everything was white and nothing was left. It was going to be wiped off the map, and all that mattered was what we did before it happened.

I found myself driving through Mary's neighborhood on my way out of town. Hadn't planned to, but there I was, just the same.

The place was deserted. Dirty sidewalks and boarded-up windows. Birds pecking at scattered trash, pausing to stare with beady eyes as I crawled by. A couple of them stretched their wings out silently. An eeriness not helped by the steadily thickening mist.

I pulled in across the road from her apartment. Debated whether I should say goodbye. Something about wanting to apologize for what I'd said.

Mary was the only person I'd met here who hadn't wanted something from me. The only person anywhere, in a long while. I'll admit to never truly knowing what we had—a passing acquaintance maybe, or the beginnings of a friendship, or maybe even the start of something more—but she'd been straight with me. And I reckoned that deserved more than just slinking off into the night.

I could see her apartment from the car. The lights were off. I stared at the living-room window, hoping for the telltale glow of a television, but there was nothing.

I sat there for a while, just watching, and a sense of dread fell over me something fierce. I told myself she was probably working at Stingray's, but that didn't shake it. So I popped open the car door and climbed out.

Birds scattered as I closed in. I peered through the apartment window and my reflection stared back. Pensive and pale. Some might chalk it up to an overactive imagination, only I'd never really had one to overact.

I went to knock on the door and with a physical churning in my stomach I saw the lock was splintered. I pulled my Smith and Wesson and pushed my way inside. Yelled that it was the police but no one yelled back. I flicked the lights on as I moved through.

It was cold in here; a breeze coming from an open window. No signs of a struggle that I could see. No upturned table, no broken glass. No bloody trail to follow. I wasn't sure if that was a good sign or not.

I went quickly from room to room. There was the smell of coffee and a faint popping sound that I couldn't place until I reached the living room. Her record player in the corner, an album spinning slowly, the needle skipping over the inner circle. I wanted to turn it off but it might be evidence.

In the kitchen I found the back door wide open. Mary's apartment opened onto a backyard, I remembered that now. Outside I could see the faint outline of branches shifting in the wind, and beyond that the stars. I called her name but she didn't answer.

Stepping outside I let my eyes adjust to the gloom. Moonbeams faded in like stage lighting and I saw something on the wet ground. A misshapen lump wrapped in what looked like carpet. It might have been anything, but it wasn't. Even from here I could see them.

Bare feet.

Gravel crunched under my shoes. I knocked over a flowerpot and it rolled in a tight little circle. Cold, clammy air pressed against my skin and peeled my gun from my fingers. The feet were white—pale white—but they were clean. That meant she'd been carried.

Closer now and I could make out what she was wearing. It wasn't carpet, it was a dressing gown. I started shouting her name. Stumbling over soil and trampling plants. She didn't move. She was lying on her front like she'd fallen and when I reached her I fell too and I clutched at her arm and rolled her onto her back.

Now I could see her neck. Bruising around her throat. Thick, dark, ugly bruising. I could see where he'd had his hands, where he'd placed each finger. A rag in her mouth to stop her crying out.

But worse than that were her eyes.

Two sockets, scooped bare and gaping open in a soundless scream that I was only too happy to fill.

Another wasted day.

I've stopped answering their questions now. We're getting too close to the Main Event, the reason I'm here, the point of no return. We're so near they can smell it. Cumstain's like a dog in heat. Guy's got the wild eyes, all crazy and rolling around in his sockets. I picture him going home and beating ten shits out of his hotel walls. For a moment I feel for the guy—God only knows who he's got breathing down his neck—but then I remember my broken arm and that takes care of that.

Tubby has looked a little embarrassed these past couple days. It's hard to tell, but I think I can see it. The way he stares at me, at my broken arm. The way he jumps to attention whenever Cumstain enters the room. A nervousness. Guy knows what his buddy did was wrong, but he also knows what I did and why I'm here. Part of him maybe even thinks I deserved it. Poor Tubby. His little brain just wasn't built for such complex thoughts.

After the interview, Rookie took me back to this plastic seat in the corridor, just down from the main door. We've never spoken about it, but I think ever since Cumstain bolted over my window, Rookie's been leaving me for as long as he can in front of that door. It's the only chance I get nowadays to see the outside world.

It's snowing, but not heavily. Drops of the stuff stick to the glass and a car passes with its headlights on. Across the street I can see the parking lot, and beyond that an intersection, each exit leading off into the darkness. Someone's not closed the door properly, and every so often I get a waft of cool air. I picture myself slipping through the door and melting into the shadows. Just spreading myself out and disappearing into nothingness.

Rookie turns up and locks the interview room. He heads my way with his keys in his right hand. Time for me to settle in for the night. I'm about to say something when Desk Girl walks by on my left. She's carrying a pile of folders, and she gives Rookie this howler of a smile before she trips over her own feet and nearly goes flying. Couple of the folders slap onto the floor. Rookie is on the scene in a flash; crouched down, keys on a nearby table and scooping up the spilled folders. Desk Girl laughs, embarrassed, and the two of them amble off to the lobby.

Everything lines up in a straight shot, just like in the movies. The keys fill my vision. I can even make out the little silver one with the black trim. Slow zoom on the one next to it, the word Ford *printed in blue. Pan up and the main door beyond comes into sharp focus. A car drives past and I can hear the tires splash and its wake smells of pine.*

I glance over at the lobby. Desk Girl is sorting the folders into stacks on the counter. Rookie is leaning over and they're chatting. I can't hear what they're saying but there's laughter and his back's to me.

One second to reach the keys. Snatch them up as I go, no time to stop. Worry about uncuffing myself once I'm in the clear. Two seconds to reach the front door. It opens outward, throw my weight against it and barrel through. Four seconds to cross the street. Seven seconds total to the parking lot. Rookie is close behind, no doubt, but I give him two seconds before he manages to find his feet proper. I'll be at his car before he finishes crossing the street. I already know what direction I'll take once I reach that intersection. East, because why not. I just need to make the car.

And maybe he'll choose the right direction. Maybe he's a fast runner. Maybe he closes the gap, and that's alright. That's his job. I reckon

214

he'll get shit for leaving the keys out, and, hand on heart, I do feel bad about that. And I don't want to have to hurt him. I don't want to force him to shoot me, either, almost as much as I don't want to get shot. Kid's got a soft heart, he'll carry that with him. Way I see it, there's no outcome that doesn't end with Rookie getting screwed.

And then Rookie is back and I look up and see him reach for the keys on his belt but of course they're not there. He looks alarmed for a second, sees them on the table and snatches them up. I watch his brain putting it all together; what might have been.

"It was the shoes," I tell him, leaning back in my chair and grinning. "No laces. Guess they're scared I'll try something stupid. Things would fall off my feet soon as I started running. End up going through the parking lot in my socks."

He stares at me, and I wonder if he can see through it. I mean, sure, the shoes are garbage, and I probably *would* end up slicing my foot on some broken glass, but maybe that wasn't the reason I stayed. Maybe I'm just having too much fun. Course, lines like that don't exactly make me sound normal, and I learned long ago to keep that sort of thinking to myself. Learned it's easier to act normal than to actually be it.

Rookie doesn't say anything as he takes me down to my cell. Uncuffs me and slides the bars home. Keeps giving me these side-looks. He's pondering something alright.

I laid it on too thick with the shoes. Kid's probably thinking I've got nothing else going on in my life 'cept these conversations. Christ. Last thing I want is anyone feeling sorry for me.

Chapter Thirty-Seven

Things moved pretty quickly after that.

Within what seemed like a few minutes, Mary's backyard was milling with activity. Paramedics ushered me away to one side where I stood, watching silently, as they crouched over her. They pressed their fingers against her bruised neck and murmured to one another. Patrol officers cordoned off the area and asked me questions I couldn't quite seem to hear.

It happened about thirty seconds after the EMT guys arrived on the scene. I saw one of them lean down close, tilting his head to press his ear against Mary's chest. There was a babble of chatter and suddenly Mary began spasming.

I heard the sounds of medical kits being torn open and voices shouting, and then there was a terrible howling and Mary started clutching clumsily at her face and trying to sit up.

I don't remember much after that.

Chapter Thirty-Eight

Mary's room was loud with mechanical clicks and the sound of sighing, heavy and regular. Rainbow-colored wires ran out of her arm and into a monitor that gave off gentle, rhythmic chimes. White gauze was wrapped across her face in a narrow strip where her eyes had been. The blinds were closed, the light dim. As though such things mattered anymore.

I stood in the corner and watched her sleep. Tranquilizers helping her sail the deep black.

It would be so easy. A second, nothing more. A kindness. A warm hand and a gentle pressure; her body wouldn't even fight me. She'd welcome me—she'd *thank* me. I know I would. Drift off into the darkness and fade peacefully into whatever lay on the other side.

I wondered if that was how it had been for Rachel.

I stepped closer as the door opened. A nurse walked in. She didn't see me at first; went straight to Mary's bedside and scribbled notes on her chart. When she turned to leave she spotted me. Jumped and clutched at her chest.

"Oh, you scared me," she said.

"Sorry."

"You shouldn't be in here."

"The nurse at the desk said it was alright."

A lie.

"Well I'm afraid it's not. This lady needs her rest. You're going to have to wait outside."

One last glance at the lady in the bed. She looked different. Her pink streak was missing.

I sat in the waiting room alone for nearly an hour. Just sat and stared at the wall. I didn't want to close my eyes because when I closed my eyes I could almost see it. And when I tightened my fists I could almost feel it. The warm, slick sensation of blood coating my knuckles. Of something solid breaking under someone else's skin. The taste of it all splashed across my tongue. I thought of his name and pictured myself sliding two fingers into his eyes until they burst apart like grapes and not stopping until I hit brain.

When my cell rang I didn't recognize the number.

"You," I said.

Simon made a humorous noise down the line. "Did you really think it was over, Detective?"

"You sick freak. I'm going to kill you for this."

"You'll do nothing of the sort."

"She wasn't involved!"

"Which is exactly why I had to do it," he said. "Don't you see, Thomas? I'm the one in control here."

"Simon, where are you?"

He paused. "You asked me once what I did with them after. Do you remember? Hmm? Well I'm looking at them right now. They're looking back, in fact. Do you hear me? I have them, Thomas. In a plastic bag."

I made a noise, something halfway between a moan and a growl.

"I'm leaving town," Simon continued, "and this is my farewell call. I am sorry things didn't work out between us. But please, don't come looking for me. It would be a great shame if these were to end up someplace that caused you a degree of . . . incrimination."

I said nothing. There was nothing to say.

"For what it's worth," Simon said into the silence, "I did enjoy our conversations."

Chapter Thirty-Nine

Joe was waiting for me at the hospital entrance. He fell into step beside me as I walked to the parking lot.

"They say you were the one who found her," he said. "I didn't know you two were close."

"I'm not sure we were."

"Well, I'm sorry to hear it all the same."

I nodded. All I could think of was Simon.

"You know where he is?" Joe asked.

I paused, turned to look. He was watching me.

"No. But I have to try."

"I'm right here," he said. "Ask me for help."

"Joe . . ."

"Don't be too proud—"

"It's not about pride."

"No, it's not," he said, his voice surprisingly gentle. "You want Jacobs caught? Ask me for help."

I swallowed. Imagined Simon behind the wheel of a car, or boarding a train. Pictured him hitchhiking out of town and blending into a crowd and vanishing out of my life forever.

"What'll it cost, Joe?"

"A lot. Your cut of the robbery for starters." He smiled sadly, then added, "Is it worth it?" and shrugged.

I leaned back against the door of my Impala and breathed in and out, deep. The air was cool and damp, but I could feel beads of sweat breaking out across my forehead.

"I keep trying to work out why I'm here," I said. "Seems like I get given a new reason every day now."

"Who says you were sent to Cooper for a reason?" Joe said. "Sometimes things just happen. Good, bad, whatever. There's no grand plan for any of us. And if there is, somehow I think Cooper got left off the list."

"We both know how this ends," I said.

Joe gave a bitter laugh. "Sooner or later we all get our hands dirty, son."

"Mine have been dirty for a while now."

"Yeah, well, I guess some filth just sticks."

I looked over at him. "He took her *eyes*, Joe. He took them while she was still awake."

"Doc says she's going to pull through."

"He should have killed her," I said. "It would have been kinder."

"Ask me."

"Joe . . ."

"As soon as you leave here, I won't bring this up again. You need time to decide? Get a coffee. But drink it fast. You need a reason? Go stand at her bedside."

"I got plenty of reasons."

"Then ask me."

"Can Marchenko help me find him?"

"You're goddamn right he can."

Chapter Forty

I was going to start with a defense for what I did next, but that'd make me a liar, and I've lied enough. No more excuses, no more half-truths, no more secrets. Not that it matters anymore.

If anyone was hoping this was a story of redemption, well, I guess you're just shit out of luck.

It wasn't difficult to track down where Mansfield was staying.

Cooper only has a handful of motels, and none of them were looking to make their lives any harder. And why would they? I'm a cop. Looking for another cop. The place she was staying at gave me her room number. A little bit of pressure and they gave me the key, too.

I'd weighed my options on the drive over. Seemed all I had was a revolver and a ticking clock. Mansfield was tough, but she wasn't stupid. She wasn't about to lose her life over some stolen cartel money.

I pulled my gun before knocking. No answer. I let myself in, tossed the place. The room was small—nothing more than a double bed and a toilet, really—and I checked every inch of it. The mattress, the dresser, the tiny two-person table that sat under the grubby window. After ten minutes, I knew the money wasn't there.

I thought about calling her. Sending her a picture of her room from the inside. Only I couldn't be sure she wouldn't show up with a couple of squad cars. So I decided to wait. Pulled up a chair in the corner of the room and sat with my feet on that little table, my revolver on my lap.

I wasn't nervous, sitting there. Wasn't impatient, wasn't agitated or on edge or anything. I was resigned, maybe, although I'm sure I don't know what that really feels like. Unless it's the absence of feeling, in which case yeah, I guess I was resigned.

She turned up forty minutes later. I'd barely moved. By then it was late, her bedside clock reading 1 a.m. It was Thursday, and I'd been in Cooper for just about bang on two weeks. It was hard to believe so much could happen in so little time.

I heard her car pull up outside, heard her quiet engine go quieter, heard her door slam and her footsteps approach. Then the jangle of change and the rumble of the vending machine. A man's voice, too low to make out. I wondered if it was the guy on the front desk. *Your friend was here earlier.*

Her gun was raised when she finally entered the room, but so was mine.

"Drop it," I said, and I pulled the hammer back with an audible click. "Don't turn around, or I'll cripple your spine."

She was caught out, her body angled the wrong way, gun pointed toward the bathroom. She glanced over at me, just with her eyes, then she spread her palms and placed her handgun on the floor.

"Kick it over here," I said, and she did. I bent down and picked it up. Another Glock.

"I thought you were leaving town," she said.

"Just tying up some loose ends."

"Judging by the state of my room, I'm guessing you're after the money." She curled her top lip in disgust. "I'm disappointed in you, Thomas."

"I'm sure you are. Now close the door and sit on the bed."

"Do you have any idea how stupid this is?"

If she was scared, she didn't show it. I stood, waved my gun a little. "Door. Now."

Mansfield did it, her eyes on me and glaring the entire time. I kept my distance.

"Take out your handcuffs," I said.

And she did that, too.

It was hot in here, and I couldn't work out if it was the heating or me. I wiped at my forehead.

"So what's the plan?" Mansfield asked. "Take the money and run? How long do you think you'll last before I find you?"

"Long enough."

"Whatever you're going to do? Don't. If you need help, then let me help. You want to talk about our deal? We can talk about it, you and me."

"I just need the money, Mansfield. Now where is it?"

"I don't have it."

I shook my head. The revolver was swaying a little now. "Then things are going to go very badly for you, Detective."

"Thomas, I don't understand—"

"You don't *need* to understand. You just need to tell me—"

"Is this really what it's all about? *Money?*"

"Dammit, Mansfield!" My arm went straight. Anger steadying my aim. "None of this is about the money."

She stared at me for a moment, and when she spoke her voice was low. "No it isn't, is it. You were stressed the other morning but nothing like this. I know you called in the attack yesterday. That bartender's gotten you all worked up."

"Her name's Mary."

"Do you know who did it?"

I said nothing.

"What happens when you get him?" She edged closer. My silence making her courageous. "You going to kill him?"

"I'm not a murderer."

"Tell that to Kevin Foster."

"You think that was me?"

"Wasn't it?"

I paused. Felt that new urge start to build. Not the anger—not this time. The intoxication of unburdening myself. Of letting it all spill out. I was so tired of keeping everything to myself.

My fingers danced along the side of my revolver. "Joe shot him. With this, actually."

Mansfield didn't miss a beat. "So why protect him?"

"I didn't have a choice."

"You do now. You've got your bullet, Thomas. Joe doesn't have anything on you. Not anymore."

She closed the gap between us farther still. Her gaze running straight along the barrel of my gun.

"Why don't we take this conversation outside?" she said. "I've got a Snickers and a can of soda by the vending machine. Still got enough change to buy you some dinner."

"I'm not hungry."

"What's the money for? Work with me, Thomas. You siding with Joe? With Marchenko? That your plan?"

"Does it matter?"

"Jesus Christ," she said. A sudden hardness in her voice. "You really are an idiot. You want to track down whoever attacked your friend? I'm right here!"

"Mansfield—"

225

"I'm serious! Put that gun away and let me make a couple phone calls. We'll get an APB out on this guy. We'll have him picked up by the end of the day!"

Now I thought about that. Hand on heart, Debra, I really did. Simon Jacobs's grinning face in the back of a squad car. In the bullpen back at the station. Orange jumpsuit and metal shackles. Pictured him safe and sound in a cushy institution for the criminally insane. Three square meals and cable TV and conjugal visits. Book deals and HBO specials. I pictured it all.

"Empty your pockets," I said quietly.

She tried to press forward. I pushed her onto the bed.

"I told you I'd read your file," she said. "You *want* to kill him, don't you. It's . . . some kind of sick thrill for you."

"Empty your pockets, Mansfield!" I snarled, and I leaned forward and placed the Smith and Wesson against her cheek.

For a moment she didn't move. Maybe she was trying to work out if I would actually do it. Guess something in my eyes answered her question. She reached into the inside pocket of her suit jacket and pulled out the plastic bag of money. Dropped it onto the bed. I almost wept.

"How long can you keep this up?" she said. Her eyes on me as I snatched up the bag. "This pretense that you're being played. By me, by Joe. *You're* choosing to work with people like Demyan Marchenko. *You're* choosing to dish out this . . . vigilante justice."

"That's enough."

"You know, I was wrong about you. Joe wasn't using you after all. He was *grooming* you."

I glared at her. Stepped back and leaned against that little table under the window.

"So what happens now?" she asked.

"You handcuff yourself to the radiator," I said. "I'll make sure Morricone knows where to find you."

226

I waited until she was secure, then at last I put my gun away. Collected hers, too. Went to the door and stopped, turned back. She was across the room and on the floor, her arm at an uncomfortable angle. I went over to her. Reached out to adjust her cuffs and she shrank back. I wondered how she saw me then, in that moment.

Stepping over her and into the bathroom, I grabbed a face cloth and stuffed it into her mouth.

I thought about saying something in parting. An apology, maybe, although somehow an apology didn't seem appropriate at the time.

I'd never have hurt you, Debra. You do know that. It's easy to say now, I guess, after all this is over, and I'm sure it doesn't come as much consolation. But if this story has taught you anything—and if you've read my file like you say you have—then you know that I don't hurt women. I'm just not like that.

So I'll say now what I couldn't say then. Which is that I'm sorry.

Chapter Forty-One

And so once again I found myself on the long road out of town.

Joe's Ford was warm, and the faded leather seats soft, and as the dashboard clock glowed the start of a new day I battled an adrenaline comedown and opened a window to stay awake. Outside it was cold and the sky was black. Clouds so low they seemed to skirt the tips of the tallest trees. Branches straining to take root and spread across the sky. I tracked streetlights as they stretched out behind us, their glow feeble and growing feebler as we hit the open expanse.

A straight shot along the narrow highway, flanked on both sides by bare fields and the sound of an engine's roar. A thin veneer of freedom. Stretched tight over a cartel's grip.

Up ahead now I could see the exit. The dirt track and the dark farmhouse. The distant barns where Demyan Marchenko was undoubtedly waiting, sitting in the back of a black car near invisible against the night. Joe slowed, tires crunching as we bounced off the road, and I remembered being dragged through the corn and forced down onto the cold earth and my heart beat that little bit faster.

"Joe," I said.

Marchenko's car came to life ahead of us. Joe glanced at me but said nothing. Dimmed our headlights and brought us to a gentle halt.

I climbed out into the cool night. The ground was hard, and my shoes slid on the frozen surface, and when I closed my door with a soft click I suddenly felt exposed. We shouldn't have gotten out first.

But then doors swung open and three men emerged from the car. The driver and his friend dressed in cheap, shiny suits; Marchenko in dark jeans and what looked like a leather biker jacket. A moment later there was the machine-gun fire of high-pitched yapping and Rocket came bounding out to join us.

"We must really not keep meeting like this," Marchenko shouted to us in his stupid broken English, waggling a finger in amusement. "People will be talking."

"It's cold, Demyan," Joe said. "Let's make this quick."

"You think this is cold?" Marchenko said, grinning. "You should come to my country for Christmas. Nights so cold they would make your nipples fall off."

He laughed, and his compatriots along with him. Even in the dim light I could see his stained teeth. They were mesmerizing.

He leaned back against the hood of his car. "You Americans and your comfort zones," he said. "You would live forever inside them if you could, I think."

Rocket was going crazy now. Racing in little circles, bouncing up on his tiny back legs and barking at the moon.

Joe pointed at the dog. "Really, Demyan? This isn't the time. Leave Rocket in the car."

Marchenko looked surprised. "Rocket *is* in the car," he said, and right on cue, manic barking started up from the back seat. "This is Rex," he said. "Rocket's brother. Rocket I bought for my daughter, Rex I bought for her mother. A peace offering. But now she says she hates dogs too, and so I have both."

"Marchenko . . ." I started.

The Ukrainian laughed and waved his hand through the air. "Alright," he said and snapped his fingers. The driver lifted Rex and tossed him into the car. There was the brief sound of tiny animals snarling before he closed the door.

"Demyan, this is serious," Joe said. "You told me not to return without a solution. Well here we are."

"Yes, here you are," he purred. "And here *I* am. Tell me, Joe, do you think I *want* to be here?"

Joe was smart enough not to give an answer. Marchenko dug around for his cigarettes before continuing.

"For six years I have been in charge. And how many times have I been to Cooper? Three? Four?" Marchenko shrugged, pausing to light up. "You view this as an insult, maybe. A sign that I don't care. That I think of Cooper as a little piece-of-shit town."

His men laughed again. Marchenko himself was smiling, but the more I stared at his face, the more plastic and fixed it became. I felt sick.

"But really, I am not needed here. I trust the people to do their job. I trust you, Joe. My money is taken, and you take it back. Like Robin Hood, yes? Of course, the day my product stops moving, the day my farms are raided, perhaps that is the day things will change. But until then? Please, do not see my absence as a sign that I do not care. Or that I hate your piece-of-shit town. And believe me, Joe, it *is* a piece-of-shit town. So when you see me here, now, waiting in this frozen field for you to arrive, do not insult me by saying that this is serious. I *know* it is serious. If it were not serious, I would not be here. If I did not trust you, I would not be here." He spat onto the ground by his feet. "If I did not trust you, you would be dead."

Joe glanced over at me, but I couldn't read his face. He turned back to Marchenko.

"I didn't mean to disrespect you, Demyan. It's just . . . we want to make a deal."

Marchenko's grin returned, and his eyes swung onto mine. "Continue, please," he said.

I took my cue. Swallowed my fear and my disgust and took a step forward. "I need your help," I said. "I need to find a man."

"Easy now, Detective, buy me a drink first."

Another eruption of laughter, another grand unveiling of yellow teeth. I saw red and reached out to grab hold of his leather jacket but Joe stopped me.

"Calm down," he hissed, his face flushed and inches away. I stepped back, my fingers twitching at my sides.

Marchenko said nothing for a moment. Then, "It must be difficult for you. To come to me like this. To ask for my help. To beg."

"Demyan," Joe said.

"No, let him have his moment. It will not last long. He wants to fight me? Let him fight me. He may even win. Although if he did, I would not be in a position to help him anymore."

"If there were any other way," I said, "I wouldn't be here."

"Then I am glad there is not another way." Marchenko walked forward and patted me on the shoulder. Like a dog. "If you want my help, you will have it. At a cost."

I reached under my jacket and his men jumped. I pulled out the plastic bag of money and pressed it against the Ukrainian's chest.

"There," I said. "That's my cut of the robbery. It's yours if you help me."

Marchenko took the bag from me and smiled. "This is a fine gesture, Detective. Only it is not enough."

"What?"

"Money is just part of it," he said, and handed the bag to one of his men. "The other part, it is more valuable to me."

"And what's that?"

"Your obedience."

I thought briefly about telling him to go to hell, but then I thought about Mary. And I thought about Simon, and what I would do to him when I had him.

"Alright," I said.

Marchenko laughed then. "Relax, Detective. This is not personal. This is just business, remember? Now, please, who are you trying to find?"

I went back. When I was older. Back to Eudora.

Rookie never asked how the story ended. I figured he just didn't care; that, or he assumed it was over when my mom came to take me away. And it was, mostly. But mostly isn't all, and there's still a little bit left to tell. An epilogue, you might call it. A bookend to my grandparents' messed-up lives that started that fateful day when Eddie picked up that first bucket of red paint from the hardware store.

I used to wonder how he chose it. Imagined him standing in the aisle, staring up at the rows of crimson and maroon, trying to decide whether Cranberry Crunch *sounded too lively for what he had planned. Or whether* Raspberry Bellini *would clash with the steel hook and wrist restraints.*

Years had passed since I'd left. My mom was six feet deep, had been for a long time.

So I went back. Back to the sticky heat and the gentle hum of the cicadas and the house on the edge of the cornfields. I got there just before dusk. When the light was amber and the shadows long.

I waited in that cornfield for hours. Stood and watched the glow from the living room flicker and change; Nancy was watching television. I imagined her rubbing that stinking paste over her gnarled fists and I smiled and peeled an ear of corn and ate it for dinner. They would find the cob afterwards, find a whole bunch of them, all piled up next to a patch of trampled crops, and they'd know that whoever did it had waited here for the light to fade and the house to settle.

I never saw Eddie. Not then, not when I was in the corn. I knew he was there—his rusted SUV was parked outside—but I'd hoped to catch a glimpse of him. When he was unaware. You can learn a lot about someone by watching them when they think they're alone. People don't pretend then. They're real.

When darkness finally came it was as black and enveloping as I'd remembered. I watched the light blink out in their bedroom, waited another half hour just to be sure, walked the short distance around the house to the rear porch, took the spare key from under the loose board, and let myself in, moving through the kitchen, the dining room, the living room, the utility room where I knew Eddie stored his hunting rifle—leaning in the corner just in case he had to grab it quick, like he was some sort of frontiersman—and I picked it up and a box of ammunition, too, loading it slowly, careful to keep the noise down before I left the room, creeping along the hallway and up the stairs, rolling the soles of my shoes on the wood to stop it from creaking, and as I stood outside their bedroom door I had to wipe my palms down the front of my jeans I was so sweaty, so nervous, like the first time I'd had sex, and when I stepped into the room I saw their sleeping forms and their faces lit by the moon and I remembered the animals I'd placed there and how Nancy had screamed when she'd woken and how she'd slapped me over and over and I gripped the rifle tight and I saw her stir, saw her eyes twitch, saw them open, saw them focus, saw them widen, and when I finally squeezed the trigger the right half of her face jumped onto the wall.

Eddie woke then. Of course he did, the thunder of the rifle in the quiet room was enormous, and when he saw what was left of his wife he started screaming. Turned out he wasn't so tough after all.

I wasn't sure if he knew it was me. It was dark and he wasn't wearing his glasses, so I stepped up close and let the moonlight fall upon my face and I saw recognition—horrifying, disbelieving—blossom in his eyes. He was screaming still, this awful, high-pitched, feminine yowl that was more like a dying cat than a big, strong man, and I jammed the barrel of the shotgun in his open mouth and pushed it back so far he started choking on it.

I led him down the stairs. Half dressed and with his fat stomach hanging over his pajama pants. His bare feet sliding on the wooden floor. His hands trembling as they gripped the banister. He was still making noises, only now it was this guttural clucking sound which was fucking irritating but at least it was quiet.

When we finally reached the red room—straight past the kitchen and on your right—Eddie turned, started making noises like he was trying to talk only he'd forgotten how. I forced the barrel of the gun into his mouth until he quit. When I took it back he threw up all over his bare feet. Nancy had made spaghetti for dinner.

I wasn't sure if I'd need to break the lock to get in, but as we stood there together—one man half naked and sobbing, his feet covered in drying puke and blood and his own teeth; the other calmly waiting—as we stood there together I saw it swinging from his neck. The key on the silver chain. I wondered if he'd used it since I left. If he preyed on the young boys from town or if he liked to drive out farther afield to avoid suspicion. I pictured him parked outside a school, or a church, or a playground on a hot day, the air-conditioning blowing cool air as he sat in his rusted SUV with the window down and his sunglasses on. Pictured him with ice cream and bags of candy and promises of rides home and I reached over and yanked the key from around his neck and the chain snapped clean in two.

I unlocked the door and swung it open. The room hadn't changed much. Walls of bright red, the same cross still on the wall. He'd upgraded the chains that hung from the ceiling. They gleamed in the dim light, as though they'd been polished.

He begged then. Nothing that I could make out, just general blubbering. I pushed him inside wordlessly. Set the rifle down to one side and strapped him into the restraints. He started screaming when I did that, started pulling back with his arms and shaking his head from side to side, sending flecks of blood back and forth across the room like a garden sprinkler. His feet danced a merry jig as he struggled and I almost broke out into a song. I wasn't worried about him escaping. Eddie had spent his life building this prison.

So I watched him squirm and howl and cut his wrists as he jerked and scratched, and he made one hell of a racket but that was alright. It was ten miles to the nearest neighbor, and I would be long gone before they came sniffing around.

I stood in the cornfield for a while afterwards. The warm breeze ruffled my hair a little, and for the first time in my life I had to force myself to leave that place. But before I did I heard a wailing sound; a long, high note drifting on the wind. Just the once, and right toward the end. Course it was hard to hear much of anything over the sound of the fire, and looking back now I figure it was as likely a nearby prairie dog as it was Eddie, but I sure did like the idea of him screaming as he burned.

Chapter Forty-Two

I didn't have to wait long. Blurry eyes told me it was just after 5 a.m. when the call came through. I'd been asleep for less than three hours, and yet I'd never been more awake.

Revolver and recorder; I was packing light. I'd get a confession out of Simon if I had to slice it out of him. I'd slept in my shirt and khakis and I didn't bother getting changed. Grabbed my coat and my keys and gunned it down the street to the edge of town.

The weather had only gotten worse in the few hours I'd slept. Thick fog drifted between the low-rise buildings, the sky scraping along the ground. My headlights didn't stretch more than a few yards. I might have been driving into a brick wall. I might have been driving into nothing. Cooper didn't have long left.

Marchenko and Joe were waiting for me, side by side. The cartel boss yawned as he sucked on a cigarette. Tossed it away half smoked as I squealed to a halt.

"Where is he?" I demanded, pulling on my coat.

"In the trunk," Marchenko said, and one of his men popped it open. I leaned over to peer inside and there he was. Bound at the hands and feet, gag tied around his mouth. His eyes were closed, blood pooling from a fresh head wound.

"He alive?" I asked.

"Don't worry, Detective. He's alive." Marchenko smiled at me and I didn't like that. "Although I look in your eyes and I wonder for how long."

"I'm no killer," I said.

"Neither was I. Until I was."

"Help me get him in my car."

Two of Marchenko's men helped me lift Simon's unconscious body from one trunk into another.

"Thank you," I said, somewhat grudgingly.

He nodded. "Please, it is my pleasure. I just hope you remember the terms of our arrangement."

"I remember."

"I will be watching, Detective. From Omaha I will be watching. And soon I will call on you, yes? When I need your help. I will call on you and you will answer."

"I said I remembered."

Joe had been standing watching the entire time, a look on his face like he didn't know what was coming next. I was about to get in my car and drive off when I thought of her.

"You need to go check on someone," I said to Joe, and told him about Mansfield.

"Jesus," was all he said. I think that was maybe the first time he realized I wasn't planning on coming back. He held out his hand in a peace offering. I stared at it for a moment, then turned the ignition and vanished into the mist.

I drove for a long while. Emerging out of the gloom and onto the highway where the sky was clear. Foot down, engine screaming. Behind me, Cooper was engulfed in fog. A great column of it rising up and into the sky. The morning sun seemed to shimmer along its surface, wrapping itself along the grooves and curves until the entire town was lit up like it was on fire. I tracked it in my rearview mirror until it burned my eyes, and I didn't look back after that. I didn't want to see whatever came next.

Ahead of me I could see the bulge in the horizon that marked the start of the Pine Ridge. I thought of how Mary had described it. Canyons and rivers, full of color. Cottonwoods that went orange in the fall. A strange oasis of beauty in an otherwise flat land. A beauty Mary would never see again.

I knew I wouldn't return to Cooper; I doubted there would be anything left to return to. Nothing but dirt and highway and those cornfields, and whispers of something that once was and maybe would be again. Cooper had served her purpose, though if you were to ask me what that was, I couldn't tell you. You might listen to this and think I'm crazy, and that's alright. I suppose that's as valid a theory as any.

Chapter Forty-Three

I drove for nearly an hour before we got there.

It was gradual at first. The land rising slightly, the cornfields giving way to the trees. All of them bare except the pines. Those stood tall, towering over my car as I snaked farther into the quiet woods.

It felt right, being here. I lowered the window and let the morning air wash over me. If everything had to come to an end here, in this place, then I thought I could accept that.

I was pretty sure that Simon was awake. At one point I could have sworn I'd heard him banging and yelling back there, but it might just have been the Impala on her last legs. My final trip in her and I didn't even say goodbye. In any event, you turn the radio up loud enough and it solves all sorts of problems. *KBBN Rock Radio: when country music can't quite mask the screams of a man tied up in your trunk.*

I turned off onto a side road. The morning sun blinking through scattered branches above us. When the road started to rise steeply, I pulled over and killed the engine. Climbed out, the roadside gravel crunching beneath my shoes.

It was going to be a beautiful day. One of those real winter stunners that creeps up out of nowhere. I could smell pine, crisp and fresh on a light breeze. It was like I'd been locked away and was being released for the first time. I'd never known it could all be so breathtaking.

I was calm then. Calmer than I thought I'd be. After everything I'd done since I'd got here, torturing a confession out of a killer didn't seem so bad. But shit, ask me that again when I'm finished. Maybe you'll get a different answer.

A sharp thumping erupted from the trunk. I looked over and started to undo my shirt. The wind on my bare skin making me shiver. I strapped the recorder to my belt. Ran the delicate wire up my back and let it dangle over my shoulder. Slipped my shirt back on and threaded it carefully through a buttonhole. When I was done, it was practically invisible. I pulled out my Smith and Wesson and cocked the hammer. Walked around the car and stood next to the trunk. Took a breath, unlocked it, and swung it upward.

Simon was awake, alright. He stared up at me through a pair of cool, blue eyes, but his hair was a mess and I was betting it wasn't from keeping still. I hoped he'd been writhing around in there for the last few hours. Like a snake. A glance at his crotch and I was disappointed to find he hadn't pissed himself.

I waved the gun at him to make sure he knew who was in charge, then reached into the trunk and rolled him out. He landed heavily on the gravel, wheezing sharply through the dirty rag tied over his mouth. I pulled my switchblade and sliced the ropes binding his legs, closed the trunk and leaned against it patiently. Waited for him to stumble to his feet. When he did he turned and stretched his neck lazily, his expression blank. I blinked and saw him in Mary's bedroom, sitting patiently on the edge of her bed as she rinsed her hair in the shower, and I rolled the gun around in my hand and struck him across the face with it. He grunted and dropped to one knee. A little blood splattered onto the road. When he looked up, I think he might have had understanding in his eyes.

I pointed the gun at him. "Move."

We left the road, trudging upward between the trees. I kept a few paces behind him, the barrel of the revolver aimed square at his back. Underfoot, the forest floor was soft and littered with needles. The earth here so unlike the frozen ground of the cornfields.

The climb was slow. Whether Simon was genuinely finding it difficult or he was just stalling I wasn't sure. It wasn't warm but I was tense. By the time we reached the top I had broken out into a sweat.

From up here, you could see out across the surrounding hills. Pine trees that stretched from rocky outcropping to canyon edge. It felt like another world compared to what I'd just driven through.

What happened next was stupid. I should never have relied on Marchenko's men to tie his hands. I should have checked them myself when I let him out. Bastard had almost an hour to loosen his bindings, and what he didn't manage in the drive and the short hike, he did while I was standing there admiring the view. I wasn't even looking at him.

Footsteps and labored breathing from beside me. I turned just as Simon threw his body against mine. I cried out, falling sideways, my revolver tumbling into the woods. On my back now, my hand scrabbling for the switchblade in my pocket but he was already on top of me. His strong legs straddling my chest, my knees thumping uselessly against his back. I swung for him but he batted me away. Delivered a blow to the side of my head. My vision swam and I tasted blood in my mouth and then he hit me again and I felt my nose break.

I howled. Then his hands were on my throat. I clutched at his mouth, my fingers scrabbling for his eyes. His big, blue eyes. He stretched his neck back, keeping them just out of reach as he tightened his grip. I could feel my entire body weakening, my strength failing. He was still gagged and there was blood trickling from his forehead where I'd struck him.

It happened quietly. A gurgling in my throat and the rustle of pine needles under my back. I stopped fighting. My hands fell away as everything around me faded to black.

Chapter Forty-Four

I remember waking. Briefly, and before he really got started.

The first time I was moving, my face scraping along the forest floor. Pine needles stabbed at my skin. The smell of them burning my nose. He was dragging me, both feet under one arm and a stout branch over his shoulder. I twisted, tried to grab hold of something solid. My fingers scrabbling at the earth.

Simon stopped to glance back. Let my body drop. I saw my chance to escape, started to move and he swung the branch like a pickaxe at my legs. A pop as my left shin cracked, and I screamed and blacked out.

The second time, everything was still. I was sitting, propped against a tree. I tried to lean forward but couldn't move. Simon had used the ropes from his hands to bind my arms to the trunk.

He must have broken my other leg while I was out. It lay twisted beneath me, bent at an awkward angle. I tried to move it, felt bone shift in a way it shouldn't under my skin. Pain shot up my thigh and I squeezed my fists to stop from passing out again.

Movement to my left. I looked around and Simon was there, and the branch came crashing across my face and took most of my teeth with it. My tongue split and my vision cracked in two. He might have done more but I don't remember.

When I came to for the third time I stayed awake. I'd been out for a while. The sun was different, the shadows longer. The pain in my legs was unbearable. My vision blurry and dark in one eye. There was vomit down my front and a strong smell of piss.

I couldn't feel my mouth, couldn't move my tongue. There was blood at the back of my throat and when I swallowed I felt a couple of teeth slide down too. I started crying.

Simon was sitting in front of me. On a tree stump, the branch by his feet. Blue eyes shining. He must have been there the whole time but I never noticed him until he stood up. In my cracked vision he was an eight-foot giant made of shadow and ink. I whimpered and tried to back away. I knew I couldn't but it was a reflex. My limbs screamed with the effort and I reckon I probably did, too.

"You know, I really did want to work with you," he sighed. Something metal in his hand. My switchblade. It was covered in blood.

I tried to say something. Not sure what. *Please*, maybe.

"You were talking in your sleep before," he said. His face seemed to shift and melt as he spoke, and only his blue eyes remained constant. "You seem stressed, Thomas. I don't think you're cut out for this line of work."

He crouched down until he was at my level.

"I wanted Mary to be a warning to you," he said, reaching down to pick something up off the ground. "Of what would happen if you came after me. But I guess we can both see how well that turned out."

When he brought his hand up he had something in his fist, and when he opened it I saw what it was and it saw me too. "You'll just have to be a warning to everyone else," he said.

He tossed it onto my chest and it rolled down my front and got caught in the dried vomit. Then he straddled me and my bloodied switchblade gleamed in the dying light.

"I'm going to take your other eye now," Simon said calmly. "Try not to scream."

Chapter Forty-Five

He left after that. Nighttime in the afternoon. Left me tied to the tree.

I could hear his footsteps as he walked, the crunch of pine needles fading until the forest had swallowed him whole.

I sat for a long time before I thought of it. I could feel the sun set and the temperature drop. Heard the rustle around me as twilight fell. I think something ran over my foot. The pain was still there, but somehow it was less. Maybe there's only so much the body can register, or maybe I was just getting used to it. I'd lost all feeling in my hands, had pins and needles something fierce in my arms.

The recorder.

I wasn't even sure if it had survived the ordeal. Wasn't sure if Simon had spotted it and smashed it against a tree somewhere.

With what felt like the last of my strength I spat out a couple of teeth that were sitting near the front of my mouth. Managed to get my tongue moving. Thought back to how this had all started. Back to DC, back to Rachel and the bag of pills and driving down that long highway, cracked and uneven. *Welcome to Cooper*, it had read.

I started to talk. Stumbling at first, and not without some serious pain, but as I went on it got better. Not sure when it was I started now, but I reckon I can feel the warmth of the morning sun on my face so I must have lasted through the night. Don't think I'll last another but that's alright. I've got it all out. Everything I did, every bad thing. Might be whoever listens to this finds some use for it, but even if not, well, it got me through the night and that's a night longer than I thought I had when I started.

Mary had closed her eyes when she'd talked about this place. I wondered what she saw. If she was seeing it now, asleep in her hospital bed. It would have been nice to come here with her. In the fall, when the cottonwoods had gone orange. Spectacular, she'd called it. And somehow, despite everything, I managed to picture the colors forming around me, and I realized I was smiling.

One final message, and then I'm done.

I just bet this damn machine's broken.

Rookie comes to collect me today. He can't bear to look me in the eyes. I try to crack a joke on the way up, a real classic I heard back in Duluth that never left me. Why can't Stevie Wonder see his pals? Because he's married.

But Rookie isn't really feeling it. His top button is done up and his tie is pulled tight, and just before we reach the top of the stairs I notice he's shined his shoes.

Two men are waiting for us in the corridor. Both dressed in snappy suits, freshly pressed, with shirts so white I have to avert my eyes. I'm passed over to them and they lead me the rest of the way. I try to flash Rookie a smile but he can't walk away fast enough.

They take me to a room—a different room, thank Christ. Still small, though; two chairs and a desk between them. I sit down on one and they uncuff me, ask if I want anything to drink and I say is a double Jimmy on the rocks out of the question and they say I'm afraid so, sir, and I'm not expecting to be called that, and I don't like it, so I tell them I'm fine and they leave me alone.

I wonder where Tubby and Cumstain are today. Maybe they got taken off the case. Maybe they quit. Just woke up this morning and realized they couldn't crack me. That they've been wasting their time trying. These new boys on the scene, clean-shaven and pressed suits, might be my deal has finally come through.

Luckily I don't have to wait long to find out. Door opens and a woman walks in who I've never seen before. She's short, with these big, stocky shoulders and a scrunched-up face. Her nose makes me think of a cartoon pig. She gives me a cold look, closes the door, and pulls up a chair. She's got a paper folder in her hands and she slides it onto the table. I get so excited I feel my legs bouncing.

She tells me she's Detective Pig Nose from Omaha. Something about working a connected case back in Cooper and being kept on to wrap everything up. I dunno, I kind of lose interest. The paper folder is all I can seem to focus on. Just open it, Pig Nose. Just open it!

She keeps on talking but I barely hear her. My eyes keep darting to the folder, my fingers dancing along the edge of the table. I lean forward and I guess I must look like I'm going to make a grab for it because Pig Nose pulls her gun and sets it next to the folder. All casual like. Barrel pointed right at my chest. I give a giddy laugh and sit back. I say Relax, Pig Nose, Piggy Piggy Pig Nose, and I hold my hands up.

Pig Nose stares at me with those cold eyes for a long while. Says that if this had been left to her we'd have an answer by now. Says she doesn't usually make deals with people like me. I say gee, you kill a couple girls and no one bats an eyelid. You kill a cop and—

She slaps me. Hard across the face. I blink and jerk back, nearly knock myself off my chair. Pig Nose says I may have gotten the district attorney to agree to keep the death penalty off the table, but if there's any justice in the world I'll get shanked in the showers good and proper and left to bleed out down a dirty drain. I laugh at that and I swing back on my chair. I already know there's no justice in the world and I tell her that.

Then Pig Nose spins the folder around and opens it up. Pushes it across the table for me to read. I lean forward and she takes her gun back but I don't care about that. I'm hardly about to risk what I've been holding out for these past few weeks. Pig Nose explains it to me as I read, like I'm stupid. Says that the agreement only stands so long as

I cooperate with their investigation. Once I'm finished reading, I nod and she gives me a pen and I sign it. She closes the folder and moves it to one side.

She says they kept up their end of the bargain.

Says it's time for me to keep up mine.

I say sure, what do you want to know.

She says she wants to know what happened in the woods. Says she wants to know what happened after. Says she wants to know where it all took place. Maybe I look confused or something because she asks me if any of this is getting through. She reaches into a pocket and unfolds a map. Spreads it across the table between us.

"I want to know where he is," she says to me. "You understand? I want you to take your finger and I want you to point to him on this map. You show me where he is, or I take that agreement and shove it down your fucking throat. Now point. Goddamn it, point. *Where's Thomas?* Where did you leave his body?"

❖ ❖ ❖

And so I tell her.

I tell her how I was picked up by two greasy Russians as I tried to leave town. How they trussed me up like a prize pig and left me in the trunk of a car. I tell her about Thomas, about finally waking up and waiting patiently for him to let me out. She wants to know where and I tell her to hold on now, don't get snappy at me, I didn't mean nothing by that prize pig comment.

I talk about how Thomas beat on me a little when he stopped driving. Cut my head with his gun and I've got the marks to prove it, see? Pig Nose wants to know what I'm laughing at and I tell her that I can't understand why everyone's so interested in this guy. I mean, he's a shit heel of a cop and Pig Nose says he's still a cop and I say oh so it's like some old boys' club and she bangs on the table and says just get to the goods or some such.

Then it's onto the hill, and how I got my ropes undone and managed to knock him out. I explain how he was going to kill me up there and what I did next, well, it was self-defense, wasn't it. Any jury would see that. Pig Nose asks what I did next and I tell her about his broken bones and so on. She doesn't say anything then but I see her gripping the edge of the table so hard her knuckles go white.

After that I talk about how I made my way out of the forest and back onto the main road. How Thomas's piece-of-crap Impala refused to start. How I managed to flag down a lift from some chump in an SUV with an exhaust that rattled all the way to the next town. Chadron, it was. Bought myself a bus ticket for California because I was just about sick to the back teeth of this weather and fancied myself some sun. Course I didn't even make it out of the state before your boys picked me up about an hour and a half into the journey. I'd just spent fourteen dollars on snacks and a copy of Hustler too, and wasn't that just a waste of money.

Pig Nose shakes her head. It's not enough, she says, and pushes the map toward me. Show me where Thomas took you, she says. Show me where you left him, she says.

I look down at the map. Tell her I never was a Boy Scout. She points to something and says that's Cooper, alright? That's Cooper and this is the highway leading out, just here, you see that? This is where Thomas would have taken you. Now you follow that road a while and you hit the Pine Ridge National Forest. Do you get this? Is this too hard to understand? You need to show me where in those woods he is. Where did the man in the SUV pick you up? He dropped you off in Chadron, and you were pulled from your Greyhound just outside Wyoming so that narrows it down but goddammit just point out the spot on the map so we can all go home.

And I sit there for a while. A long while. And suddenly I'm not sure if I can remember. I mean, obviously I can remember, *but what happens once I tell her? Everything comes to an end, doesn't it?*

Wasn't something I was rightly expecting to feel, and I thought I'd planned this thing out pretty well.

But there's just no getting away from it. I've enjoyed my time here. And maybe some people would say that's a sign of how shitty my life was before now, and they'd probably be speaking the truth. Or maybe I feel like I've just had enough. Little Jesse Kane and my mom, they taught me to go out on my own terms.

So I take a deep breath, sit back, look Pig Nose dead in the eye, and tell her where she can stick her fucking map.

◆　◆　◆

Couple days pass. Nothing much happens.

I'm starting to think maybe I made a mistake, got caught up in the moment. I've been told I do that sometimes. I'm just about to start the last chapter of my book and I'm practically reading each letter aloud to stretch it out.

And then the door swings open. I pause, eyes glancing upward to see who's come to visit me. I can hear voices talking in hushed whispers. A woman's voice, at that. Telling someone she'll be fine. I close the book and sit up straight, intrigued.

Tap tap tap.

Something is tapping against the sides of the stairwell. I see feet, pumps by the looks of them. Slip-ons, no laces. The beginning of dark jeans and a white stick going tap tap tap.

Holy shit, I think to myself. She's come to visit me.

And true enough, after a slightly fumbling descent of the stairs, Mary is standing in front of the cell door. Walking forward until her stick clinks against solid steel. She stops then. Takes a step back.

252

She's not changed much—beyond the obvious, I mean. No pink streak, mirrored sunglasses. I think back to how all this started. To the first time we met. Standing in the falling rain, watching her through her window. The music in her living room and the hushed sound of my wet shoes rolling along her wooden floor. It all seems such a long time ago now.

She stares forward, or at least does an uncanny impression of someone doing so. Her jaw set; a look of defiance.

"Simon Jacobs," she says. Her voice is strong.

I slink back slightly into my bunk. I don't want to speak to her.

"Simon Jacobs!" she says again.

I wish I hadn't sat up after all. My brain keeps telling me she can't see me but damn if it's not unnerving. I start to stretch back out again, hoping she'll get bored and go away.

My book slides off and clatters to the ground. Mary's head tilts at the sound.

"I can hear you in there," she says. "And I know you can hear me. So I'm just going to say what I came here to say and then I'm going to leave."

I thought I heard her voice crack a little on that one. I keep quiet, my heart racing.

She says that she didn't know Thomas very long. She says they weren't close friends, but they might have been one day, and that she doesn't have many of those back in Cooper. She says she knows I was with him at the end, and that she doesn't care for what went on between us and that's fine. At the end of the day it's none of her business. She says that what I did to her she won't ever be able to forgive. She says she doesn't know if she'll ever be able to move on. That her legs are covered in bruises just from trying to move around her apartment. She says she can't work her record player anymore, and that's maybe the worst thing of all. She says that Thomas was lost and that whatever point I was trying to make by killing him is made, and that there's nothing left to gain *from leaving him out there in a shallow grave, or worse, in none at all. Left for the animals to strip right down to his bones. She says Thomas was troubled, and that was alright because so was she. And that she hadn't ever thought about what would happen if she met someone as messed up as she was, hadn't ever thought about how it would end, but even if she had it wouldn't be like this.*

Don't let it end this way, she says.

Then she starts to cry. There's footsteps from above and a guard comes down to see if she needs help but she waves him away. She's strong. Stronger than I thought. She stands there for nearly a minute, waiting to see what I'll say.

I say nothing.

After the longest time she nods. Sniffs. Says that she had to try. Turns and starts to walk away. Tap tap tap. *I watch her leave and I think about what she said. The part about two messed-up people meeting. I guess spending the last few weeks here talking about my past has affected me more than I thought, because that part makes me think of my mom.*

So I watch her climb the stairs, her body slowly disappearing from the top down. I get to my feet to keep her in view. And then, when all that's left is the tip of her cane and the cuffs of her dark jeans and her slip-on pumps, I step up to the bars and press my mouth through the gap.

"Wait," *I say.*

Epilogue

It's been a few months now since it all happened. Life, I guess, is starting to normalize. It's not the same, obviously. But nothing ever will be. My therapist tells me I need to find that "new normal"; a way of living that I can cope with. That I can look back over as I lie in bed at night and think: *This was a good day*.

I'm getting there. It's slow going. Today was better than yesterday, yesterday better than the day before. I think the worst thing about it is the bruising. Not on my neck—that doesn't hurt anymore—but on my legs. My shins ache constantly. I've knocked them into everything from the coffee table to the TV cabinet. I don't even know why I still *have* a TV cabinet. I should get rid of it, I know, only then it would feel like the cabinet won.

So I'm just going to have to learn to get my bearings properly. I'll get there. And I'll work out a way to listen to my records, too. I can work the machine well enough, I just don't have a clue what I'm putting on. Lionel Richie has been spinning on my turntable for the last three weeks now I think, and he was just an accident. (I was hoping for Pink Floyd.)

But maybe that's not true, maybe the bruises aren't the worst thing. Sometimes I can still see his face. I still see faces even though I can't, you know, see faces. Other people talk about it happening at night. When they go to bed, when they close their eyes. And maybe that's how it is for them.

For me, I see his face all the time. My eyes are always closed, always ready to spot him looming over me. Sometimes I'm in bed—in my head, in my memory, I mean. Other times he's pinning me down in the shower, or the yard, or dragging me through my home toward the back door. Often it's different locations. Like he's sitting at the bar in Stingray's. Or pressing me against the flimsy fence that runs along the river. Pressing me so hard I pray for it to break so I can drown in the dirty water. Never has the creaking of an apartment sounded so much like footsteps. I can still cry, and when I lie in bed at night sometimes the tears pool in the backs of my sockets.

Those are the bad days.

Today is a good one, though. I managed to go from my bedroom to the bathroom without stubbing my toe on something. I managed to make myself toast and a cup of tea without spilling anything. I managed to put the radio on and for a short while it was almost like it had always been. Like I might have just been relaxing with my eyes closed, listening to music.

There's a knock on my front door and I jerk upright so hard I send the mug tumbling down my front. I swear, loudly, and reach for my stick. I'm not sure what time it is, but it's Sunday, I know that, and I'm not expecting anyone. My brain throws up images of him standing on the other side of the door, and my heart goes into overdrive and it's hard to breathe.

Another knock. Sharp, tight. Someone official. I make my way to the door on trembling legs that I bash against that damn TV cabinet, only this time I barely feel it.

I swallow to clear my throat. "Who's there?" I shout.

"Ma'am, it's Detective Mansfield," comes the reply. "I'm sorry to drop in on you like this."

I recognize the voice. We've spoken before, she and I. Her first name begins with a D. Dana, maybe. My fingers still want to go for the peephole. I take a steadying breath and undo the chain. Slide back the deadbolt. Step away and smile and swing open the door.

"Good morning," I say. "Dana, isn't it?"

"Debra," she says. "I hope I'm not intruding."

She's looking at the tea stain down my front, I realize. Or maybe she's not. I brush at it self-consciously. "Not at all. Would you like to come in?"

"Thank you."

I hear her as she moves inside. She's shorter than me, I can tell. I wait until I'm sure she's in then close the door, rattle the chain, and slide the deadbolt home. I give a slight smile.

"Force of habit," I say.

Debra makes a noise like she might be smiling.

"Cup of tea?" I ask, then wipe at my damp clothes. "I was just about to make myself another one."

"Why not," Debra says.

So she stays for tea. It's nice, having her here for a bit. She doesn't stay long, maybe a half hour at most, but I like her. She doesn't treat me like some precious object that might break apart at any moment, even if that's how I feel sometimes. She asks if I want help with anything. I say no and that's that. We sit at the kitchen table and drink tea and talk and I even put out some cookies, although neither of us eat them.

She asks me how much I know about what happened after. I tell her the truth: "Just what was on the news."

"You know we found the recorder," she says. "On Thomas's body."

"I know."

"We couldn't have done it without him."

She's talking about Joe Finch. Thomas had spilled everything out onto that tape, everything that had happened in Cooper. It was his final confession. I wonder if it made any difference in the end. I don't believe in any of that stuff about what goes on after death, but I don't know about Thomas. I guess I don't know a lot about Thomas.

"This is all very interesting," I say. "But you didn't come here to tell me this."

"No."

"You've found something."

"Yes."

"Something on the recording."

"Yes."

"Something for me."

Debra doesn't say anything, but I know what the answer is. I hear a rustle as she reaches into a pocket and then a dull clink as she places something metallic on the kitchen table.

"He left you a message," she says. "After he was finished. I've had it copied for you. They put it onto a tape, made me bring you this little player. Who has a tape player anymore, right?"

Then her fingers are on mine, and I jump at the touch. She presses the device into my palm—feels like a Walkman; I remember those—and closes my hand around it, shows me where the Play button is. I ask her if she's listened to it and she tells me yes. I think I start to cry then, but maybe it was a little sooner.

◆　◆　◆

Debra leaves shortly after. Says her goodbyes and shakes my hand. Tells me to take care and wishes me luck. I wait until she's gone, until a minute has passed and then ten minutes have passed. Now I'm sitting at the kitchen table and an hour has passed and I'm holding the Walkman in my hand and there's a fresh cup of tea in front of me and those cookies, too, but I don't think I can eat anything. I think about him, about the time he'd needed help and we'd talked, and we'd walked along the river and through the darkened streets and swapped our sad stories, and my finger finds the button and presses down. A hiss of static, and then I'm transported to the wide forests of the Pine Ridge. Here the light is warm and the ground is soft, and in my own private imagination I'm sitting next to him, leaning back against a cottonwood tree with my head on his shoulder and the sun on our faces, and I listen to the message that he left for me when he was alone and I was asleep.

ACKNOWLEDGMENTS

Thanks first and foremost have to go to my agent, Jamie, for seeing something in my manuscript when others didn't. The work you put into the revisions helped improve the novel no end, and hopefully by this point I've received my vaccine, lockdown is over and I can legally buy you a beer. Thanks also have to go to everyone at my publisher, Thomas and Mercer—Sammia, Dolly, Jack; you guys have been awesome to work with and have always had time for my newbie questions about the whole process. A shout out to Sophie for her PR work and to Gemma and Sadie for their copy-editing wizbotery. A huge thank you to David Downing, the unsung hero of this book. The work you did on the developmental edit was nothing short of transformative, and you're clearly some sort of magician.

I also have to say thanks to the friends and family who gave their time to read my book and offer their thoughts   James, Karen, Sara, Celanne and Sube (and anyone I've forgotten . . .). Marco—cheers for all the support and writing discussions we've had over the years! Thanks to my mum for far too much to mention here, but specifically for spotting the writers' group advert online—the spark from which this novel was born. And finally thanks to my wife,

Lucy, who suffered through countless vomit drafts and listened to my endless stressing that the book wasn't working/it was crap/ the whole process wasn't going to amount to anything, all without once threatening to divorce me. Oh, and for making us get a dog (hi Scout).

ABOUT THE AUTHOR

Tariq Ashkanani is a solicitor based in Edinburgh, where he also runs WriteGear, a Kickstarter company that sells high-quality notebooks for writers, and WriteGear's podcast Page One. He had no formal writing training or consultation prior to writing *Welcome to Cooper*. He is currently working on a follow-up thriller, also set in Cooper, called *Follow Me to the Edge*.